Psychic Surveys Book Eight

The Weight Of The Soul

Psychic Surveys: Book Eight

The Weight Of The Soul

How far will you walk down a dark dark path?

SHANI STRUTHERS

STORY
LAND
PRESS

ISBN: 978-1-8382204-6-4

www.shanistruthers.com

Storyland Press
www.storylandpress.com

In the midst of death, life persists. In the midst of untruth, truth persists. In the midst of darkness, light persists. *Mahatma Gandhi*

Acknowledgements

A huge thank you to all the people involved in the creation of this book. My beta reading team once again came up trumps with some wonderful suggestions, which were all taken on board. Kate Jane Jones, Sarah Savery, Louisa Taylor and Lesley Hughes, you are marvels, every one of you. Special thanks also to Rob Struthers for going over in such painstaking detail the first polished draft and for all the brilliant amendments you make. Then it's off to super Ed, Rumer Haven, you are such a joy to work with, as are you, Gina Dickerson, thank you so much for yet another brilliant cover and for formatting. Finally, thank you so much to all the readers who breathe life into these characters every bit as much as I do.

Prologue

WHO was Edward Middleton? Was he sane? Or was he the balance? In a family where madness had gained a stronghold, manifesting so greatly in Ruby's father and great-great-grandfather, had he – her grandfather – somehow avoided what she sometimes thought of as a disease, this longing for power and status at any cost? A willingness to trade your soul, not to the highest bidder, to the lowest. To those mired in the darkness.

In the bedroom of her and Cash's new home in Sun Street, Lewes, Ruby squeezed her eyes shut, but only briefly. This preoccupation with a man who was a part of her family, but whom she knew next to nothing about, was becoming an obsession, and all because of a photograph. One not given to her by her grandmother Sarah – she'd had no photographs of Edward Middleton that Ruby knew of – but found in a building that housed the most depraved entities the Psychic Surveys team had ever encountered. Blakemort, of course. A photograph the house intended her to find, even though Blakemort had no connection to her family that she was aware of.

In black and white, it was of a man standing outside the house, wearing slacks and a buttoned shirt, hair neatly combed. A handsome man, who was smiling, looking pleased to be where he was. As if anyone could be pleased to be there. Anyone in their right mind.

On the back of the photograph was an inscription: *With love, Edward Middleton.* Handwritten, the words were large and looped. In among other photographs found at Blakemort, of the post-mortem variety so favoured by the Victorians in mourning, there it was, one of him, very much alive.

The other photographs she'd archived, along with reams of notes on Blakemort, all that had been seen and said there. How her hands had loathed to type such words, but documentation was a vital part of this business. It helped her, usually, to clarify matters, and it was something her great-grandmother Rosamund had also done – written extensive notes regarding the paranormal, both personal experiences and those of others. Most of these records were kept in the vaults of the London Psychical Society, an institution that Rosamund had been a founder member of.

So, yes, archiving those terrible photographs, once the police had vetted them, had been necessary. The one of Edward Middleton, however, never made it into police hands. She'd kept it separate. Not even shown the Psychic Surveys team, Theo, Ness and Corinna. Or her husband, Cash. Instead, she'd stashed it away in the drawer of her office desk, under a heap of papers, pens, staples and paperclips. It was safe there. In the drawer, but also on her mind. Always.

Obsessed?

Ruby shook her head. She mustn't be. She had to focus on all that was good in her life, of which there was plenty.

Hendrix Christopher Wilkins had been born three months prior, and what a whirlwind time she and Cash had had of it since! Ruby had been dreading the birth, and certainly it was dramatic. A fifty-hour labour followed by an emergency caesarean. Edge-of-the-seat stuff but also not something she wanted to dwell upon, just the joy of him being born, finally, the relief that they had both made it through a dangerous time of transition. He was beautiful! Perfect! His tiny face screwed up, red and angry, his fists punching at the air. Cash had been the first of them to hold him, and his face was also a vision. Full of wonder, bursting with pride.

Sure, it had been a tough three months that followed. Perhaps because of the traumatic birth, Hendrix cried a lot, Ruby and Cash doing their best to soothe him, often through the night as well as the day. But he was here, he was healthy, and he'd settle soon enough. Exhaustion, raw edged right now, would also settle, become a memory to laugh at. "Do you remember, Cash," she'd say, "all those nights we paced the floor with him? How tired we were, how we could only dream of sleep!"

It was good. All good. They'd made it through the pregnancy, and now they'd make it through the agony and the ecstasy of becoming first-time parents – all those scenarios no one ever told you about, that weren't noted in any books, how normal life got…obliterated.

Normal. There was that word again. As if anything about her life, her history, was normal. Regarding her own father, he didn't know he was a grandfather.

And nor would he. Ever.

Her mother, though, Jessica, and Jessica's partner,

Saul, were over the moon. As for Jed – the spirit dog that had been Ruby's constant companion for so long, nearly four years now – not so much. He'd appear regularly and sit by the baby's cot, stare at it, his head inclined to one side. But he seemed concerned rather than happy, his tail not wagging but static.

"It's okay," Ruby would say to him as Hendrix insisted on screaming the house down around them. "I know this sound hurts your ears, but he won't be like this for long. It's a newborn thing; it has to be. He'll grow out of it."

Jed would continue to sit there, looking like he didn't believe a word.

"And you know something else," Ruby would add, "just because we've got Hendrix, it doesn't mean I love you any less. It's just…Cash and I have two best boys now."

It was late. The dead of winter. January. Such a bleak month. And, incredibly, only Ruby was awake – Cash slumbered soundly, Hendrix in his arms, occupying the space that used to be hers and also flat out, his cherub mouth open, snuffles escaping him. She should of course adhere to the advice her mother *and* Theo had given her: sleep when the baby slept, no matter what time of day or night it was. And it was good advice that she usually followed, but tonight, at just gone three a.m., she was lying there, wide awake. Admitting defeat, she got up to head downstairs to the kitchen, padding softly like a thief in the night, grabbing her dressing gown before leaving the door ajar.

In the kitchen, bright lights temporarily blinded her as she flicked the switch and pulled her dressing gown tighter, painfully aware of just how rounded her stomach was still. It was going to take time to get back to her pre-pregnancy days, something she accepted. Something she wasn't helping either as she headed straight to the biscuit jar, opened it, selected a bourbon and proceeded to eat. That was quickly followed by another, Ruby popping the kettle on in between, waiting for the water to boil.

Once it had, she made a cup of tea – chamomile, which she hated the taste of, but it was supposed to aid sleep, and the plan was to return to bed eventually.

Cup in hand, she sat at the kitchen table, relishing the warmth of the mug between her palms. That was when Jed appeared. He'd been in the bedroom previously, a dark shape in the gloom, sitting by the bed – her side – as if guarding her. Now he was here, in the kitchen, as if seeking to guard her still.

She placed her cup on the table and reached out, wishing she could stroke him, reassure him further. "What is it, eh? What's wrong?"

If only he could talk, but all he could do was continue to stare, his dark brown eyes as deep and as soulful as ever.

A shiver ran through her, and eventually she stood.

"I'm just taking another look, that's all," she said. "Just…another look."

As she'd stolen out of the bedroom, she stole out of the kitchen, back up the stairs and up another flight into the attic room, Jed behind her.

How many times had she done this – taken a look? Studied the photograph, examined it. Too many times to count, and always when she was on her own, when

Cash was preoccupied, only once when the baby had been with her, and, oh, how he had howled! Worse than usual, making her put it straight back. Now, though, she had free rein.

Rather than using the main light, she opted for the lamp, the glow it cast slightly yellowish as she opened the drawer the photograph resided in, as she searched for it.

Even if Cash found it, he wouldn't know what it was, *who* it was; he'd likely think nothing of it. Best to hide it, though, just in case, although deep down she hated there was this secret between them. It felt wrong somehow. Dirty.

The photograph now in her hand, Jed whining slightly, hopping from leg to leg the way he always did when agitated, she told him again everything was okay. To keep calm.

Was she calm?

After a fashion. Her hands weren't exactly trembling, but there'd been a slight shake to them initially. She'd never, *never* handle the photograph without putting in place protection. White light, of course. Wrapped around her like a blanket, one made of steel rather than wool. Good intent was also important but harder to summon. It was curiosity that inspired her, not a simple yearning to know but a burning desire.

Are you the *Edward Middleton, or is this some sort of sick joke?*

Something intended to torment her, long after the walls of Blakemort had been razed to the ground. *There will always be another Blakemort.* That's what Theo had said, or words to that effect. And this time it needn't be something made of bricks and mortar but on paper instead, a simple square that you could hold in your hand, an image, an imprint.

Edward Middleton – whom her sweet grandmother had known whilst living in London, who had fathered Jessica. As soon as Sarah had realised she was expecting, she'd left London and bought a house in Hastings. A woman of means, thanks to her parents, she'd been able to do that despite the times, the controversy that being a single mother might provoke. Not that Sarah would have given a stuff about other people's opinions, Ruby thought with fondness. She'd been a woman who'd carved her own path in life, who'd been strong and independent, who'd taught Ruby everything she knew: how to respect the spirit world, to see it not as something dark and terrifying, because it wasn't, not necessarily, but something natural that existed alongside the material. She'd been a kind woman, gentle, with psychic abilities of her own, who'd shielded Ruby and also Jessica – the latter as far as it was possible, as Jessica had been a wild teenager. She'd been rebellious. Traits inherited from whom?

Were you wild and rebellious too, Edward?

Sarah hadn't told Edward she was pregnant, not at first. Why, Ruby didn't know. This was knowledge only recently learnt, when the issue had been forced during an argument, the one that had preceded Sarah's death.

A tear choked Ruby, rather than a frisson of fear. How she missed her grandmother! She wished she were still here, not just in memory but as someone living and breathing. Gran would have been able to solve this mystery, to identify the man in the picture, a man she'd professed not to have loved, hence why she'd left him rather than married him. Although, at some point she'd relented and written to tell him about Jessica – a letter that had subsequently been returned, *No longer at this address* written on the envelope.

With Jed still whining, still agitated, Ruby studied the photograph further, not the man but the house behind him. Even though the photograph was black and white, she could see how grimy the walls were, windows like blackened eyes glaring back at her. Nothing was right with the house; everything was off-centre, a repellent structure that didn't want you anywhere near it, but once you *had* discovered it, it wouldn't let you go. Ever.

It was the window she homed in on. Was there a shadow behind it? She'd puzzled over this before. A figure of some description? The boy whose kingdom Blakemort was, who'd held dominion there? Or someone else. Someone…taller, with longer hair. Gran's hair had been long when she was young. Had she worn it free and easy, past her shoulders?

It couldn't be Gran.

No way.

Why not?

If she *had* been there, with Edward, would she have kept that information to herself too? *For your best interests, Ruby.* She didn't doubt that, but a house like Blakemort left an indelible mark. How could someone as pure as Sarah have stood it?

If *it's her.*

The possibility of it began to plague her too. She could feel her lip curling, forming a snarl. That bloody house! And that bloody boy, beautiful but full of hatred.

A cry, a scream.

Hendrix had woken.

Shit!

She could hear Cash too, calling out for Ruby. "Where are you?"

"Coming," she replied, although so low he likely wouldn't hear, her eyes still on the picture and Jed not just whining but barking. "Okay, okay," she told the dog. "I'm putting it back, see?" She rose from the chair, feeling weary again. Even more confused.

The image of Edward Middleton remained in her mind, standing outside Blakemort and smiling. The figure at the window too, also smiling, and the smile of the beautiful boy.

And all of them so insincere.

PART ONE

Ruby

Chapter One

THE end of an era. That's what it was.

Lazuli Cottage was to be sold at last. The house where three generations of Davis women had lived: Sarah; her daughter, Jessica; and Jessica's daughter, Ruby. For a while, all Jessica and Ruby had done was talk of the possibility, but now it had been registered with an estate agent, the ball well and truly rolling.

It was a beautiful cottage in the Old Town of Hastings, a *homely* residence despite some of the events that had taken place there over the past few years. Dark events but, thankfully, transient. It was a place where the light belonged, instilled by Sarah, who'd fought so hard to keep it in place, to protect her own. Those walls housed such history, such love, but with Sarah gone it was time to move forwards and for others to love it now, a family, perhaps, that could grow there, that could flourish.

"Imagine that," Jessica had said when she and Ruby had met there soon after that decision had been made, their aim to give it a thorough clean before estate agents came to value it. "There'll be laughter again, there'll be excitement at Christmastime and birthdays. The smell of baking will be in the air. Gran loved to bake, didn't she? She was the best cook."

Ruby had closed her eyes and tried to do just that: imagine, the shape of future residents wispy, like ghosts themselves. Jessica was right, but, nonetheless, it was hard to let go. All those memories... But to leave a house empty, which Lazuli Cottage was, for the most part, wasn't something to be recommended, Jessica living full-time with Saul in Bexhill, and Ruby in Lewes with Cash and Hendrix. The absence of life and energy could attract things other than a happy family. Gran would have hated for the house to remain stagnant; she would have feared that for it.

And so, a 'For Sale' board had been erected and people shown around, most of them sighing at how sweet the cottage was, according to Dawn Keate, the estate agent.

"This won't take long to shift," she'd told them with a gleam in her eye. "Cottages in the Old Town never do."

She was right. An offer had been placed two weeks later, only five thousand below the full asking price. Silly not to bite their arm off, to accept. The money from the sale would come in useful, Jessica's half providing an income for her, and for Ruby it meant she and Cash didn't have to rent in Lewes; they could buy. Hence the move from her flat in De Montfort Road to a house in Sun Street, one with an attic in which the new Psychic Surveys office would reside. Ruby had laughed at that. Once upon a time, she'd dreamt of ground-floor offices in a prominent position in the High Street, of placing the business of spirituality alongside other businesses. Bringing it out of the darkness and into the light, an everyday thing. Because that's what it was. She and the team could *see* that. Some people, however, could only experience, and it was those they helped. Those confused by it, who didn't understand, who were frightened. Possibly the haunted.

That dream, however, had not borne fruit. Ruby didn't mind too much; she accepted not all dreams could. An attic office in her home was fine for now. It was handy. She and Cash, who also worked from home, were sharing the parental load, accepting that working hours could prove interesting, at least until the baby settled into some kind of routine.

Cash and Ruby had been able to afford a deposit on their new home – one that was free of spirits, Ruby had told Cash, having performed a psychic survey beforehand – but the proceeds from Lazuli Cottage would ease mortgage payments, that was for sure.

Gran's house, meanwhile, had to be cleared of all her furniture, clothes and papers. Some items would be kept, some would be sold, others heading to charity. Regarding the papers, Ruby would go through them thoroughly, decide what to shred and what to file.

The Saturday that had dawned was a chilly one. Neither Cash nor Ruby were working, although on recent weekends they had tended to. Ruby had been awake since early morning, pacing the floor with Hendrix, wearing a hole in the carpet of the living room if she didn't stop sometime soon. Cash was upstairs enjoying a lie-in.

"Shhh, quiet, little one," she soothed, the baby

wriggling in her arms, red-faced, suffering a bout of colic, most likely. "Come on, now, settle down."

As soon as Cash managed to stir himself, she'd hand the baby over. Whilst she'd like to grab more sleep – she'd only had around three or four hours in total – she'd take advantage of the childcare opportunity to head over to Hastings and continue the clearing. She already knew Jessica couldn't come, not today; she had a cold.

That was handy too…

Cash, come on, wake up. It's your turn now.

It was gone ten before he put in an appearance, Ruby at her wit's end.

"How can you sleep through it?" she yelled the moment he appeared in the living room. Jerking her head upwards, she continued, "It's not like we're sound-proofed or anything."

Cash only smiled – a great big soppy smile that made him look about ten rather than thirty, that dissolved any anger building in Ruby, any resentment.

She held out the baby. "Your turn. I'm off to the cottage."

He took the baby and immediately began cooing. "Oh, my little sweetheart, how are you? Oh? Not too happy so far, eh? Don't worry, Daddy's got you now. It's a boys' day today. We're going to have such fun!"

God, he was good with Hendrix, who – annoyingly or mercifully, depending on which way you looked at it – immediately began to still in his arms.

"How d'you do it?" Ruby asked, baffled. "Get him to settle like that. Oh, look, look! He's closing his eyes! He's going to sleep. At long bloody last."

Again, Cash's grin was wide. "You've got your magic ways, and I've got mine."

"Thank God," Ruby said, her smile a little weaker. "And you'll be okay today without me?"

"Sure! We'll be fine. We've got motor racing to catch up with, then we'll head out for a walk down to the Grange. Afterwards, we'll come back and fix something to eat."

"Cash, he doesn't eat, remember? He drinks milk."

Cash winked. "Ah, but he can watch while I eat. I can teach him what an art form it is."

A burst of laughter escaping her now, she left the living room and her two boys and headed to the bathroom to get ready. Gazing at her reflection in the mirror there, she felt like a kid now, felt like stamping her feet. It wasn't fair! Cash looked great, his usual self, a tall man with chiselled features and dark eyes that gleamed. She, however, was a wreck – limp brown shoulder-length hair, green eyes that were far from gleaming, and skin that was pale and blotchy. She could do with trowelling some makeup on, concealer and a bit of blusher, at least, but she was too tired to bother. And also too eager to be on her way.

She was out of the house in under twenty minutes, sans makeup, having blown the still sleeping Hendrix and Cash a kiss on her way out. In the car – not her beloved old Ford anymore, a newer model on lease – she turned the heat up to max soon after the hybrid whispered into life.

As she drove the familiar roads from Lewes to Hastings, she couldn't help but think how much life had changed, but it might have changed more if she'd stuck to her guns; she could have been out of a job too. Because that's what she'd been planning to do, give up Psychic Surveys, hand the reins over to Corinna, Ness and Theo. Step back. And all because of Blakemort. She was so glad she'd changed her mind. Whilst she loved her baby, *infinitely*, she suspected full-time childcare might push her over the edge. She was a working woman, running a spiritual domestic clearance business that had boomed since its conception a few years back. It was a job she'd been born to do. Gran had told her that.

"You have this ability," she'd said. "As far as I know, all the women in our family have had it to varying degrees. It's a gift, Ruby. Don't deny it, use it – to help, not only the dead but the living too, treating both with love and respect. Above everything comes love."

And Ruby had paid heed to those words, found others with abilities similar to hers – like calling to like in action – and created a team to be proud of, that she couldn't *not* be a part of, she realised. No matter how dark the job was at times. How dangerous it got…

The journey was relatively quick, the only real traffic on the road on the seafront of Hastings itself. Parking the car a short walk away, she hurried towards the cottage. Although chilly out, the sky was bright enough, with what she thought of as the Hastings soundtrack accompanying her – seagulls circling above, their cries as shrill as Hendrix. Before reaching the front door, she delved into her pocket for the key, hesitating only slightly before inserting it into the lock. Once inside, she closed the door behind her and took in the silence of her grandmother's absence.

Sarah Davis, aka Gran, had died in somewhat harrowing circumstances in this house, in the kitchen, during an argument involving Jessica. Despite this, her spirit had flown; Ruby could sense that she hadn't lingered, wasn't grounded by distress. Her eyes welling with tears as she stared down the hallway to the very spot in the kitchen where Gran had collapsed, she also forced a smile. The Great Halls of Learning was where Gran had said she'd wanted to go on the other side. She could hear her voice now as she described them.

"Ruby, they're beautiful! Walls made of white marble that tower above you, and shelf after shelf is filled with the most amazing books, the kind where you'll find answers to every question you might ever have had about the mystery of life and, of course, death."

"But how do you know that's what they'll be like?" Ruby had asked. How old had she been, ten or eleven? Maybe older.

Gran had shrugged. "I just know," she'd answered, tapping at her chest. "In here."

I hope that's where you are, Gran. An already wise woman becoming wiser.

Ruby continued onwards to the kitchen, where she'd make herself a cup of tea before heading upstairs to Gran's bedroom to go through the bureau there. Oh, for some of Gran's homemade shortbread to go with the tea, the tin they used to be kept in – an old McVitie's tin with several dents and worn edges – packed away but on the list to come to Ruby's house.

A few minutes later and she was upstairs, placing a full mug on a coaster on Gran's bedside table. There were so many papers in the bureau that stood in front of her, kept under lock and key when Gran was alive, including papers written by Rosamund and which both Jessica and Ruby had now mostly read. There were a few other bits to sort through, though, and this she intended to do, pulling up a chair and opening the bureau.

The contents of the bureau also included letters from friends, Ruby scanning the contents, the chatty tone both comforting and saddening her further. Then there were bills. Everybody kept a fair amount of those, ranging from telephone to electricity and gas. Some had handwritten sums on them, which made Ruby's heart ache. Although Gran had come from money, she'd used it to buy this house, for a start, but also Gran couldn't work when Jessica had had her breakdown, so she'd stayed at home and looked after her instead. Savings only lasted for so long, and this was proof of it. Not that Gran had ever let on she was worried about making ends meet; she'd just kept sailing the ship, over rough waters and smooth.

With a sigh, Ruby bundled up the papers and put them into a box. She'd store them at home for now, unable to get rid of them, to erase the evidence of a life well lived.

A couple of hours passed, Ruby having emptied the bureau and now packing away clothes that would go to charity. Primarily, though, she was searching. Hands checking the backs of drawers, the side panels too, for anything that might have been kept there, secreted away. She was on her knees too, checking beneath the rug for any floorboards that might be loose, tugging at them sometimes, but they held fast.

Eventually, the tea having turned cold, Ruby failing to have even sipped at it, she sat on the edge of Gran's bed, wondering at what she was doing. Trying to find evidence, basically. Anything to do with Edward Middleton and Blakemort. That Gran might have known about a house Ruby had only encountered *after* Gran had died, it seemed…incredible. But the incredible was what Ruby dealt with. All the time.

Where else would Gran have kept something that she'd wanted to remain private?

Ruby's head tilted as her eyes glanced upwards.

The attic, of course.

There wasn't much up there to dispose of. Ruby and Jessica had already gleaned that much from poking their heads up there on an occasion prior to this, but that was *all* they had done. They hadn't ventured up there fully because…well, because there'd been so much else to do in the main body of the house. Was now the time to rectify that?

Her heart began to hammer in her chest at the very thought.

What have you hidden up there, Gran? A place no one usually went. Certainly not Ruby as a child or a mother who'd remained, for much of Ruby's childhood, in a near catatonic state, venturing only from bedroom to bathroom to living room and back again. It was therefore a safe place, a haven. Somewhere that had to be examined more fully whilst it still could be, whilst the house was still in their custody.

Her heart still beating wildly with anticipation, Ruby stood. She was feeling clammy, though it was cold inside the cottage, the heating having been off for weeks.

Would the attic be a colder place still?

She took a step forward and then another.

Whatever was up there, was it best left alone? Illusions remaining intact, not shattered.

Illusions?

Ruby screamed.

Her mobile had burst into life and scared the shit out of her.

Oh, Cash! Trust you! What is it, is it Hendrix? Is everything okay?

On reaching her phone on the bedside table, beside the cold mug, she saw it wasn't Cash trying to get in contact but Theo.

Accepting the call, she spoke. "Theo? What is it? Are you okay?"

"Hello, darling, all good here, thank you. But…I've been talking to someone."

"Alive or dead?" Ruby quipped, quickly recovering from the fright of earlier.

"That's just it," Theo answered. "They seem to be neither."

Chapter Two

THEO had listened to the woman in front of her describe what she felt was happening to her – or rather, *not* happening. Concerning the latter, the woman meant death.

Her name was Carrie-Ann Kendall. She was thirty-four years old, unmarried, with no children. Of medium height, she was on the slim side and pretty, with blond hair in a short, easy-to-manage style. She had blue eyes, rather faded in colour, which Theo told Ruby was the first thing she'd noticed about her, that had made her take her claims seriously.

"My eyes are faded, but at my age, that's what you'd expect," continued Theo with her usual black humour. "After all, I've got one foot in this world and one in the next!"

"Not true!" Ruby protested. Theo might be in her early seventies, she might have suffered from heart problems, but she had the willpower of a Trojan, something Ruby was grateful for. Theo wanted to stay in this world, populated with the people she loved, her friends and her family, including ever increasing amounts of grandchildren, for as long as she could.

On the phone to Ruby, and in response to her protest, Theo chuckled. "Look, this is a little difficult to explain. You need to meet her. She's free later this afternoon if you are."

"I'm at Gran's," Ruby told her. *About to go into the attic.*

"Oh, I see. No problem, sweetie. I'll get back on the blower—"

"No, it's okay," Ruby decided. "If she can see us later today, let's go for it. I'll come back here another time."

"Okay," Theo conceded. "Just us, or shall I include Ness and Corinna at this stage too?"

Ruby thought for a moment. "It's Saturday, so let's fill them in on Monday. I know Corinna's flat hunting with Presley, and Ness, well, Ness is probably with Lee."

"Ah, yes, they do spend most weekends together nowadays." Laughter had returned to Theo's voice. "Going great guns between them, isn't it?"

"It is. It's brilliant. She seems like a different person."

"No longer dour, you mean?"

Ruby gently chided Theo, laughing too. "She's not so bad!"

"You haven't known her for as long as I have," Theo retorted. "But, yes, she's a heck of a lot better. Positively kittenish, I'd say! The power of love, eh? It's a marvellous thing."

A few minutes later and Ruby had rung off, agreeing to return to Lewes for the meeting with Carrie-Ann Kendall. She'd need to leave soon, within the next hour. Time enough to have a quick look in the attic, at least.

It was a plan she put into action, but not before hauling black bin bags full of clothes downstairs to the living room. She'd call one of the local charities during the week, arrange a time to get them picked up along with other bits and pieces. Before returning upstairs, she grabbed a quick glass of water from the kitchen and downed it in one. Then, taking the stairs two at a time, she sought out the rod that hooked into the hatch and opened it, the ladder unfolding.

For a moment before climbing the ladder, she stared upwards into what could only be described as a yawning chasm. It was dark and foreboding. Attics weren't her favourite thing, not since Blakemort, where she'd encountered the beautiful boy, where he'd…*threatened* her. But, as she reminded herself, the last attic she'd been in, one in Barcombe, was where something rather lovely, rather touching, had happened. It had been where she'd encountered another boy – not so beautiful but covered in burns. Christopher. He'd been stuck in the attic for a long time, since the 1940s. A little boy who'd played with matches, whose panic-stricken guardians had buried him somewhere out in the vast countryside. An evacuee, one whose own parents were dead. No one would come looking for him. That's what his guardians had banked on, and they'd been right. Just a little boy, confused, angry and hurting so badly. It had been Ruby and Ness who'd mainly dealt with the case and Ruby who'd managed to send him to the light, promising him she'd name her baby after him, that he might not have a consecrated grave, but he'd be remembered. He had hugged her burgeoning stomach, Hendrix kicking inside. Hendrix Christopher.

So, yes, attics weren't always something to be dreaded. She'd had an attic office too for several years, replaced by another office in the gods in her new home. But both had been light, airy and frequently inhabited.

The very opposite of this one, cramped and confined, a refuge not for humans but spiders, moths and beetles. Naturally repellent.

At last she climbed, beating back any further trepidation. Fully inside, she sought to find the light switch and quick. Her hand flailing for the cord, she wrinkled her nose. It had that musty attic smell, the stench of things long forgotten. Locating the light cord, she pulled it, then sighed. What was it about attic lights? They were always so weak! Certainly this one was, the naked bulb unchanged for an age.

Despite the gloom, her eyes scanned an area filled with shadows and cobwebs. Her gaze becoming fixed on one corner, she squinted. Was that a box there? A blanket box, it looked like, on top of which lay a stack of magazines and some shallower boxes, jigsaws, perhaps. Whilst recovering from her breakdown, her mother had completed so many jigsaws, losing herself completely in a world that, like her own, needed piecing together. There were a few other items surrounding it, small items of furniture that Gran clearly couldn't bear to part with but that had no place downstairs either – a pair of bedside tables and a small corner wall cupboard.

The blanket box, though. That was where her gaze returned, her senses prickling.

As she climbed fully into the attic and placed a foot carefully on a timber joist, it creaked, a sound she ignored as she continued to tread her way across the joists, her breath becoming shorter.

What can you sense? What can you feel?

It was hard to gauge. As every psychic knew, fear and trepidation could muddy the waters, imagination running riot. She believed in the light, wholeheartedly, was visualising it even now, but to be human was to be flawed, and that frisson of unease that sat in the pit of her stomach refused to budge.

Games. Jigsaws. They were piled on top, magazines too: *Oh Boy! My Guy. Jackie.* Most likely those belonging to her mother as a teenager. Covered in dust, all of them. She reached out, intending to lift them off the box and place them on a joist beside it.

Did you mean for me to find this, Gran? Or was I never supposed to?

Gran was always so protective of Ruby. She'd taught her about the light from a young age, about the good in people and in spirits too, that most were grounded because of trauma, sadness and fear of what lay beyond. What she hadn't taught her about, what Ruby had had to discover for herself, was non-spirit, entities from the lower realms that could find their way into this one by being summoned. She hadn't been taught this because Sarah had seen the damage that knowledge of such entities could wreak – via Jessica. For so long Ruby hadn't known what was wrong with her mother, just that she was ill. But naïvety could only last for so long. Her ability was like a flashlight, alerting those in the darkness that she was near, those that wanted help as well as those that sought to use her. Over the years, Ruby had had experience; she had learnt, and she had grown. She was naïve no more. But how far had Sarah gone in her efforts to protect her and Jessica too? Just what kind of man had she been involved with once upon a time?

The answers might be there in that box, a box that

Sarah might have disposed of if she'd lived to tend to such matters.

Ruby's fingers tingled. She could also feel the blood pumping around her system, causing her heart to race again.

What's in there? What the hell is in there?

Her entire body jerked as her breath caught in her throat.

It was the phone. Again.

Oh, for pity's sake!

One hand retrieving it from her back pocket, she noted this time it was Cash.

"Ruby? Ruby? Are you there?"

His weary voice and the baby's manic cries were the sounds that greeted her.

* * *

"Ah, Ruby, there you are! Come in, come in," Theo said, standing aside so that she could pass. "Carrie-Ann's already here. She's on her third cup of tea, quite awash with the stuff."

"Sorry I'm a bit late," Ruby replied. "After Hastings, I had to rush home quick and see to Hendrix. He just wouldn't stop yelling. Cash was losing the plot."

"Ah." Theo nodded gravely. As a mother of three, she understood well enough the trials and tribulations that a newborn could inspire. "All okay now, though?"

Ruby shrugged, a somewhat rueful gesture. "As well as can be. Cash is usually so good with the baby, but...I don't know. His cries were, like, terrifying. That's the way Cash described them. He honestly thought something was wrong with him. He's asleep now, though. They both are, crashed out on the sofa."

"Good, that's something, at least. Well, come on in and meet our prospective client."

Carrie-Ann was already standing when Ruby entered the living room. Theo had described her well, especially the eyes, which seemed to lack any vitality.

On seeing Ruby, Carrie-Ann smiled, but, again, it didn't reach the eyes; they remained sad instead, and confused.

"Thank you," she said to Ruby. "Thank you so much for agreeing to see me."

"You're more than welcome," Ruby said as Theo indicated for them both to sit.

In the brightness of the living room, sparsely furnished because Theo adored 'sacred space', Ruby took a seat on the sofa beside Carrie-Ann, Theo occupying the matching white leather armchair opposite. There was a jug of water on the table, flavoured with lemons. Ruby helped herself to a glass whilst waiting for the woman to continue.

"I'm not mad," she said, something both Ruby and Theo were used to hearing from their clients. "What I'm telling you, or rather what I've told your colleague"— here she averted her gaze to smile gratefully at Theo— "is what I feel is true."

"Because of what the clairvoyant said?" Theo responded.

"And because of the near-miss I had." Carrie-Ann's eyes now back on Ruby, she apologised. "Sorry, I'd better fill you in."

"Yes, please," said Ruby, taking a sip of water. "But

take your time. There's no rush." Hopefully Cash and Hendrix would sleep for a while longer.

The woman – fairly confident in manner before, now bit her lip. "Shall I…um…start with the clairvoyant?" she asked Theo.

"If you wish." Theo's smile was indulgent.

Again, Carrie-Ann turned to Ruby. "Last summer, do you remember it? It was a hot one, the sun always blazing, from March right through to September."

"Later, even," said Ruby. "October was pretty nice too."

Carrie-Ann's shoulders relaxed further. "Yes, it was. It was in early September that my friend had a hen night in Brighton. She's not from the south, she actually lives in Derbyshire, but she loves Brighton, you know, all that corny pink-cowboy-hat stuff, and so she wanted to host it down here, which was great for me as I live so close in Lewes."

"There's lots of hen and stag dos in Brighton, virtually every weekend," Ruby replied conversationally. "It's a bit of a mecca for that."

"Always so much going on, isn't there? It's a great town."

"A city now," Theo mused. "Allegedly."

All three women were smiling, the atmosphere, boosted by so much space and white furnishings, tranquil.

"So, yeah, like I said, we all bundled over to Brighton for a raucous girls' weekend, laughing, gossiping, dancing, eating and drinking, and Debbie – my friend – also had another surprise in store for us. She wanted us to see a clairvoyant, and she was going to foot the bill.

Her future looked great, but for some of us, it wasn't so great. We were either in between jobs or hadn't found Mr Right yet, that kind of thing. I guess…" Carrie-Ann paused. "I guess she wanted us to have hope in the future, to be assured good things were waiting round the corner."

Ruby frowned. So what had Debbie done, she wondered, in order to achieve this aim, bribed the clairvoyant? She remained quiet, however, let Carrie-Ann speak.

"And so, on the Saturday morning, off we went, all six of us, to the pier, where the clairvoyant had one of those gypsy-style caravans. Debbie went in first, came out glowing and giggling. The rest of us were waiting on a bench nearby, huddled together and drinking coffee. She'd been about twenty minutes. Shelley went in next, and she too came out chuffed with what she'd heard, then Pennie, Jayne and Anna. All of them were so happy and astounded too. This guy – Leon Vasilescu – really seemed to know stuff about them. He seemed to…connect."

"Leon Vasilescu," Ruby repeated. "Exotic handle."

"He's Romanian, apparently. Of Romany descent. Spoke very good English, though."

"Fair-haired, by any chance?" The sarcasm in Theo's voice was evident.

"It was dark. His eyes were too," Carrie-Ann answered.

"So what happened when you saw him?" Ruby asked, growing more curious.

Carrie-Ann lowered her head, her shoulders slumping. Her hands were in her lap, and now one reached over to the other and started scratching at the skin there.

Noting her anxiety, Ruby checked if she was okay.

"Yes…thank you…just…can I have a moment, please?"

"Of course," replied Ruby, catching Theo's gaze, noting the concern there too.

Carrie-Ann took a deep breath. "I was due in last, just the way the cookie crumbled, you could say, and we were all excited about what I was going to be told, what nuggets of information he knew about me. Or should I say, my friends were excited, because actually I was getting more and more nervous. My stomach was tying itself in knots."

Theo leant closer. "Would you like some water, Carrie-Ann?"

She shook her head. "No, thank you. I'm fine. Could I…sorry, could I have a tissue?"

Immediately, Theo rose and headed over to a sideboard on which there was a box of Kleenex. She brought it over, and Carrie-Ann took one and dabbed at her eyes.

"If this is difficult for you…" Ruby began.

Carrie-Ann lifted her head. "Difficult? It's downright weird. All of it."

"So what happened?"

The woman shifted in her chair, dabbed once more at her eyes, then blew her nose. "All right, okay. I'm fine now. I can do this. So, right, I…I went over to his…caravan. It was nice enough on the outside, kind of what you'd expect of these things, predominantly red and green, a few steps leading up to it. There was a board outside, one that had quotes on from people professing how fantastic Leon Vasilescu is, how he's helped them with his insights, got them back on the right track, that they wouldn't entertain the idea of seeing another clairvoyant. Why would they? When they'd found the real deal. So, yeah, it was my turn to enter. At the top of the steps, I knocked on the door, and a voice from inside told me to come in. I pushed the door open. It was dark in there, the glow of a Tiffany-style lamp really helping to set the scene, moody, you know. A bit cheesy too, if I'm honest. I thought, here we go, let's get this over and done with, then we can head to one of the bars elsewhere on the seafront and get the party started. Before I could open my mouth, however, even smile at him, he shook his head. *Violently* shook his head. Oh shit!"

Carrie-Ann's entire body had tensed again, and, as a result, Ruby tensed too. Where was Carrie-Ann going with this?

"Sorry…for swearing," was her next comment.

"Don't be. It's fine," Ruby assured her, desperate to hear what was coming next but not wanting to rush Carrie-Ann either. Some stories took time to tell.

On another deep breath, she resumed. "He chucked me out," she revealed. "He…literally chucked me out. He stood up, his head still shaking from side to side, and said I shouldn't have come. No, no, his exact words were 'You shouldn't be here.' There was fear in his eyes, bewilderment and even anger. 'You shouldn't be here!' He moved towards me, saying that same thing. Just…repeating it."

"What did you do?" Ruby asked, aghast.

"I left. What else could I do? I opened the door and

hurled myself down those steps, just wanting to get away from him, from what he was saying. I thought he might follow me out, repeating those same damned words, but he didn't. Instead, he slammed the door shut and bolted it, actually *bolted* it. There's a small window in the door, and he pulled the shutter down too. He wanted nothing to do with me. Absolutely nothing. All my friends were waiting on that nearby bench. What the hell was I going to tell them? How could I even begin to explain? I couldn't. I just…I told them he'd had a phone call and that it looked like it was an emergency. That he'd apologised, but there was no way he could see me right now. Debbie was disappointed, but, like she said, c'est la vie. Anyway, they seemed to accept it, and we headed off the pier, towards the town. God, it was hard getting through the next few hours."

"I'll bet," said Ruby. "That was a terrible thing to happen."

"It was," Carrie-Ann agreed. "But that's not the worst of it."

Ruby gazed at Theo briefly before replying. "What's the worst of it?"

The woman was ashen, her faded eyes filling with tears again.

"The worst of it is, I knew what he meant. Exactly. And he's right. I should be long gone."

Chapter Three

RUBY'S mobile had rung again whilst she'd been at Theo's. It was Cash, most likely. He'd obviously woken up, and Hendrix too.

She should really answer it. What with Hastings as well, she'd been gone such a long time today, guilt setting in about that, but what she was hearing from Carrie-Ann fascinated her. Plus, there was another part to the story. No way she could leave without hearing it.

"Ruby," Theo said on hearing her phone, which was in Ruby's bag on the floor beside her, "do you need to get that?"

Ruby gave a shake of her head. "I will, but…not right now." She then returned her gaze to Carrie-Ann. Psychic Surveys specialised in domestic spiritual clearance – the removal of grounded spirits from people's homes. That was their bread and butter, as the saying went, and, like Vasilescu, they had plenty of people testifying to how good their work was. Not on a billboard, nothing as crude as that, but on a website and Trustpilot. Strange, then, as she relied on the same word-of-mouth recommendations, that she should doubt those who'd recommended Vasilescu. Doubt his reaction too. The drama of it. Was that even his actual name or something he'd grabbed off the internet because it fit the bill? How cynical she could be. And yet, it galled her when people were as dismissive about her.

The phone becoming silent, she gestured for Carrie-Ann to continue. Only with the full story could they work out if she needed their help or not.

"I was involved in an accident," Carrie-Ann told her. "Early spring of last year, the end of March. A freak accident, I guess you could call it."

Ruby was shocked. "I'm so sorry to hear—"

"I'm not after sympathy," Carrie-Ann said. "This is more than that. Much more."

Quiet now, Ruby simply nodded.

"I'd gone sailing with some friends, just off the coast of Devon. It was a beautiful day, late spring, like I said, but feeling more like summer. The sun was shining and the water like a millpond." Unexpectedly, she laughed, although the sound held no amusement at all. "There's a saying, isn't there? 'Ne'er cast a clout till May be out.' You heard it?"

Again, Ruby nodded.

"There was no sign of bad weather on the horizon and nothing forecast either, but, even so, the weather turned. Dramatically. The blue sky suddenly darkened, and there was thunder in the air, and lightning; it just rolled in from nowhere. None of us had realised how far out we'd sailed, too busy having a good time, I suppose. And, yes, before you ask, we'd been drinking, a lot. It was Jem's boat, and immediately he turned us back towards the coast, reassuring us it'd be okay, that we'd make it easily enough. We didn't, though. We were struck by a bolt of lightning, and then I think we hit something, a rock. The boat capsized, it was chaos, and we were just…in the sea. There were four of us, and I was the only one not wearing a life jacket. I was supposed to, but I'd got so warm that I'd taken it off. Didn't think there was any harm in it. I started to sink. I'm a reasonable enough swimmer, but in the panic it was like I was being dragged under, like the tide was impossible to fight against."

Carrie-Ann closed her eyes as she relived the memory, Ruby enthralled, Theo too, even though she must have heard this tale already.

"I…I started to see things, visions, you could say, episodes from my life, basically, things that had happened. Not always big things but stuff you'd think of as inconsequential – Sunday tea with my grandmother, kicking a ball around a park with my brother, that kind of thing. I guess they're not so inconsequential in the end, those times. They matter. It all does. They're fragments of a whole. I was choking, breathing in water, but looking at these scenes calmed me somehow. I was *enjoying* watching my life flash before me, and I wasn't in pain anymore; my lungs no longer felt as if they were burning. It was like…I'd detached from myself, become an observer in more ways than one."

"A near-death experience," breathed Ruby.

"Not quite," murmured Theo.

"I'd gone limp, and I could hear voices, as though from far, far away, coming from one end of a long, long tunnel. They were my friend's voices, from above the waves, calling for me, telling me to hang on, but also other voices, ones I didn't recognise, although…I *did* recognise them; they were somehow familiar too. 'Welcome!' they were saying. 'It's so good to see you again.' Sorry, could I take another tissue? I'm so sorry about this."

Carrie-Ann's body was shaking with the force of her sobs. Alarmed, Ruby moved closer, reaching out a hand to lay on her arm and stroking it gently.

"It's okay," she said. "I can imagine it was an incredibly emotional experience. Near-death experiences often—"

Carrie-Ann stopped dabbing at her eyes. "It wasn't a near-death experience!"

Confused, Ruby glanced at Theo. What the hell would you call it, then?

"This is where it gets weird," Carrie-Ann said, the face she pulled plus the shrug of her shoulders now giving her a childlike quality. "I heard voices trying to save me and voices welcoming me, and I didn't know what to do. Which ones to pay attention to. All the while, my body was continuing to sink. But my friends, they're, like, my best friends, more familiar to me than the others, and so...I followed them. From being an observer, I started to drift back towards my body. That's when the other voices began to change."

Again, Carrie-Ann paused, the ensuing silence in Theo's living room heavy with expectation. And something else too, unease. *Ruby* felt uneasy, what the woman was about to say – what Ruby was consequently going to hear – something new to her, another aspect of the paranormal previously unconsidered.

"The other voices got louder. There was concern in them...and alarm. 'No!' they were saying. 'Stop! Don't do that. You *can't* do that. Come on, now, come to us. It's your time.' Over and over they said that. *It's your time.* A cacophony of voices, screaming at me, begging me. But…" Carrie-Ann swallowed. "I ignored them and kept on drifting. Then, bang! I was in my body. I began to move my arms and legs, flailing, kicking, forcing myself upwards. Hands grabbed me, helped me, dragging me closer to the surface until, eventually, I broke through the waves and took a big breath of air. I wasn't dead. I was alive! And the blue skies were back, the sun trying to shine. I…I don't remember much. Well, not a thing, actually, after that. We were rescued. Another boat had witnessed what had happened and come to help. On shore, ambulances were waiting to take us to hospital. I was kept in for days. It was all a blank for so long. I think…I think because I didn't want to remember, the trauma of it. But, lately, it's been different. I've been hearing the voices, the ones that told me not to come back. They're…as clear as anything."

"Okay," Ruby said, still unsure where this was going. "But it's just a memory, right?"

"We don't think it's that simple, Ruby," Theo answered.

Before Ruby could respond, her phone rang again.

"Shit! Sorry. You know what, I'll turn it off, okay? So we don't keep getting interrupted."

Reaching into her bag, she located the phone, noticed it was Cash having called a second time; he'd sent a couple of texts too, asking where she was, saying the baby had woken up and was, once again, ballistic. As sympathetic as she was, there was no way she could answer, not yet. *Sorry, Cash,* she thought, switching the phone off. She then turned her attention back to her colleague and the woman who still had a tale to tell.

"So, if it's not a memory, if it's not a near-death experience, what is it?"

"A mistake."

"A mistake?" queried Ruby, confused further.

Carrie-Ann nodded. "Exactly that. I shouldn't have returned to my body. I should have listened to the voices welcoming me, telling me my time was up." She tried to laugh. "I've always been stubborn, though; it's one of my worst traits. 'You always think you know best,' my mum says. 'You've got an answer for everything.' I thought I knew best on this occasion too, but I was wrong. Just like I've been wrong before."

Leaning back into the sofa, Ruby couldn't help but speak her mind. "Carrie-Ann, how do you think we can help you?"

"I think, for now, just believing me will help until we can figure out what else to do."

"Believing your—" Ruby omitted the words *near-death*, as they seemed to rile Carrie-Ann "—experience?"

"No, believing me when I tell you I shouldn't be here, that I should be dead. And that the clairvoyant, Leon Vasilescu, sensed that straightaway. It was why he couldn't read my palms, couldn't tell me about my future, because I don't have one. None at all."

* * *

Only later that evening, with Cash in bed already and Hendrix beside her on the sofa, not crying for once but lying there gurgling, could Ruby fully process all that had happened that day, principally what Carrie-Ann Kendall had said.

The woman was, in her own opinion, the walking dead, or a version thereof. And Theo believed that to be the case too, her opinion being that the woman was somewhere in between. That she was caught there.

Ruby turned to Hendrix and studied him, thoughts continuing to rumble through her head. New life was such a miracle. The hope of it, the sheer enormity of potential. But death, in its own way, was a miracle too, the shedding of one stage and the embracing of another. Nothing lasted forever despite how much you wanted it to. Only the soul. There was a theory expounded by those in the paranormal world that each of us was born with an allotted time, what Theo, with her trademark humour, called a 'sell-by date'. If Carrie-Ann was to be believed, it was proving true. She'd not only had her time but *exceeded* it, and Leon Vasilescu had realised. From the moment he'd set eyes on her.

Mad. Quite mad. But if Theo was convinced…

Ruby leant into the sofa, praying Hendrix would carry on cooing rather than crying. God, she loved him when he was like this, could just sit and watch him all night long, adoring the sweet roundness of his cheeks and eyes as dark as Cash's, dark hair sprouting on his head too, little tufts of it. Whatever time he'd been allotted – and she hoped it was a very, very long time – she wished for every minute to be magical, for him to know about neither hardship nor heartache, although of course he would.

With one hand on the baby's stomach, she gently rubbed it in a circular motion. So, what they knew of their client so far – and she *was* a client; they'd agreed to take her case on board – was that she'd had an accident in which she'd nearly drowned, a pocket of weather responsible for it, a freak storm conjured out of seemingly nowhere. She'd had, no matter that Carrie-Ann herself had denied this, a near-death experience. Her spirit had left her body, and she had heard voices – familiar voices – calling to her, welcoming her, but she'd fought against them. She'd done so because she was worried about her friends and the grief and the guilt her death would cause them. A nice woman, Ruby concluded, thoughtful. Perhaps…too thoughtful.

Fast forward a few months and she'd gone to see a clairvoyant, whose reaction, to Carrie-Ann's mind, although rather alarming, was spot on. *'You shouldn't be here.'*

The trip to Brighton's pier for Debbie's hen do had been in September. The accident had taken place the previous spring.

"Why has it taken you this long to seek help?" Ruby had asked.

The answer was a simple one. "Because I didn't want it to be true."

The bleakness in Carrie-Ann's voice, her heartbreak, couldn't be disguised. Ruby had felt like her own heart was breaking to hear it.

Carrie-Ann had then elaborated. "After the accident, I didn't feel the way I used to. I know things like that can take a long time to get over, but this was different." She'd raised a hand and tapped at her chest. "Even before Vasilescu said what he said, I didn't feel like I belonged anymore, and I was…sluggish. To move felt like wading through mud. Even now, it requires effort. It's so…tiring. Also, look at my skin, my complexion."

Ruby had leant forward.

"See how grey I am?"

Ruby wouldn't exactly describe it as grey, but there was very little colour to it.

"And my eyes, they used to be such a bright blue, so bright that people would comment. Now they get duller by the day."

The eyes were something Theo had commented on, and, yes, they lacked any spark. The last thing Carrie-Ann had pointed out was her hair.

"It keeps falling out, in handfuls sometimes, when I'm in the shower and washing it. My hair was a vanity of mine. It used to be thick, luxuriant."

"Have you always been…slim?" asked Ruby, her eyes briefly travelling over the woman's body.

Carrie-Ann shook her head. "Not really, not like this. I've been losing weight, although it seems to have stabilized now. And before you ask, because I know you will, I don't have any underlying health conditions. I've been to the doctor, had a full-on check, blood tests, the lot. There's nothing wrong with me, except…"

Her voice had trailed off, but it didn't matter. Ruby got the gist.

Regarding how they could help her, the clairvoyant was a natural starting point. They would need to speak to him, try to get him to explain to them the reason for his reaction. Other than that…well, it was something to discuss with Ness and Corinna too, get their take on it. Monday morning they'd convene in the attic at Sun Street, Cash busy on Sunday putting shelves up, transforming it into a more work-like space.

The attic… That was of course another thing to investigate – Gran's attic, and the blanket box to see what it contained.

"Oh no, no, don't do that again, don't start crying."

A blissful period of calm had come to an end. As she picked up Hendrix to soothe him, she couldn't help but think how fleeting they always were.

Chapter Four

"OH, hi, Ness. You on your way to mine?"

A chilly Monday had dawned, the radiators in the house in Sun Street not quite up to speed yet, causing Ruby to shiver a little as she'd reached for her phone.

She was in the kitchen again, the baby on her hip, the phone on loudspeaker. Having fed the baby, she was trying single-handedly to butter a slice of toast as the clock rapidly counted down the minutes to ten o' clock, when the team would arrive.

"Change of plan, I'm afraid," Ness answered.

"Oh? Something come up?"

"I'm afraid so. For all of us."

The piece of toast now erratically buttered, Ruby took a bite. "What do you mean?"

"I had a phone call this morning. It's a bit of an emergency, I'm afraid. Some strange happenings at a house in Poynings, and it seems to be coming to a head. I've notified Theo and Corinna, and they're on their way. Can you make it too? Sorry for the short notice."

All four of the team fielded calls to Psychic Surveys now, not just Ruby, and a situation like this was sometimes the result. With the phone still on loudspeaker, she glanced at Hendrix, then towards the front room, where Cash was working on his latest IT project. Would he watch him for a couple of hours, even though, strictly speaking, it was her turn? She bit down on her lip before answering. "Give me the address, and I'll meet you there."

Ten minutes later and she was in her car, embarking on the short journey to Poynings. She winced slightly as she remembered Cash's face when she'd asked him to look after Hendrix, how torn he was. He had no problem with looking after his son, that wasn't the issue, he relished every moment, but he was up against a deadline.

"I won't be long," she'd promised. "It's just an initial survey, so a couple of hours max. And…you know…he might sleep." God knows he hadn't through the night.

She tried not to think of her job as more important than his – certainly, she didn't earn as much at it – but, she had to confess, she *did* think it was more important. Deep down. A grounded spirit usually meant a distressed spirit, and that had to be addressed. Okay, she could let the other three members of the team sort this case out, they did work separately on occasion, but from the little Ness had told her, this sounded like quite an extreme case, and four psychics were better than two or three. They'd have more of an impact. After sussing the case out, they could all head back to Ruby's to discuss the more unusual case that had landed in their laps.

First, though – and it was with excitement that Ruby thought this – there was the Poynings case to deal with. Excitement because she was following her vocation.

"Oh, there you are!"

As she drove, Jed materialised in the front seat, not staring at her but out the windscreen, his tail wagging, excited too.

Ruby had a good feeling in her bones about this one, a feeling of success.

Corinna, Theo and Ness were already parked outside the house that Ness had got the call from, two of them having hitched a ride together and Ness having brought her own car. Parking alongside them, Ruby climbed out of the Ford with Jed at her heels.

"A cold morning," Theo said, Corinna stamping her feet on the ground to prove it.

Ruby smiled to see them all – the team, complete. With Jed too. God, she was glad to be a part of it, couldn't believe she'd once entertained the idea of walking away from Psychic Surveys for good, turning her back on her own business, on these people, even. What a dark, dark tunnel that would have led her down, one with no light at the end.

"So, what have we got here?" Ruby said, addressing Ness.

"Poltergeist activity, it would seem—"

"To the untrained eye," Theo interrupted.

Ness glanced haughtily at Theo, not caring for her behaviour. "As I was saying," she continued, "*alleged* poltergeist activity: doors slamming, items being lifted and hovering midair, also being projected, furniture moving, the usual thing."

"Any teenager in residence?" Corinna asked, her green eyes sparkling.

"Actually, no," Ness replied, "not this time. It's a couple, Mr and Mrs Masters. From the sound of Mrs Masters on the phone, she's not young either, more middle-aged."

"And they called just this morning?" Ruby double-checked.

"That's right. They'd heard about us via word of mouth and found our details on the Net. The events they've been experiencing have gone on for some time, about four or five months, but after the supposed entity smashed a particularly precious piece of china, the wife's decided she's had enough."

"And the husband?" enquired Theo.

"She didn't say. But my feelings are he's a bit of a sceptic."

"Oh joy," muttered Theo. "How I love a sceptic. At least proving them wrong."

Ruby grinned. "Best crack on."

Ness led the way, down a long winding path in a well-kept garden that Ruby imagined would look glorious in spring when tulips and daffodils were in bloom.

Rather than a doorbell, there was an iron knocker, which Ness rapped against the wood. The door opened a moment or two later.

Mrs Masters was indeed middle-aged, a small, neat woman with hair that might have blazed as red as Corinna's once but was now gentler. The look on her face on seeing them was one of utter relief as she ushered them inside.

"Do you know," she said, indicating for them to go straight through to the kitchen, "I had no idea what the hell I'd let myself in for, who the hell was going to turn up on my doorstep. Whether Noel was right all along. But...well, it's marvellous you're here. Thank you. Thank you so much. All that's happening, it's sending me mad, quite mad."

In a large, airy kitchen Noel Masters was waiting, looking less relieved to see them. Dark-haired and large in stature, there was an undisguised wariness in his eyes.

"Morning," he said with a sigh, clearly champing at the bit to add more but likely having been warned on pain of death by Mrs Masters to keep his mouth closed. Jed took one look at him and promptly disappeared. He was clearly unimpressed too.

Mrs Masters asked them to sit and then set the kettle to boil, several china coffee cups already laid out. "You'll want to know the whole story," she continued whilst she busied herself, "although, to be fair, I don't know where to start. Not exactly. We love this house, don't we, Noel? Been here a year now, love the village too. We don't want to leave, but…well, we want *you* to make whatever else is here leave. I know of someone who's used your service, a friend of a friend, really, but word filters down, and they were very impressed. The testimonials on your website are impressive too. If they're real."

"Oh, they're real," Ruby assured her, not begrudging the comment at all. After all, she'd wondered the same thing about Leon Vasilescu – was *still* wondering.

At last the coffee was brought over, a cafetière, and the team told to help themselves. Mrs Masters sat, as did her husband.

"The name's Susan, by the way. No need to keep calling me Mrs Masters. Not now we're—" she gave a slight laugh "—working together."

Both Theo and Ness had been glancing around as Susan spoke, trying to tune in, glean what they could.

Ruby had been doing the same, and most likely Corinna. There was something in the air, a heaviness despite so much bright white décor.

Susan began to explain, basically repeating all that Ness had already told them, apart from one detail. "We have an attic room. That's where the activity normally takes place."

"The attic?" repeated Ruby, perhaps a little too robustly.

Susan stared at her. "I know it's clichéd—"

"Oh no, no, it's not that," Ruby replied. "Is activity confined to the attic?"

Susan looked at Noel, who just shrugged. "Yes," she answered. "It seems to be."

"What was this house before?" Theo's expression was curious.

"Before? Um...well, it was built in 1864—"

"Sixty-five," corrected Noel.

Again, Susan laughed. More of a brittle sound this time. "Ever the pedant," she said with a raise of her eyebrows.

Noel, who was frowning anyway, frowned some more.

"Look," he said, speaking more than two words at last, "there's no great history attached to this house. It's just a family home, okay? It hasn't been a rectory, a school, or the bloody post office. Just a home. *My* home."

"Okay," said Ruby. "Fair enough."

"And it's her that sees and hears stuff more than me."

"Her?" Theo repeated, sarcasm in her voice, perhaps for the disparaging way in which he'd used the term.

More of an atmosphere building, Ruby started to explain the way Psychic Surveys worked, that they would walk round the house and investigate each room, see what they could sense before moving up towards the attic. She was little more than halfway through her spiel when Noel Masters scraped his chair back against the lino and stood.

"I'm off," he declared.

Susan stood too. "Where are you off to? I thought we agreed—"

"This"—with a sweep of his hand, he encompassed all of them—"is women's work. I've better things to do with my time, I'm afraid."

"Noel!" There was a plea in Susan's voice, one he ignored. "This is unfair. This…problem, it affects us both."

"Do you know what?" As if a switch had flicked in Noel, he immediately ignited in anger. "If word gets out in the village who these people are, and I don't care how normal they look, they'll think we're mad, do you know that? This is a house, Susan. Pure and simple. We came here for a fresh start. Now that the kids have grown. And it's been a bloody nightmare ever since!"

Before Ruby or any of the team could intervene, before Noel could show his displeasure further by striding from the room, a loud crash resounded through the house, like that of a plate hurled across a room. An attic room.

"Oh my!" Susan exclaimed.

"For God's sake," Noel swore. "This is…" He shook his head, refusing to say exactly what 'this' was before indeed leaving the room. "Call me when this is over," he shouted before progressing to the front door, opening it and slamming it behind him.

Ness also rose from her chair. "Susan, are you okay?"

"What? Yes. Yes, I'm fine. Thank you. Sorry. About him. I'm so sorry."

Ruby rose too. "Do you still want us to go ahead with the survey?"

The woman had lowered her eyes, but now she raised them. "Oh yes! Definitely. It's my money I'm using, so he can't complain."

Whilst Ruby doubted that, she nodded, Corinna and Theo also on their feet now.

"Would you like to stay here in the kitchen whilst we carry on?" asked Ruby.

"Oh no! I'd like to accompany you if I may."

Theo shrugged. "Sure."

Noel and Susan's home was immaculate. In the living room, cushions were placed just so, as were ornaments on shelves and the mantelpiece. The carpet beneath them was gorgeous, cream in colour and thick piled, the kind you could sink your feet into. Ruby would love a carpet like this, but with Hendrix now in residence, it was indeed the kind of flooring that would have to wait. Just a few feet in front of her was a framed picture, three children in it, taken during teenage years. The kids seemed happy, relaxed, their arms around each other's shoulders, but of Noel and Susan together, there were no photographs at all.

Ruby stood, absorbing the atmosphere. There was a heaviness for sure, but more residual than intelligent. She glanced at her colleagues and then at Susan, noted the woman's expression, her expectancy. With her present it was hard to say what was on her mind, but Ruby projected a word that had sprung to mind, hoping one of her colleagues would catch it. *Sterile.*

It was Ness who locked eyes with her and nodded.

Also downstairs was a second living room – an office, Susan explained, used by Noel, who was an accountant.

"That figures," Ruby heard Theo mutter, a slight grin on her face.

The office was almost as large as the living room, clearly much occupied, more so than the other rooms, various papers dotted all over the desk.

After the downstairs accommodation, they climbed the steps to the next floor. The house comprised three bedrooms, more neat, sterile environments, in particular the master bedroom. Everything was so artfully arranged but…uptight, somehow, restrained, the counterpane on the bed without a crease on it.

Last but not least was the attic, up another flight of stairs, Ruby wondering what she might find there. Aside from the noise they'd heard earlier, all had been quiet since Noel had left, something that didn't entirely surprise her…

"Shall I go first?" Susan asked.

"If you like," Ruby replied.

They filed upwards, Susan at the helm, opening the door then standing aside.

Sure enough, on the floor was what looked like a jug, now in pieces.

"Oh dear," said Susan, hurrying towards it.

The first thing Ruby noticed about the attic was how small a space it was, certainly compared to Noel's office downstairs. Also, that it was quite untidy – scrub that, *very* untidy, crammed as it was with knickknacks, furniture, books and other items.

Perhaps noticing the surprised expressions on their faces, Susan immediately started to fuss, picking up larger pieces of the smashed jug and placing them on the table.

"This is your space?" Ness checked. "Entirely?"

"It is, it is. Noel has his, and I have mine. And voila! This is it."

An overstuffed, cramped attic.

Susan bent again to pick up more pieces of the jug. "This was a wedding gift," she explained. "From his mother."

Theo raised an eyebrow.

"Do you...feel anything?" Susan wanted to know. "A ghostly presence."

Corinna had her eyes closed and was tuning in, Ruby about to do the same when Theo spoke. "Are you happily married, Susan?"

For a moment there was silence – Ruby unable to believe how bluntly Theo had asked such a personal question, and Susan clearly taken aback too.

"I really don't see what that has to do—"

"Because I don't think you are."

"Theo!" It was Ness rebuking her rather than Susan. "What are you doing?"

"I have to say, this isn't at all what I was expecting," Susan added, still flustered.

"I'm sorry," Ruby began, but Theo cut in again.

"There's no ghostly presence here, but what there is, in this room, is a lot of energy, a lot of anger and resentment, feelings that are otherwise kept repressed."

"Theo!" Ness tried harder to get her colleague's attention, but Theo was having none of it. Nor, it seemed, was Corinna.

"She's right," the youngest of the Psychic Surveys team said, having opened her eyes. "You've heard of the term *poltergeist*, Susan?"

"Poltergeist?" Susan repeated, one hand at her throat, rubbing at the skin there. "Well, yes, I have. That's what I thought this might be."

Theo elaborated further. "A poltergeist is a German term for a noisy ghost, usually held responsible for disturbances such as the kind you've mentioned – the slamming of doors, objects being moved, being thrown, even. But there's a theory, and it seems to hold some weight, that a poltergeist is actually a physical representation of the energy held within a person. It has built up to such an extent that it demands an outlet. In finding that outlet, it can affect the physical environment and produce certain…phenomena." Having delivered this explanation, Theo eyed the broken jug. "Interesting that it was that piece which was hurled. A piece given to you by your husband's mother."

"Ridiculous!" was Susan's retort. "I loved that jug! It was very expensive, I'll have you know. And I love my husband…the life we've forged. A good life. We've been blessed with three healthy children, all of whom have good careers, and we're well-off too; we want for nothing. We're happy. We are! Very happy! I'm not responsible for…for *this*!"

No sooner had she uttered the last word than another object, on a shelf close to where Ness was standing, began to rattle and shake.

Theo's eyes widening, she yelled, "Duck!"

All of them did. The object, a candlestick, pewter and therefore heavy, shot upwards before flying across the room, straight over Ruby's head.

"Shit!" said Ruby, realising how much that would have hurt had Theo not shouted her timely warning.

Theo was furious. She turned to Susan and issued another caution. "Stop this, right now. And no, don't bother to deny it. You are responsible for what's happening. Entirely."

Susan was red-faced with anger too, and Ruby looked around her, wondering what was going to come hurtling their way next – there was no end of ammunition.

"Look, perhaps we can get out of here, go downstairs and discuss this," she suggested, but neither Theo nor Susan moved, nor even glanced her way. Ruby couldn't believe it; the pair were having a standoff! And, yes, on another shelf, another item was shaking, an ashtray that looked to be made of marble. It lifted off the shelf, not shooting upwards this time but levitating bit by threatening bit.

"Theo! Susan!" Ruby tried again, was about to force the issue when Ness stayed her.

"Wait," she whispered.

With one eye on the ashtray and one eye on the warring pair, Ruby held her breath, saw Corinna doing the same, although a smile was playing around Corinna's lips, one that showed she had supreme confidence in Theo and what she was doing.

More silence, and Ruby's nerves stretched to breaking point.

A crash resounded, the ashtray not flying forwards but smashing back down on the shelf.

"That was another fucking wedding present," Susan said before bursting into tears.

Chapter Five

IN the comfort of another attic, Ruby's own in Sun Street, the Psychic Surveys team gathered around Ruby's desk, mulling over what had happened that morning.

"It was a risk I took, admitted," Theo said, her cheeks as pink as her hair from the exertion of climbing yet more flights of stairs. "But we had to make her see the truth of what was going on, acknowledge how deeply unhappy she was."

"Noel Masters is in for a shock when he finally comes home," Corinna said, grinning.

Ness was smiling too. "Yes, he will be. But perhaps there'll be relief too. You can't be happy on your own in a marriage; it does take two. And, as Theo says, Susan was *very* unhappy. She kept up a front, tried to control all other areas of her life, her spotlessly clean house another physical representation of that, but the heart…well, the heart wants what it wants. In this case, an escape. As painful as it will be for them to part, it will also give them the opportunity to start living again, hopefully a life with a bit more contentment."

"When one door closes," Ruby mused.

"Another one slams in your face," Theo finished, causing them all to laugh. "So," she continued, "after wrecking a marriage this morning, it's on to our next case. Rather a peculiar one, with…um…sadly, no opportunity for a better future."

Ness frowned. "What on earth are you talking about?"

"Ruby," Theo said, "care to do the honours?"

Ruby shifted in her seat. "Right, well, where to start? That's the question."

Both Ness and Corinna also shuffled in their seats, as if in anticipation of what Ruby was going to say. And well they might because, if Carrie-Ann was to be wholly believed, then what Theo had just said was correct – there'd be no grabbing a second chance by the scruff of the neck for her. When the team had left the Masters', after Susan had finally faced up to the truth of her marriage and how the bitterness had been building inside her and manifesting, she'd looked different – younger. There was a light in her eyes that hadn't been there before. The truth could be painful, but it could also set you free. With Carrie-Ann, it could set her free too, certainly, but she was thirty-four, *only* thirty-four. Right now, though, wasn't time to question the big mysteries, just explain the case to her colleagues.

Fifteen minutes later and Ruby was done, she and Theo sitting back in their chairs, waiting for Ness's and Corinna's reactions.

"Well," Ness said finally. "This is most unusual."

"Are you sure she's not…" Corinna began, her voice drifting off as her cheeks flushed.

"Delusional?" queried Theo. "Is that what you were going to say?"

Corinna nodded. "Well, you know, she could be.

56

Just a little bit."

Theo denied it. "She's the sanest young lady I've ever met. I consider myself an excellent judge of character, and to that end I'd say she was no liar. She's telling the truth."

Ruby agreed. "I'm with Theo on this one."

Corinna was still gobsmacked. "So, let me get this straight. She's alive, but she should be dead. Her body's still functioning but only just. It's catching up with the truth, even though her mind is taking its time. She's…fading."

"That's right," said Ruby, "she is. Week by week, day by day."

Ness exhaled. "And what are we supposed to do about it? How can we help her?"

"Surely you don't think we should kill her!" How wide Corinna's eyes were.

Theo guffawed. "No, dear! Of course not! We might be guilty of wrecking a long-term marriage, but murderers we are not."

"Then how?" Corinna urged.

"We help her to understand her situation better." Theo paused briefly to give the question some thought. "She's defied her fate, and some think that's a dangerous thing to do because it upsets the equilibrium, the precarious balance of things, hence the alarm in the voices on the other side when Carrie-Ann started to backtrack, and Leon Vasilescu's alarm too, perhaps. Basically, what was meant to be hasn't transpired. Although, what also needs to be considered is whether it was *truly* meant. If so…if so…"

"If so, what?" Ness challenged.

"Then I guess we help her to understand her situation, that's all. Help ourselves understand, too, the continuing wonders of the paranormal world."

"Do you think it's a unique case?" Ruby asked.

"That would need to be researched," Theo answered, "but certainly I've never come across something like this before. Ness, have you?"

There was a hint of the old Ness as she replied, a sombreness about her. "Only anecdotally on the radio once, decades ago, but no, not really."

Ruby bit her lip. "It could be we're out of our depth with this one."

"Out of our depth?" It was Theo challenging now. "Even if that were so, where does that leave poor Carrie-Ann?"

"It's just...we're helping her to die, essentially," Ruby protested. If she felt uncomfortable with that, she could see by their faces that Ness and Corinna did too.

"She's right," Ness interjected. "We usually deal with either the living or the dead; there are clear-cut boundaries. With Carrie-Ann, those boundaries have become blurred."

Theo sat back in her chair. "What if fate, or whatever you prefer to call it, has got itself all mixed up, had a blip, so to speak, and Carrie-Ann is the end result? What if this is actually what fate has decided for her – she *is* still meant to be here, for a certain period of time, for a reason? She's meant to do something...*meaningful* before the Grim Reaper finally has his way."

"She may have already done that something, that unfinished business or whatever it is," Corinna pointed out. "This happened last spring, remember."

Theo nodded. "Indeed. She may well have, but…one thing we can ask her to do is map out her life post-accident, try to recall every interaction, no matter how small, how insignificant, to see if she knows of any positive impact she's had."

"Bit of a tall order," Ness declared.

"It is," agreed Theo, "and heaven knows I've no idea what went on yesterday with my own life, let alone the week before or any time prior to that, but she's far younger. She should manage well enough. It's something constructive for her to do, at any rate."

"Does she work?" Corinna asked.

"Not since the accident, apparently," Ruby told her. "She was in admin at Southern Water, but she hasn't felt able to return since. I think she's on disability."

"Poor thing." Corinna's voice was sombre too. "When do we get to meet her?"

"This week, if that's okay? I'll make an appointment."

"We can meet at mine again," Theo offered before adding, "Fewer steps."

"Absolutely," replied Ruby. "Another thing we have to do is check out the clairvoyant."

"Leon Vasilescu," mused Theo. "Do you think that's his real name?"

"It's his working name," Ruby answered. "And the only one we have."

Ness shrugged. "That should be easy enough to do. He works on Brighton Pier?"

"That's right."

"In winter as well as summer?"

"Not sure," Ruby admitted.

Corinna waved her mobile. "Have you googled him yet?"

"I've googled his name, but that's all. Yesterday was frantic with the baby."

Corinna sighed. "Ah, I can't wait to give him a squeeze when we go back downstairs."

"Only if he's awake," Ruby replied. "Believe me, if he's asleep, he's best left that way!"

"What did you find when you googled his name?" Ness was not so easily sidetracked.

"I'll show you," said Ruby, tapping on the keyboard, then manoeuvring the screen so that the other three could see it.

Variations on Vasilescu's name came up but none that were easily attributed to a clairvoyant who worked on Brighton Pier.

"Oh," Corinna said, "not very helpful."

They then looked at Brighton Pier's website. Bright, lively and modern, as you'd expect, but there was nothing about a resident clairvoyant.

"Odd," murmured Ness. "Fortune-tellers are really quite the thing in a seaside town. I'd have thought there'd be something on there, if not about him, then about them in general. Try googling *Brighton clairvoyants* instead."

Ruby did. Several came up, but none with his name. Checking out their profiles, they were mainly women. One was a man, though, a David Daynes.

Theo shook her head when Corinna mentioned him. "Not him. I know David. Thoroughly nice chap, not one ounce of psychic talent, though."

"Oh," Corinna replied, deflated.

"We're going to need to visit the pier," decided Ruby. "Go straight to source."

"Today?" said Theo.

"Uh-huh."

"So sorry, love, I can't," she continued. "My grandchildren are visiting this afternoon."

"No worries," Ruby said, glancing at Corinna, who was also shaking her head.

"You know what? I can't go this afternoon either. I've got another flat in Brighton to view with Presley. From the details, it looks amazing, really quirky."

"That's great!" enthused Ruby. Presley was Cash's older brother, and he and Corinna had been a couple for a while now.

"Oh dear," lamented Ness.

"Ness, what is it?" asked Ruby.

"I've a private client coming to my home for some chakra healing. I can always try to rearrange, though."

Before Ruby could respond, an almighty cry tore through the house.

"Hendrix is awake!" Corinna said, clapping her hands in glee.

"Glad to see someone's excited about that." Ruby sighed and stood up. "Right, that settles it. The baby's awake and needs some fresh air. And what could be better than sea air? I'll take him to the pier; maybe Cash will come with me. But, Theo, could you phone Carrie-Ann, ask her to do what you suggested, map out her life since the accident, and also arrange a time that Ness and Corinna could meet her too?"

"Absolutely, dear girl," said Theo, huffing and puffing as she rose from her chair.

Ruby also clapped her hands.

"That's sorted, then. Here we go again, eh?"

Chapter Six

"RUBY, seriously? I've got a deadline on this."

"Oh, Cash, come on. You know you can't resist a trip to the pier."

"I can in January!"

"But Hendrix will love it."

"At three months old? I doubt whether he'd give a damn."

"Cash, please! Come with us. You can work when we get back. We make our own hours, remember? Such is the beauty of being self-employed."

Cash's shoulders slumped. "Oh, for goodness' sake."

"Look, I've tried ringing the number for the pier. It goes straight to answer machine."

"So, if the mountain won't come to Mohammed…"

"That's right. We go to the mountain."

Whilst Ruby cradled Hendrix, Cash contemplated further.

"Is the ghost train open?"

"No idea."

"The helter-skelter?"

"Not sure about that either."

"The teacups?"

"Could be."

"The burger stall at least?"

"Definitely."

"In that case, you're buying. And on the way, explain this latest case to me again because, I don't know about you, but it's doing my head in trying to work it all out."

"I will, although don't worry your poor fevered brow about it too much, okay? This is my domain. IT is yours, which is something I can't get my head around either."

After a couple of abortive attempts to leave the house – Hendrix had vomited on the first occasion, then explosively overfilled his nappy on the other – they were on their way, driving into Brighton, the boot of the Ford stuffed with the baby paraphernalia that accompanied them everywhere.

Even Jed had come along for the ride, on the back seat beside Hendrix, just...staring at him as the baby continued to fuss and squirm and yell. She'd heard that some children loved the soothing motion of cars. Hendrix wasn't one of them.

"Remember the days when we could just race out the house, you and me, drop everything and be gone within a couple of minutes?" Cash said, still ruminating on how long it had taken them to leave. "Wonder if that'll ever be the case again."

"Of course it will. Babies grow."

"But if we have more babies?"

"Hey, back up a bit. I'm fine with just the one, thanks."

In the passenger seat, Cash turned to face her. "You don't want a whole football team?"

"Do you?"

He actually looked tired today, eyes slightly puffy

and his skin, a few shades darker than hers courtesy of his Jamaican heritage, with a sallow tinge to it. "You bet," he said, his smile becoming a grin. "I love having a family. It's brilliant, isn't it?"

"It is." Ruby smiled too, although not as widely. It *was* amazing to have created this family of theirs, wonderful, surprising and magical. But families, as she knew well enough, could be a curse as well as a blessing. What was in that blanket box in the far corner of the attic? When would she get a chance to go back to Hastings and find out? That was next on her list of priorities. It had to be. Soon the house would no longer be theirs, and if it held any secrets, it would keep them.

With that in mind, she asked Cash what his plans were that week.

"My plans? Work, work and more work. What about you?"

"Work," she replied, adding, "And childcare," when Hendrix emitted a scream. She sighed. "I think we might have to pay for childcare, you know."

"Seriously? What with? All our money's gone on the house. There's nothing left."

"We'll have the money from Gran's house soon," she pointed out.

"Not to waste on childcare!"

If he was getting riled, she was too. "It's not a waste! It's a necessity!"

Still, he wasn't having it. "It's working out, isn't it? And occasionally our mums can help out, but...he's our responsibility. I don't want him going to a nursery or a nanny."

"Cash—"

"Ruby, for now, whilst he's still so little, let's sort it out between ourselves, okay?" He glanced in the rearview mirror. "We've got this, we have. Being able to work around Hendrix is another advantage of being self-employed, right?"

"Okay," Ruby complied. "We'll leave it as it is. For now."

Cash nodded, satisfied, Brighton coming into sight, one long straight road leading all the way through town to the seafront.

"Breaking him in young, eh?" he quipped after a short while.

"What do you mean?"

"Well, he's one of the team, isn't he?"

"Oh, right," Ruby replied, her heart not exactly leaping at that prospect, especially as Jed had started whining the moment Cash said it.

* * *

The pier in January was a different beast to what it was in summer. Far lonelier, like going behind the scenes of an abandoned film set. With more clement weather the crowds would rush to Brighton, to the seafront especially, and the pier, to play the slot machines, gorge on candyfloss, ride the ghost train Cash loved so much, and, of course, visit the clairvoyant to have their palms read. Right now, though, with the skies grey and the wind picking up, there was barely a soul about.

"It doesn't look promising, does it?" Cash observed.

"Still worth a shot," insisted Ruby. "Besides, as I was saying to the team, the sea air is great for Hendrix. Look,

I think he's settling."

"The sea air would knock anyone out." Cash yawned. "You sure he's warm enough?"

"He should be. You've dressed him as though he's heading for a polar expedition, not Brighton Pier!"

"Same thing sometimes, don't you think?"

Ruby smiled. "Maybe."

With wooden slats beneath their feet now rather than the hard surface of the seafront, Ruby gazed down between the cracks, at waves crashing against the pier's rusted cast-iron legs. Beside them trotted Jed, occasionally running ahead but quickly returning to Ruby's side. It only took a couple of minutes for the gypsy caravan to come into sight, situated just to the left of the amusement arcade. The latter was open; the former had a 'Closed' sign in the window. The breeze whipped round Ruby's head as she approached, her hair getting in her eyes, temporarily blinding her.

No clairvoyant in residence, nor any signage advertising one.

"Hey, mate," Cash said, addressing a young man, tall and slim and dressed in a red sweatshirt with the pier logo in one corner. "Do you work here?"

The man nodded as he came to a halt. "Yep. Can I help you?"

Cash thumbed towards the caravan. "Just wondering about the clairvoyant. Doesn't work in winter, does he?"

"No, mate. Not much call for it."

"Shame," Cash said as Ruby came to stand by his side. "He was really good. You know…um…what's his name again, Ruby?"

"Leon," she answered, studying the young man in

front of her and the bemusement in his eyes, "Leon Vasilescu. But then you probably know that."

The man shrugged. "Haven't got a clue, actually, just started working here, and I'm usually in there"—he thumbed at the amusement arcade—"so, yeah, don't know."

"Is there someone who does?" Ruby pressed. "A manager?"

"Yeah, yeah, Phil's around somewhere."

Without explaining where that somewhere was, the man turned to go.

"Shit!" Ruby swore under her breath, causing Cash to lay his hand on her arm.

"Wait with Hendrix. I'll find Phil. He must be in the arcade. Everywhere else is dead."

A minute or so later and Cash had disappeared through the arcade doors, the less-than-helpful man having been swallowed up by them too.

The baby squirming now and then but otherwise quiet enough, she wheeled him back towards the caravan, Jed already having bounded ahead to sit outside it, his head to one side as if listening to something. The roar of the sea? Or an echo from the past.

"What is it, boy?" she asked. "What's wrong?"

He whined but otherwise kept staring outwards. Making sure the brake on the buggy was on, testing it twice, Ruby reached out and laid her hands on the caravan's wooden slats, having also made sure there was no one in the immediate vicinity to question what she was doing or to raise an eyebrow. January had its good points; she would have looked a fool doing this if anyone saw. With her eyes closed, she tuned in.

All she could see was the darkness behind her lids. All she could hear was the baby continuing to fuss, emitting those little noises she regarded as warning signs, the ones that proceeded a full-on bellow. She had to be quick about this so she could tend to him again, roll his buggy backwards and forwards, get him to settle properly.

Come on, come on, is there anything to sense here?

Still nothing, just unremitting darkness, the world having vanished with an action as simple as the closing of the eyes. A tunnel of darkness, which she travelled further down.

Who are you, Leon Vasilescu? How did you know about Carrie-Ann? How?

No insight, nothing. Not yet.

Push yourself further, Ruby. A little bit further…

"Whoa!"

She staggered backwards a step or two, not a voluntary movement; rather, she'd been forced back, the darkness not aiding her to see but turning against her, rising up to form a wall or a wave, one which rendered her temporarily powerless, likely because she hadn't been expecting it, hadn't prepared for any kind of backlash.

A backlash? Is that what she'd experienced? She'd been trying to see, to glean what she could. Had Leon Vasilescu realised that – installed some sort of psychic security system to prevent intruders? And retaliated.

"Whoa!" she repeated, but this time under her breath, the baby screaming in earnest now as she opened her eyes and reached into the pram, patting at his chest, trying to calm him. He refused all attempts, Jed adding to the cacophony as he barked and growled, having sensed what had just happened, no doubt. A flock of seagulls circled overhead, crying out too, her head beginning to ache, feeling like it might explode. And then another sound intruded, her name being called.

"Ruby! I found Phil, found out about Leon – well, a bit, anyway. Ruby, are you okay? What's wrong with Hendrix?"

On reaching her, Cash delved into the pram, undid the straps that restrained Hendrix and picked him up. "Hey, come on, now, there's no need for that. Daddy wasn't gone long."

Ruby blinked, took a deep breath, tried to get her bearings.

"What did you find out?" she said, torn between a desire to know and a desire to put as much space between herself and the caravan as possible.

"Leon isn't Leon. His name is Dave Lane," Cash answered, still rocking Hendrix. "Leon's like his 'Madame Fortune' name."

"English, then, most likely," replied Ruby, "not Romanian or Hungarian or whatever."

Cash shook his head. "More likely Croydon. Also, he's not coming back to work on the pier, although he was due to. He'd booked the space for a good long stint."

"Why not?"

"Phil doesn't know. Only that he took off last September, vanished overnight, packed his stuff, and that was it."

"Really?"

"Really. They never heard from him again."

Chapter Seven

"DO you think he's dangerous?"

Ruby considered Theo's question before answering. "I think he's got a gift. He's not a charlatan. All those testimonials about him are correct."

"And clearly the two of you managed to connect." Ness too looked thoughtful. "At the pier, he felt you reaching out to him."

"I presume so. And if it was him, he didn't like it, not one little bit."

"He prevented you from connecting further?" Corinna checked.

"He did, but I don't know if the fact he succeeded was a true measure of his psychic ability or because I wasn't prepared for it. Next time, I will be."

"Next time?" quizzed Theo.

Ruby nodded. "Well, as the pier has long since drawn a blank with the address they had for him, it looks like reaching out is the only way I'll be able to forge a connection again. According to Phil, one of the managers, he was popular, brought in the punters. Word spread about how good he was, then his punters spent money on food, the rides and slot machines – that's how it all works. He'd been there for about three months before he hightailed it, leaving pier management very disappointed."

"And he hightailed it in September?" Ness asked.

"That's right," Ruby replied. "Mid-September, likely after Carrie-Ann and her friends were there. Oh, there's the doorbell. That must be her. Theo, shall I do the honours?"

"Please, save my old legs a trip."

The team had gathered at Theo's house, where they'd already agreed they'd host Carrie-Ann rather than in Ruby's attic office, Ness and Corinna intrigued to meet her. Prior to her turning up, Ruby had also informed them of the clairvoyant's real name: Dave Lane, a common name compared to the exotica of his alias, which might very well hamper them trying to find him, taking up time and resources. Although, strangely, when Ruby had typed *Dave Lane, Brighton* into the search bar on Facebook, not one had come up.

Ruby opened the front door. "Carrie-Ann! Hi. Come on in. The team are in the living room, waiting to meet you."

The woman had a smile on her face that tugged at the heart rather than lifted it.

"Go on through," Ruby continued, closing the door behind Carrie-Ann, unease in the pit of her stomach at how much the woman had changed since the last time she'd seen her. It had only been a couple of days ago, and yet she'd aged, her eyes more sunken than before, her cheeks hollower. Whatever had happened to her, whatever was *still* happening, was it accelerating? Death was a natural process, a timely process; how long could anyone expect to cheat it? The body would have its way even if the soul tried to defy it.

On entering the living room, on seeing the expression on Theo's face, the only other member of the Psychic Surveys team that had met Carrie-Ann up until now, Ruby knew that she was thinking the same and was also struggling to hide her surprise.

Corinna and Ness stepped forward, each of them shaking Carrie-Ann's hand before Carrie-Ann was invited to sit.

"Thanks for seeing me again," she said. "I promise I won't be so emotional this time."

"It's fine," Ruby assured her. "Here's the…um…box of tissues, just in case. Ness and Corinna have been brought up to speed with what happened to you and what you've been experiencing since your accident."

"And you believe me?" Carrie-Ann eyed both Ness and Corinna. "You don't think I'm certifiable?"

"Not at all," Ness replied. "And if we can help you, we will."

"Thank you." This time Carrie-Ann's voice was a whisper as she lowered her head, maybe in need of those tissues after all. Jed appeared, sitting at her feet, trying to offer what comfort he could. It was just a shame Carrie-Ann couldn't see him, although she shifted and looked at the spot where he was now slumbering, something Ruby noted with interest.

"Carrie-Ann." Theo's voice was very soft, very soothing, almost hypnotic. "We've been putting our heads together, thinking about your…situation." How careful she was to avoid the word *case*. "It's an unusual one, as we've said, possibly unique. I've mentioned to you already on the phone that one of the things we thought of was that you might have returned for a reason. A very good one."

"Yes, I've been thinking about that, about all the interactions I've had, as you put it. I'm trying to get my head around it, jot everything down, but could you explain again?"

"Of course, dear. You returned, you forced yourself to, not wholly because you were afraid of how upset your friends would be if your demise had indeed occurred but because you still had to impact on someone else – in a good way, I mean, a meaningful way. Unfinished business. Maybe even unfinished business that was not apparent at the time but has arisen since. It could be your higher consciousness realised this, if not fate itself. Now," Theo continued sagely, "there is a flaw in this argument if you believe souls spend only an allotted time on earth, a time span that we've perhaps chosen beforehand because, for example, we need to learn a certain lesson or repeat a certain experience. Once that lesson has been learnt or that experience completed satisfactorily, then we can fly. There's simply no further need to be here."

"Is that what you believe?" Carrie-Ann asked Theo.

"I always have," she admitted, "but you've made me, made all of us, wonder. You see, we don't doubt you; we believe what you're saying, and so that's rather thrown our beliefs into the air. However, there is such a thing as free will. You know what that is?"

"In simple terms, yes, but esoterically…"

"Okay, free will is, as the name implies, the freedom to make our own decisions, to act in a certain way. There are many paths we can follow in life laid out before us, a route map, if you will, and we stand at the helm, deciding which route to follow. I've researched various near-death experiences, for want of a better term, and so has my colleague Ness. It's an interest of ours. Ness, would you like to add something about what you've found?"

Ness nodded, smiling at Carrie-Ann before she carried on. "Regarding near-death experiences, it's often the case that people are given a choice. They cross the bridge, reach the end of the tunnel, soar upwards towards green pastures – the experience is often unique too – and once there, they want to stay but know they can also return, that they have the freedom to do that. With you, the experience seems to be a little different."

"I was told not to come back," Carrie-Ann said so quietly it was almost a whisper.

"Exactly," Ness replied. "And yet you exercised free will, and, well, here you are."

"I am, but...I don't feel I belong, not anymore. I have a roof over my head, but I'm homeless. Oh, sorry." Carrie-Ann reached for a tissue. "I said I wouldn't do this."

"It's perfectly fine," Ness said, her voice as soft as Theo's.

It took a few moments for Carrie-Ann to collect herself. "I've heard of near-death experiences," she said. "I mean, who hasn't? And after my accident, I did a bit of research into it, but there seems to be a lot of scepticism about whether it's true."

"And yet you experienced something similar in the sea." Theo wasn't posing a question, merely pointing out a fact.

"Yes, yes, I did."

Ness interjected again. "The thing is, experiences are too numerous, too detailed and too similar just to be simply dismissed as imagination. Science tends to require hard, cold facts. Spirituality, or Conceptual Science, however, won't be bound by those measures."

Whilst Carrie-Ann nodded, Theo cut to the chase. "As I said, we were wondering if your higher consciousness knew there was something that you still needed to complete, which is why we've asked you about all the interactions you've had since the accident and whether any of them seem particularly meaningful to you, besides the interaction with Leon Vasilescu, whose real name is the rather less impressive Dave Lane, by the way."

"Dave Lane?" It was this Carrie-Ann grabbed on to.

"Yes," answered Ruby. "You...don't happen to know a Dave Lane, do you?"

"What? Oh no, no, it's just...such an ordinary name, isn't it?"

"Dave Lane, the clairvoyant," Theo mused. "Doesn't really have the same ring to it."

"So he's a fake?" Hope flared in Carrie-Ann's faded eyes.

Ruby winced. She would love to tell her this was so, but if what had happened at the pier was anything to go by, Dave Lane was no fake.

Theo brought the conversation back on track. "So, you managed to do as I suggested?"

"Yes, but, to be honest, I've not had that much contact with anyone, really, since the accident. Oh, I went on the hen do. Debbie was like a dog with a bone." Again, she glanced downwards to where Jed was, Ruby growing more fascinated by this. "She wouldn't have it otherwise, but...look how that turned out. Exactly as I'd feared, to be honest, that someone would look at me, that they would...*know*."

"Did being so close to the sea make you uneasy?" Theo was curious to know.

Carrie-Ann shook her head. "No, it didn't. I visit the seafront quite a lot, actually. It's like...I'm drawn there."

There was silence, then Carrie-Ann murmured something.

"Sorry?" said Ruby, glancing at Theo, Ness and Corinna, noting the worry on their faces. "What did you say?"

Carrie-Ann lifted her head. "The weight of the soul, that's what I said."

"The weight of the soul?" Corinna questioned.

"Yes. Twenty-one grams, isn't it?"

"Well..." Theo replied, "again, another theory suggests that is indeed the case. It dates back to 1907 when an American doctor, Duncan MacDougall, professed to the world of science that the human soul had mass, and, as such, it could be weighed."

"That's it, that's right," Ness continued. "He studied a series of terminally ill patients in their last moments of life, with their permission, of course, recording various factors in minute detail, such as the loss of bodily fluids and gases at their exact time of death. He concluded that the human soul weighed three-fourths of an ounce, twenty-one grams in new money. Straightaway, there was an effort to debunk his theory, which isn't surprising. What is surprising, though, is the number of scientists who took it seriously."

"A few years after he'd expounded his theory"—warming to the subject, Theo's eyes had begun to twinkle—"he went one step further and attempted to photograph the soul as it left the body. And, by jingo, he managed it! He captured a light that, according to him, resembled that of the interstellar either in or around patients' skulls at the point of death. As I say, this all took place in the early 1900s, and MacDougall himself died in 1920. A lot of the scientists who railed against it simply waited for the theory – which had gained traction on both sides – to drop off the radar. Thing is, it never did. Instead, it caught fire, passed into popular culture. So, yes, the weight of the soul, it's a 'thing.'"

Having listened patiently to all that had been said, Carrie-Ann turned to Ruby. "You asked me whether I've always been so slim."

Ruby nodded, confused but intrigued.

"And I told you I'd lost weight after the accident, but it's since steadied."

"That's right."

"But recently there's been more change."

"Weight fluctuates—" Ruby began, but Carrie-Ann interrupted her.

"No. This is something different. I know it is. I…feel it."

"What could it be, then?" Corinna was as baffled as the rest of them.

"It's more that I'm losing my soul, bit by bit. That continuing to be here is destroying it."

* * *

Unique. Carrie-Ann Kendall's case was certainly that. What she'd said about the soul both alarming and something Ruby didn't want to believe. She was going to pursue the matter there and then – they all were, perhaps to try to reassure Carrie-Ann that what she'd said wasn't true – when they were distracted and in the mightiest of ways.

No sooner had those words left Carrie-Ann's mouth than there came a roar – not emitting from some spiritual realm, several souls having banded together to protest, screaming out that the soul cannot die, but from another room in Theo's house, her study. Hendrix was in there, previously asleep in his pram.

On hearing it, Ruby shot to her feet. "Sorry," she spluttered. "I'm so sorry about this."

Carrie-Ann was on her feet too. "There's a baby here?"

"There is," Ruby confessed. "Mine, in the other room. I had to bring him with me, no childcare. Look, do you mind? I need to see to him."

Jed had disappeared, but Ruby could hear him barking. Likely, he was in the study, having reached Hendrix before her. Turning, she hurried from the room and entered another, where sacred space was also treasured, containing only the bare necessities: a desk, a computer, a lamp, and one wall furnished with rows and rows of reference books. She was right, Jed was already there, barking, whining and wiggling his behind. In the cot was Hendrix, his face bright red and tiny fists punching at the air.

Rather than reach down and pick him up, Ruby hesitated, a wave of something sweeping over her –

despair? *Why are you so angry all the time? So restless?* Was it normal for him to be this way? Should she have him checked out by the doctor? He was like a mini ball of fury, a tornado, a tempest, one she tried over and over to placate but with limited success. He'd just fight against her, continue to punch.

As there'd been tears in Carrie-Ann's eyes, there were tears now in hers. She had to quieten him; the racket he made was ear-shattering, but still she couldn't force herself to bend over and pick him up. And she knew why. A fear of failure. A growing suspicion that she was the one making him angry, that he despised her very presence. A terrible thought, one she could never share with anyone, not even Cash. She loved this boy with all her heart. Why wouldn't he respond to that love? Why did she seem to detest it?

Shit! The tears were coming thick and fast, although, in contrast to Hendrix, they were at least silent. She had to get both Hendrix and herself under control. Sort the situation out.

"Hey, are you okay?"

From having sunk into the depths of despair, every bit as much as Hendrix seemed to have, poor Jed in just as much sorrow to witness it, Ruby gasped in surprise. Turning, she saw Carrie-Ann had come into the room.

"Oh!"

Carrie-Ann simply smiled in response, moving closer to the irate bundle.

"I had no idea your baby was here."

Ruby found her voice. "He was sleeping. I thought it'd be okay—"

"It *is* okay!" Carrie-Ann said, adding, "Do you

mind?"

"You want to pick him up? Oh yeah, sure. Go ahead."

Carrie-Ann reached into the buggy, and the moment she touched Hendrix, he calmed, the anger in him released.

"There, there," she said, murmuring those age-old words that everybody who'd ever nursed a baby employed. "It's all right. Everything's all right."

"Wow," Ruby exclaimed. "You're a natural."

"I love babies," Carrie-Ann told her, now rocking the now supremely contented Hendrix in her arms. "Would have loved to have had my own."

"Maybe you still could."

They were desperate words, hollow, Ruby wishing she could snatch them back.

"Sorry," she muttered instead.

"It's fine," Carrie-Ann said graciously.

"I wish I had your touch. It's like I…like I…" She couldn't complete the sentence.

"You're his mum. He loves you," Carrie-Ann said. "Sometimes, though, and I've seen this with my friends and their babies, the bond can be a little too intense. A little too…frightening. Perhaps that's what's at the bottom of it."

Frightened. There and then, in Theo's office, she'd been exactly that, terrified at where her thoughts had led her, anger now setting in that she'd entertained them at all. Some babies were content, others were restless. Often there was no rhyme or reason; it was just the way it was, and it would balance itself out. A restless baby might equal a happy toddler, who knew? Often in life, you couldn't have it all ways. Carrie-Ann must have noticed Ruby's continuing conflict, as with one hand she reached out.

"You're doing a great job," she insisted.

"I'm really not so sure—"

"Hey, look at me."

Ruby did as Carrie-Ann asked, tried to see beyond beleaguered blue eyes to a soul she sincerely hoped was not depleted. It didn't seem so, not right then. Carrie-Ann's body might be failing her, but what lay within was very much intact, more so than before, perhaps. With the baby in her arms, something in her shone.

"You are and will be a great mother, Ruby. Believe it."

That was all she had to do, not constantly doubt herself.

"Okay," Ruby said after a moment. "Thank you."

Carrie-Ann handed the baby over, Ruby fearing he'd start up again, but Carrie-Ann's influence lingered.

"We'd better go join the others," she said, and Carrie-Ann agreed.

The woman didn't walk to the door directly, however. She sidestepped to the right as if to avoid something, that something being Jed, who sat there wagging his tail and, unlike Ruby, not looking the least bit surprised she had done so.

Chapter Eight

HENDRIX remained calm all that day and slept a large chunk of the night too, waking a couple of times to feed but not fussing so much when Ruby returned him to his cot afterwards. That was part of the reason that when Carrie-Ann had texted her the next morning to ask if she'd like to meet, and to bring the baby with her, Ruby jumped at the chance. *Let the magic touch continue!*

They'd agreed to meet in Lewes, by the bridge over the River Ouse, heading to a nearby restaurant called Bill's for breakfast. As well as genuinely looking forward to seeing Carrie-Ann, it would give Ruby a chance to learn more about her in a more casual setting.

Whilst getting herself and Hendrix ready, Cash already downstairs in front of his computer, she called out to Jed.

"Where are you, boy? I'm going to meet that nice lady from yesterday, Carrie-Ann. Why don't you come along too? Jed, can you hear me?"

Hopefully he'd appear soon enough – ghost dogs being the type they let into restaurants – and then she could watch Carrie-Ann's reaction. She could, of course, come right out and ask her if she sensed him, but she'd rather Carrie-Ann offer the information voluntarily. If Carrie-Ann was right, and, technically speaking, she was dead or supposed to be, it'd make sense she'd be closer to the spirit world, that it would be more available to her. Acknowledging that, however, might alarm her. She might *imagine* she was seeing more than she could and not always the good stuff. It was best to let her come to terms with her newfound status as gently as possible, although, again, what she or the team planned to do about it, Ruby had no idea. As Corinna had said, no way could they assist her in completing her journey. Not that Carrie-Ann had asked, but she might…as her body failed her further.

With Hendrix now in his snowsuit, Ruby having had to fight with him to get it on, surprised at just how strong a baby of three months could be, he was now fussing and wriggling in her arms, any feeling of normality that Ruby might have experienced after a better-than-normal night's sleep vanishing. Having negotiated the somewhat steep stairs with him, she called out to Cash in the kitchen.

"I'm off now, okay? Going to see Carrie-Ann."

Whatever he was doing, he left it, entering the hallway to come and say goodbye, kissing the baby's forehead first and then hers.

"I just realised, this case, it reminds me of that horror franchise. You know the one?"

"*Final Destination*?" said Ruby, having watched one or two at Cash's insistence a year or two back. She'd regarded them as enjoyable nonsense. Now, though, she wasn't so sure. "I know what you mean, but…"

"Yeah, that's fiction. This is real life. The latter being the stranger of the two."

Ruby smiled. "Something like that."

"Do you, though, Ruby? Believe her, I mean?"

She nodded. "What I don't know is what to do about it. The rest of the team feel the same way. We've come to the conclusion that all we can do is to be there for her, to listen, try to help her understand, to see if there is a reason or if she can just...let go."

Cash sighed. "Heavy," he said.

"It is a bit, as is this baby. I need to put him in his buggy and go."

"Okay." As he gave Hendrix one last kiss, then rubbed his nose against the baby's tiny button one, Ruby felt a pang of sadness because of what she'd just said about a woman who, as far as she was concerned, was still living and breathing – but also because Cash had turned back towards the kitchen without giving her a second kiss. *Jealous now, Ruby?* No, she wasn't, but there being three of them instead of two was taking some getting used to. Everything about Hendrix was.

Before tears could prick at her eyes as they'd done yesterday in Theo's study – worse still, begin to fall – she fought once again with the baby to strap him in. Feeling hot and flustered, actually looking forward to getting outside to cool off in the January morning, she wheeled him down the narrow hallway and opened the door, calling out another goodbye.

The day was indeed a chilly one as she hurried up the hill and towards the town, a few people on the streets, hurrying just as much as she was, eager to get to wherever they were going. At the top of the high street, she now walked downhill, past the war memorial and various boutiques selling clothes, candles and books – Lewes treasure, in other words, some unusual items to be found in some of the shops, handmade by local artists.

At the bottom of the hill, entering a pedestrianised area known as Cliffe High Street, home to more generic shops like Boots, New Look and Waterstones, she continued towards the bridge. Bill's lay on the other side of it, opposite the locally revered Harvey's Brewery. Hendrix was fidgeting, her stomach was rumbling, and there was no sign of either Jed or Carrie-Ann.

As she came to a halt on the bridge, the river level high because of recent rain, she looked about her, then jumped when she heard a voice in her ear.

"There you are! Didn't you see me waving?"

Ruby turned to where Carrie-Ann had appeared, wearing a brown knee-length coat, jeans and boots, her hair tied back in a ponytail. Ruby blinked.

"You were waving to me?"

"Uh-huh, didn't you see me?"

She hadn't seen her, or anyone that remotely resembled her on the bridge. And yet…here she was. Ruby shivered and not because of the cold. *A ghost already.*

Carrie-Ann bent to look into the pram.

"Hello, little man!" she enthused, and, as he'd done the day before, Hendrix immediately quietened as he assessed the face of the woman greeting him. After a moment, his face broke into a smile, the widest Ruby had ever seen.

"How d'you do that? You just have…the most amazing effect on him."

Carrie-Ann shrugged. "No idea, to be honest. I just… It's nice he reacts that way to me. It's really very flattering. Shall we?" she continued, nodding over towards Bill's. "And it's my shout, I insist. You're not charging me for your time, which I really appreciate. It's like, I don't know, incredible to have found you, people I can actually talk to about all this."

Ruby didn't protest, felt it'd be rude to do so – and it was true, she and the team had already agreed they'd be there for Carrie-Ann but at no charge. How could they charge when they didn't know how to resolve the problem? If it pleased Carrie-Ann to buy her breakfast today, then so be it. Next time – if there was one – Ruby would buy.

Once they were seated, and after asking if it was okay, Carrie-Ann leant into the buggy and retrieved Hendrix, freeing him of his snowsuit before holding him in her arms, where he was perfectly content to be. Just as they were about to order, Jed materialized, drawn not by Carrie-Ann or Ruby's plea, perhaps, but the prospect of food. As intelligent as he was, not a superhuman but a superanimal, he still couldn't seem to fully accept that a spirit no longer consumed food and – to coin a phrase – lived in hope.

As Carrie-Ann fussed over the baby, Ruby eyed her. Had she noticed Jed appear? Right now, she'd say no, she was too occupied with Hendrix, but Ruby would monitor the situation, the memory of how Carrie-Ann had appeared on the bridge from nowhere still fresh in her mind. Just what were they dealing with here? None of them knew, including Carrie-Ann.

Eventually, with the baby now settled in her arms, even dozing, Carrie-Ann began to talk. Two coffees had been delivered whilst they waited for chefs to prepare their food.

"I've been thinking," she said, "you know, about what Theo said, all the people I've connected with since the accident, and, apart from the clairvoyant, it's my interaction with you that's been the most meaningful."

"Me?" Ruby queried.

Carrie-Ann gave a small laugh. "By you, I mean the team. Psychic Surveys. I just don't think anyone's affected me as much as you all have. Sorry, that's not much help, is it?"

"It's fine," Ruby said, smiling too. "It was a hunch, that's all."

"Something to grasp at?"

"Kind of. And something may still come to mind."

"If it does, what then?"

Unsure how to answer, Ruby looked into her eyes, saw not an emptiness but a plea. Was there any hope? That's what Carrie-Ann was wondering, and Ruby too. If only they could find the clairvoyant, speak to him, get his take on it. Although she also had to remind herself that from his reaction, he'd seemed repelled by Carrie-Ann's condition. In contrast, she had nothing but compassion for this woman, a good person, someone who'd probably never done anyone any harm, who just wanted to live life, embrace it. And then had come the accident.

"Tell me all about yourself." Ruby surprised herself as well as Carrie-Ann, perhaps, by asking. "Let's not talk about the accident, what you experienced and what we all think is going on, but about the life you had before, every bit of it."

Ruby was right. Carrie-Ann was stunned. "Every bit?

You really want to know?"

"I do, yeah, and Hendrix is asleep, so…why not?" Jed was too by now.

Carrie-Ann shifted her body slightly so that Hendrix was more comfortable, even if she wasn't, and did as Ruby asked.

Although having moved to Lewes five years back, she'd been born at the Royal Sussex County Hospital in Brighton, a town she was raised in, going to a local school there. She had a brother and a sister, but one lived in Australia now, the other in France. Both were married with kids. She had never married, although she'd had plenty of relationships, a couple of which had lasted a few years, but she'd never found the one to commit to long-term.

"I live in hope," she said, "or rather I used to. I'd have loved kids too. I mentioned that, didn't I? Yesterday? But again…not to be."

She'd enjoyed her job at Southern Water, somewhere she'd worked for many years, rising into a managerial position and making plenty of friends.

"I can't say I haven't had fun," she continued. "I have, plenty of it. Brighton's a great place to be when you're young. There's always so much going on. It's like London in miniature, don't you think? What's that saying, 'When a man is tired of London, he is tired of life.' Well, the same can be said of Brighton. Perhaps that's why people flock there!"

Whilst Carrie-Ann was talking, their food turned up, neither Jed nor Hendrix stirring. As they ate, the woman in front of Ruby – the miracle-worker, as she thought of her with regard to keeping Hendrix so content – went on to talk about her likes and dislikes, a lot of which were similar to Ruby's. She loved films, books, true crime documentaries, Indian food, Thai food and Italian. She also enjoyed walking on the rolling Downs, and the seasons too, all of them, although if she had to choose, autumn would be her favourite.

"It's the smell of bonfires, you know, and the run-up to events such as Bonfire Night in Lewes – it's amazing, isn't it? The atmosphere's always electric. I love Christmas too, not so much New Year's Eve, though; it kind of makes me sad, maybe because of the passing of time, how quickly it goes. It just…vanishes. I visit my folks regularly, at least fortnightly – they live in Reigate – and I just…try to have fun, to be thankful for what I've got because, although I may have the odd off day, as most people do, I *am* thankful. I…" From being so enthused, her voice cracked a little. "I don't want it to end, not necessarily. I'd love to go on and on, live to old age, have a cottage by the sea somewhere, maybe down in Cornwall. That's the dream, isn't it? Everyone wants to head west eventually. My friends do, anyway. But…if it has to end, it does—"

"Carrie-Ann—"

"No, it's okay, hear me out. The one thing I've learnt from my experience is that there's something other than this life. I didn't want to acknowledge it at first. To be honest, only since Leon Vasilescu have I really come to accept the truth. Before him, I tried to bury it deep, about the accident and what happened, spent so much time convincing myself it was my memory playing tricks on me, but when you know, you know, don't you?"

Ruby nodded as she bit into a corner of croissant.

How could she argue with that?

"So, yeah," Carrie-Ann continued, "I'm no longer fooling myself anymore, only my friends and family, who've all been so great, by the way, so caring, assuming I'm still traumatised by what happened to me, depressed, even. And I let them think that. For now."

"You haven't discussed what we've talked about with anyone else?" Ruby checked.

"That's right, only Psychic Surveys. And that's the way I want it to stay, just until I've got more of a handle on it. But as I was going to say, I now know there's something beyond life, that all that talk, that suspicion, that *hope* is for real. I know you know already, but it's quite the revelation for someone as ordinary as me."

"I'm ordinary too," Ruby said gently.

Carrie-Ann shook her head, the food she'd ordered – eggs and hash browns – barely touched. "You're not. You're *extraordinary*. And, again, I'm so grateful for that, for how you've treated me since I reached out. Thank you. Thank you so much."

A little abashed, Ruby was about to tell her she was glad she'd met her too, despite the circumstances, when she heard someone call her name.

She turned to the right, towards a woman who'd come to stand beside their table.

"You are Ruby Davis, aren't you?" There was excitement in the woman's eyes. "It's just, I was looking at your website only this morning. That's how I recognised you!"

"Oh...um...yes," was Ruby's stuttering reply. "Sorry...can I help you?"

"God, yes!" the woman continued to enthuse. In her

mid to late thirties, she had short brown hair, almost an urchin crop, and pale eyes. "I was going to phone you, was plucking up the courage. And then I saw you here, at Bill's of all places, and I thought, 'It's a sign!'" She glanced apologetically at Carrie-Ann. "Sorry to disturb you. I know you're eating."

"It's fine," Carrie-Ann said, "don't mind me," adding as she looked at Ruby, "I didn't know you were famous."

"What? No, no, I'm not. I… Ah, Hendrix is awake. Shall I take him from you?" Jed too had stirred and was sitting up, staring at the newcomer in a confused manner.

Before she could retrieve her baby, the woman introduced herself.

"My name's Leanne Monaghan, although call me Lea. So pleased to meet you. I…um…" She lowered her voice and leant forward. "I'd love it if you could come and check my house out for me. We're sure there's a presence there. You know, a ghost. We've only been there a few months, should have got a survey from you people before, I suppose, and I would have done had I known you existed. It's just…in the spare bedroom, there's a feeling in there. It's, like, really sad. Even the cat won't go in there. That's got to mean something, hasn't it? I don't mean come right now, but soon. Please?"

Still surprised by the intrusion, Ruby nodded. "Is tomorrow okay for an initial survey?"

"Tomorrow? Oh, that's perfect. Thank you! Thank you so much. I'll give you my mobile number and address. What time shall we say? Ten a.m.?"

"That should be fine," Ruby said, plugging her details into her phone. "I'll see you then."

The woman backtracked, still grinning widely. Ruby, however, was wincing as she returned her attention to Carrie-Ann. "I'm really not famous. That was unusual."

"I believe you," Carrie-Ann replied. "Thousands wouldn't."

Holding each other's gaze for a few seconds, they then burst out laughing. "Touché," Ruby said when she was able to.

Although breakfast was over, time spent with Carrie-Ann continued, the pair of them lingering over another coffee, the baby awake but just so content, and Ruby relishing that.

Finally, it was time to go. Ruby had admin to tend to this afternoon as well as needing to get some shopping from the nearby Tesco.

"Will we meet again?" Carrie-Ann asked.

"Of course!" Ruby answered, meaning not simply as a client but also a friend. Not only intrigued by Carrie-Ann, she also found her very likeable as a person. "Any concerns, anything, basically, that springs to mind about—" she hesitated but only briefly "—your situation, we've told you we're here for you, all of us. Also, I need to buy you breakfast in return."

Carrie-Ann smiled. "I think I'll hold you to that."

The two women rose, Carrie-Ann at last handing over the baby, who immediately started to protest. Quickly, Ruby worked to secure him in his buggy.

"Sorry," she muttered, but Carrie-Ann reiterated what she'd said before, that Ruby was doing just great.

Straightening up, Ruby watched her as she left. Again, neatly sidestepping Jed. Again, saying nothing.

Chapter Nine

SOMETIMES the whole team attended an appointment, at other times just two or three of them carried out the visit. Ruby used to go alone to some of them, but that didn't tend to happen anymore, not since their experience at Low Cottage during the previous summer, or rather Corinna's terrible experience, which she was still recovering from.

Ruby had promised Lea Monaghan she'd visit her house at ten the next morning to investigate what Lea felt was a presence in the spare bedroom there. The afternoon after meeting Carrie-Ann, she'd rung round her colleagues to see who could also make that appointment. Corinna could, the pair of them heading there now, Ruby able to leave Hendrix behind with Cash and relieved about that. He might have been supremely content in Carrie-Ann's arms, a different baby almost, but after she'd left, he'd returned to his normal self – worse, really. He'd seemed more distressed than ever.

She'd had a dreadful night with him, she and Cash – both had taken it in turns to pace the living room floor with him whilst the other grabbed some shut-eye, but whatever sleep they'd managed had been sparse, to say the least.

Still, the phenomena that Lea had described was fairly standard work, for Psychic Surveys, at any rate, and Ruby briefed Corinna as they drove to Lea's house on the western edge of Lewes. She'd also mentioned the breakfast with Carrie-Ann.

"Whoa, what a case hers is, though," Corinna said, her red curls swinging as she shook her head. "I mean, what do you make of it, Ruby? Really."

"I don't know, to be honest," Ruby admitted. "I think what's bugging me is how we help her other than just listen."

"I'm sure we'll find a way. We always do."

"Hope so," Ruby murmured, desperate for that to be true, but also for what was happening to Carrie-Ann to *not* be true, that they'd got it wrong, that somehow instinct had become skewed.

According to the satnav, Lea's house was in sight, so Ruby pulled in and parked the car. A residential area with a small green in front of it, the house looked fairly innocuous as they approached it.

Lea answered after only a couple of rings of the doorbell, every bit as eager as she'd been yesterday at Bill's. "Hi there! It's so great to see you again. Come in, go straight through to the kitchen. Would you like some coffee or tea?"

Ruby and Corinna both accepted a cup of tea, experience having taught them it was the best way to break the ice with a new client and the perfect opportunity to make a crafty initial assessment of the site with the client going about an everyday task.

It was clearly a family kitchen, but Lea was alone that morning, her husband at work and the kids at school.

"I've got my husband's blessing regarding asking you to come here," she assured them. "Like me, he thinks it's fate that I was looking at your website only that morning and then I bump into you at Bill's."

Ruby smiled, couldn't contradict her. Perhaps she had a point.

Once again, Lea described what was happening in the spare room, or rather the feeling that everyone, including the family cat, Luca, seemed to experience upon entering.

"Thing is," she continued, "we're planning on a third child, so we're going to need that bedroom soon enough." She pulled a face as she told them she expected to conceive fairly easily. "Just love kids, don't you?"

Remembering the night she'd endured, Ruby failed to nod quite as enthusiastically as she could have done.

"How old is your baby?" asked Lea. "He's gorgeous."

"Three months."

"Ah, tough times for sure, but the best too when they're little like that, unable to talk or run away from you the minute your back's turned!"

Run away from her? Funny, but she could imagine Hendrix doing just that, running and running...

"You got kids?" Lea asked Corinna.

"Heck no," Corinna said. "Too young for that."

Lea waved a hand in the air. "It's easier when you're young, though." She patted her tummy. "The body bounces back. Had my first baby in my mid-twenties, the second a couple of years later. I'll be nearly forty when I have my third, but, hey-ho, so be it. I thought I was done with having kids, to be honest, but lately there's this urge in me to have one more, before it really is too late, I guess."

Small talk over, Lea got down to the nitty-gritty.

"I'm a little bit psychic myself, I think," she announced. "You know...sensitive. My husband and kids might avoid that room, and the cat, but I've tended to go in there and sit on occasion, tuning in – that's what you call it, isn't it? To whatever haunts it."

"Yes, it is," Ruby replied, glancing briefly at Corinna and how bemused she looked. It wasn't that she doubted Lea's claim at all, more the theatrical way it had been announced.

"It's a woman," Lea said. "Not sure of her age, but something happened to her, and because of that, she can't move on. I suppose the trick is to find out what, isn't it?"

"It can be," Ruby told her. "Do you know anything of the history of this house?"

"Well, it's not that old, built in the 1930s. Not sure about the owners from way back when, but we bought it off a very nice couple who were moving up north because of work. They mentioned nothing about a presence, but then, you wouldn't, I suppose; it would put people off. Do you need to look further into the house's history, then?"

"We may do," answered Ruby, "but right now, today, it's all about performing an initial survey. We'll take a walk around the house, ending up in the affected bedroom, and, as you say, try to tune in, to see what we can sense there."

Lea sat back in her chair, a look of amazement on her face. "What a talent to have! An incredible talent, but it must also be a bit...weird at times. Unsettling."

"You know," said Ruby, glancing again at Corinna, who had also raised an eyebrow, as this type of questioning was very common on first entering a client's household, "our days can be really quite humdrum."

"Seriously?"

"Seriously. There are false alarms, people thinking they're haunted when they're not. But if it is a genuine case, then often we find the spirit is willing enough to move on. All it takes is a gentle nudge in the right direction."

"Towards the light?"

Both Corinna and Ruby nodded.

"Incredible," Lea breathed. "I don't think mine's a false alarm, though."

"Maybe not," Ruby said. "Are you...frightened sometimes by the prospect of a spirit grounded here?"

Lea shook her head, wide eyes and pixie haircut making her look more like a child than a fully grown adult. "No, not frightened as such. Well, not me or my husband, anyway. My kids aren't overjoyed, though. They get spooked."

"And it's restricted to the spare bedroom?" Corinna asked.

"It doesn't go on walkabouts, if that's what you mean."

"Good," said Ruby. "That's good. So, shall we get started?"

Lea jumped up. "Great, shall I lead the way?"

"Is it possible we could do the initial survey alone?" Ruby asked, praying the answer would be yes. "It's just that sometimes it can interfere with our ability to tune in having another person alongside us."

"Oh." How crestfallen Lea looked. "I suppose it's difficult to perform with someone breathing down your neck."

"Something like that," Corinna replied amiably.

"How will I know it's worked, though?" Lea quizzed. "There are no bumps in the night, so to speak, no…ghostly footsteps running around. Nothing like that."

"You'll know," Ruby told her. "Mainly by the change in atmosphere. It will feel different, cleansed. And, of course, Luca will also let you know by being happy to go in there again."

"I suppose. Where shall I wait?"

"In here?" suggested Ruby. "If we need you for anything, we'll let you know."

Lea nodded. "Okay. Thank you."

About to leave the kitchen, Ruby's phone rang. "Sorry," she said, reaching into her jacket pocket. "I thought I'd put it on silent. Tell you what, I'll turn it off altogether."

She did so, not even checking the screen.

"What about your phone, Corinna?" Ruby asked.

"Haven't brought it with me, so no worries there."

"Okay. Shall we?"

Corinna answered by striding ahead.

* * *

An ordinary house, an ordinary job.

When Ruby had first set foot in it, she'd felt a sadness – not hers, definitely belonging to someone else – emanating from upstairs. Not the attic, thankfully, not this time, but a bedroom there. Although, thinking of attics, she resolved again to head on over to Hastings, solve the mystery of what was in the blanket box. Strange how she was both eager to carry out that task and reticent too. But this weekend she'd do it. Without fail.

Corinna calling her name pulled her away from her thoughts, back to the confines of Lea's house rather than Gran's. "This is the bedroom she was talking about, Ruby."

Her hand on the door handle, Corinna eased it open. It was a pleasant enough room containing a single bed, a bedside table, small wardrobe, and brightly coloured rug. But, yes, there was a sense of something in there, something that deepened her sadness.

Ruby and Corinna entered the room fully, then closed the door behind them.

"Not a troublesome spirit," Corinna murmured.

"No, I get sadness but also…a gentleness. How about you?"

"Same," said Corinna. "Just trying to work out if it's residual or intelligent."

Ruby was too. Not always an easy task. Sometimes the weight of someone's emotions could so heavily permeate the air that they seemed to be all too real rather than what they actually were: a lingering echo from a time long gone, welded to the atmosphere.

Although it could sometimes feel like talking to yourself if the latter were true, Ruby went ahead and made an address.

"Hello, my name is Ruby Davis, and this is Corinna Greer. We're psychics. What that means is we're able to communicate with spirits in the material world. If there is someone here in this room, someone who feels they're stuck here, who…feels sad about that too, as well as confused, lonely and frightened, we want you to know that it's safe to let us know, to talk to us. We're here only with the intention of helping you. If this was your home once, where you lived, it isn't now. You've passed. Your true home is in the light."

Standard words. Words she said on a regular basis, sometimes day after day, certainly week after week. Words that usually had the desired effect…eventually.

She waited patiently, as did Corinna. After a few minutes, she looked at Corinna. "Anything?"

"Still working on it."

"Okay," replied Ruby, closing her eyes and opening her mind wider to what occupied this room besides them, taking care to wrap white light around herself, just in case…

In case of what?

When she'd entered this room, there'd been no unease within her. This was her job, what she did for a living, some situations proving tricky, certainly, but not this one particularly. So why the unease now? It simply wasn't justified. Yet.

"I think I'm getting something," Corinna said. "Something…strange, actually."

"Strange?"

"Yeah…I…Lea feels it's a woman here, and I got that sense too when I walked in, a female energy, a young woman in her twenties, no older than that, but…that energy seems to have changed. Become…something else. Are you picking up on it too?"

"Um…" Corinna was right, the energy within the room had changed, although why and in what way baffled Ruby. There *was* a woman here, grounded, an intelligent haunting, not residual after all. But was there also something else? Something…darker?

As soon as she thought it, it was as though an energy rushed towards her, precisely that, startling in its speed and ferocity, as if it had been caged but now found release.

"Corinna! Be careful!"

Although Ruby's concern was for her friend as well as herself, she needn't have worried about Corinna, at least. This other energy was focused, laser sharp, its target one person and one person only: herself.

Despite having put the usual protection in place, she couldn't withstand it, perhaps because the element of surprise was as strong as it was dark. She simply hadn't expected anything of this kind to happen in the bedroom of Lea Monaghan's house.

Ruby was slammed into the wall behind her, the impact forcing the breath from her body. Immediately, she tried to fill her lungs, but it was like sucking dark energy deep within her, just as Carrie-Ann would have sucked in water when drowning beneath the Devon waves.

"Ruby! Ruby!"

Corinna's panicked voice was far off, distorted.

"Shit, what the hell's going on, Ruby? I don't understand!"

That made two of them – three, actually, as Jed had now materialised, his barking as panicked as Corinna's voice.

Ruby asked the same question as Corinna, albeit silently.

What's going on? Who are you?

And what was their endgame? She was still struggling for breath, her mind as black as the energy that engulfed her.

Ruby began to drift, not her body but her mind, as if the glue that fused them together was becoming unstuck. Another person had entered the room – Lea, of course, drawn by Corinna's screaming. She added her voice to the melee.

"Christ! What's happening here? What shall I do? Call the police?"

If Ruby didn't feel half dead already, she might have laughed at that. The police would be no good in this situation. *Theo…Ness…*

They were who she needed. Corinna had to call them, tell them it was an emergency.

Oh, Corinna, I know this is scary, but stop panicking. Think! Call the others.

She could see Corinna, and Lea and Jed and…herself. And she had to admit, the situation looked scary indeed. Her feet a few inches off the floor, she was pinned to the wall, her face bright red and her green eyes bulging as though whatever held her was indeed strangling her. An invisible force, full of fury.

She was further detaching, drifting away from the bedroom, entering a long, long tunnel instead. Other voices joined those of the living, calling her name, familiar voices. One in particular. *Gran? Gran! Is it you? Are you waiting for me?*

It was her, it had to be, that soft, silvery voice of hers no longer a memory but something more solid. *Gran!* If there was joy in Ruby's voice, there wasn't in Sarah's.

Oh, Ruby, Ruby, I'm so sorry.

Why? What about?

Ruby...darling...

She wanted to drift further, she really did, all the way into Gran's arms, but other voices assailed her, just the memory of them – Cash's and her baby's voice, wailing like he did all the time but not a terrible sound, not anymore, one that was bursting with life.

I can't leave them, Gran.

Ruby...

I can't.

Fight harder.

Fight harder? Was it Gran who'd said that? Hard to tell anything anymore, what was happening, this whole situation, becoming so confused.

Fight, Ruby!

She'd been fighting with darkness all her life. How much longer could she do it?

Fight!

If it was Gran, she was right. No more drifting. This wasn't the time to give up. Her family needed her. Her baby did. *You are a great mother, Ruby.* That's what Carrie-Ann had said. And with such conviction. Ruby wanted so much for it to be true.

It's the right thing to go back?

It hadn't been for Carrie-Ann. Were there voices yelling 'no, no, no' at Ruby now that she was returning? There weren't. Just Gran's voice. Resigned. Still sorrowful.

Fight.

White light would be her saviour; it always had been, always would be.

She had to wrap it around herself, layer by thick layer, wrap it around the force that held her fast as well. *You can't kill me. It's not my time.*

It was powerful, though, determined.

But not as determined as she was, Hendrix's face appearing in the midst of that white light, his beautiful face, no longer screaming or howling but smiling, the way he'd smiled at Carrie-Ann, with pure delight in his eyes. *You are a great mother, Ruby.*

She'd prove it, she would.

Another great rushing resounded in Ruby's head, and it felt like being slammed again, this time straight back into her body.

She landed awkwardly on the floor, Jed rushing forwards, as did Corinna and Lea.

"Shit, are you okay?" Lea was saying while Corinna had something in her hands. Ruby's mobile, extracted from her jacket pocket. Had thought to call for backup at last.

"Are they on their way?" Ruby asked through a throat that felt bruised and parched.

"Um…I…" Corinna stuttered. "They are, but…"

"But what, Corinna?" God, she was exhausted. How she'd be able to stand, she didn't know. As for poor Lea, what the hell would she make of all this? And her family too? If she told them. "Corinna, what is it? What's the matter? Were you also attacked?"

"No! God, no. But…you've got so many missed calls, Ruby."

"From Theo and Ness? They must have sensed what just happened to me."

"From them, but from others too. Your mum and Carrie-Ann, dozens of them."

"What?" There was no time to question further, as whatever had attacked was appearing to regroup so it could rush at her again.

No, that was wrong. Instinctively, she felt that. This was different. A second energy.

And darker still.

PART TWO

Jessica

Chapter Ten

A few days earlier…

JESSICA knew that her daughter Ruby was due to go to the house in Hastings today; they'd exchanged a few text messages about it. She'd wanted to accompany her, but she was feeling unwell, although she played this down for Ruby, said it was just the sniffles she suffered from. Not true. If it were just the sniffles, she'd have gone to Lazuli Cottage. She'd have gone because she didn't want Ruby to go there without her. Sadly, however, she was bedbound, a nasty case of food poisoning, something her partner, Saul – who was the chef of the house – was mortified about.

Saul. She still marvelled at the fact they were a couple. More than that, that they lived together, in his recently deceased father's home in Bexhill, a big old Victorian house overlooking the sea, a view she loved, that she never tired of, the ocean in all its moods.

It was this expansive vista she was staring at now, having finally moved from bed to a comfortable armchair in front of the floor-to-ceiling window in the living room. A January day, grey and drizzly, the sea was nonetheless calm, green rather than blue, a murkiness to it that was not so enchanting, she had to admit. That gave her a slight feeling of unease instead. Closing her eyes, she leant back against a cushion and wished she felt better.

Would Ruby find it, the box in the attic? One that Jessica had previously laid magazines and boxed games on in an attempt to make it look...ordinary, she supposed. A box in a corner of the attic, nothing more than that. To have covered it with blankets might have invoked more curiosity. Sometimes, it was better to hide in plain sight.

Ruby hadn't looked in the attic yet; Jessica was certain of it. There was plenty elsewhere in the house to keep them occupied, but it would be the attic's turn soon enough, which was why she had to get herself better, had to go over to the cottage herself in a day or two, venture in there and pluck up the courage to open the lid. Finally.

She had to because there was something in there. She felt it in every cell of her body, in every bone. Something...vital but treacherous too. That her mother had hidden from them both and might well have disposed of if she hadn't died so suddenly.

Jessica was feeling ill, and now she was feeling sorry for herself too, wretched, actually, as guilt overwhelmed her. The argument she'd had with her mother shortly before Sarah's death had been about Jessica's father, Edward Middleton, about a family history that had been concealed from both herself and Ruby. And she had been so angry with her for that, for doing the same thing to her as Jessica had done to her own daughter – for hadn't she concealed Ruby's father's identity too? *Because I wanted to protect her!*

That had been Sarah's reasoning too. Hadn't it?

She gave a violent shake of her head, which made her feel as nauseous as she had earlier, her vision blurring a little, probably because of the tears in her eyes.

Like her daughter, like her mother, Jessica was a gifted psychic. Unlike Ruby, she had abused that gift when younger, raised hell – literally. And it was because of Saul that she had done it. Back then, when she had first known him, both had been fascinated with the occult, Jessica seeking to impress him with her 'powers' to secure his attention. All by invoking a demon. What they had seen on that long-ago night, the pair of them, was, if not a demon, something so…negative, so…terrifying it had driven Saul into the arms of madness, a bleak and lonely place where he had stayed for many years in an institution.

As for her, she'd had a breakdown when her child was so young, aged seven. Because of the breakdown, Sarah, Jessica and Ruby had lived together in the cottage in Hastings, and Ruby had subsequently been raised by Sarah, the bond between them intense as a result. And what had she done meanwhile? Jessica? Sat and stared into space, much like she was doing now, retreating further into herself, trying to become small, to hide, not just from the material world but what existed in spiritual realms too – a place not just full of light and love but something base as well, full of ill-formed creatures created by hatred.

A ragged sigh escaped her.

She was in recovery; Saul was too. Because of Ruby, they had found each other again later in life, faced up to what had once plagued them, the Psychic Surveys team by their side and that sweet, sweet dog of Ruby's – Jed, whom none other than she and Ruby could see. When she had been at her lowest, Jed had stayed by her side, staring up at her with such love in his deep brown eyes that it had somehow healed her, made her realise she wasn't as hateful as the thing she'd tried to manifest, that she was human, and, although to err was human, there was a path back, if not to normality, then sanity, at least. A path she and Saul had trodden carefully ever since. Slowly and together.

On that path, something miraculous had happened: she'd fallen back in love with Saul, and, even more miraculously, Saul had fallen in love with her – finally. It was something she had wished so hard for in her youth, when his head seemed to be turned by anyone but her. They'd been given a future because they'd faced up to their demons; they'd stood their ground and refused to be cowed anymore.

But, as gentle a life as they lived, their mental health remained precarious.

"Darling, how are you feeling now?"

So lost in thought, Jessica flinched at hearing a voice.

"Sorry," Saul continued upon reaching her, "did I startle you?"

When he was in his twenties, Saul had had ice-white hair, close-cropped, and the bluest eyes Jessica had ever seen, like the summer sky on a breathlessly hot day. So handsome that it almost hurt to look at him. Certainly, it had hurt her heart with the indifference he'd often looked at her with. Now, though, there was such concern in his eyes, eyes which had faded, admittedly, but still burnt brightly enough for her. In his early fifties, a decade that she was fast approaching too, she still considered him an attractive man, although there were perhaps more lines on his face than someone his age should have, and his frame was slight too.

In answer to his question, she forced a smile. "I'm fine, still feel a bit sick, but I haven't actually been sick for a few hours. Let's hope the worst is over."

"Perhaps we'll lay off seafood for a while, stick to something blander."

Jessica nodded. "Whatever you say, Doc."

He pulled up a chair beside her. For a few minutes there was silence between them, nothing awkward about it; rather, it was companionable, something that they often did, sitting in silence, both of them appreciating a peace they thought would never be theirs again.

Eventually Saul spoke. "Jessica, is there something on your mind?"

She turned slightly to gaze at him. "Why do you ask?"

His smile was slower than hers. It always was. "Because I can tell."

A laugh escaped her. Not psychic, although he had wanted so badly to be once upon a time, he was intuitive, and he was right: he could always tell when she was preoccupied. Being truthful with each other was very important to both of them. As far as they were concerned, it was essential to their continuing recovery. Truth pushed the darkness aside, preventing it from taking root, from festering or becoming bigger than it should be. And yet...the truth was something she hesitated to tell him right now. Even though when it had been withheld from her in the past, and from Ruby too, it had only led to problems. They had promised to tell each other everything, she and Saul, but was there really anything to tell?

Yes, she was concerned about what was in that box in the attic – a blanket box, it looked like, a chest of some sort, marked heavily with age – but her instinct might prove wrong; there might be nothing of interest in there at all. So why worry him unduly and cause his mind to work overtime, just as hers was, becoming full of worries, doubts...and fears. She couldn't be truthful. *All I want to do is protect you!* And yet they'd already established truth was the only protection there was. Even so...

He'd asked her a question. She had to say something in response.

"Ruby's going to the cottage today to pack up more of Mum's things. I was supposed to go with her, but obviously I can't. I find it sad, that's all, that soon the house won't be ours anymore, that after so long in our family, it'll belong to someone else."

Saul nodded. "It is sad, but sometimes you have to let go. I know it's your family home, but it's also a place where the past is entrenched. Our future is here, in this home, yours and mine, where new memories can be forged, *better* memories. Some of them, at least."

This house in Bexhill had been Saul's parents', both of whom had passed, and although her part of the inheritance from Lazuli Cottage would come in useful in the future, they wanted for nothing. Saul's family was a wealthy one; he'd been well provided for, and by virtue of being his partner, so now was she. Ruby needed her part of the inheritance more, having moved to a new house in Lewes with Cash and their baby, but that wasn't why they'd decided to sell it. It was, as Saul had just pointed out, so they could move on. Not all the memories Lazuli Cottage harboured were precious ones. There had been conflict there, confrontation, and there had been death. A new family and, thus, new energy might help wipe the slate clean.

Her explanation of what was on her mind seemed to have appeased Saul, as he didn't press further. More companionable silence followed, both of them losing themselves in it.

At some point, though, Jessica must have closed her eyes and fallen asleep, as she woke sometime later. Although the chair Saul had pulled over was still in place, only his impression upon the cushion remained. He'd gone, probably down to the kitchen to make himself a drink or to the conservatory at the back of the house, where he tended to various herbs and plants – gardening being a hobby both of them adored, another gentle pastime.

A gentleness she wanted so much to continue, more time in which to heal, in which to love for all the right reasons, not simply because of lust and obsession. And it *could* continue. The box in the attic could be ignored, left there, covered up by more junk, this time courtesy of the new owners, but for one thing… If Ruby found it. If she went there today, became curious and poked her head up into the attic. If she opened it before Jessica.

And Jessica would know if she had due to the games and magazines positioned on top.

If she found something…

Ah, her child, she was talented indeed. She was strong spirited, full of ideals that Sarah had taught her, wanting to pursue goals, to make matters right. But she was also Jessica's daughter, half her blood and half her father's. Just as Jessica was half Sarah's blood and half Edward's – and that paternal half, it was too curious for its own good. Too dangerous. It would rock the boat, dig and dig, and it wouldn't stop despite the peril.

If Ruby should open the box, or if Jessica herself should, that gentle life might end.

Chapter Eleven

THERE'D been no phone call from Ruby after her visit to Lazuli Cottage, which Jessica considered a good thing. Another good thing was that she was feeling better. Saturday – when the food poisoning had been at its worst – had turned into Sunday, another day of her and Saul taking it easy, for her part recovering more fully. Now it was Monday, and she was back on her feet, the whole day stretching ahead of her.

Jessica didn't work. Hadn't done for many years. At first due to the breakdown and the lingering effects of it, and now because, she supposed, she still lacked confidence. No way she wanted to put her psychic skills to work as Ruby, Theo, Ness and Corinna did; her talent was something she sought to keep in retirement. Perhaps in the not-too-distant future, a voluntary job in one of the local charities might be the way forward, again something gentle that wouldn't tax her too much or be stressful. Just a way of filling the days other than just pottering around the house, walking with Saul along the beachfront, and gardening and reading. Keeping occupied was always best, although she'd learnt to balance activity alongside plenty of rest too.

Saul was busy today, hooking up with a friend, one he'd met in one of the hospitals he'd been in, and who was also in recovery. It was therefore a perfect time to head to Lazuli Cottage and continue sorting out Sarah's belongings and some of her own too, which were still there. And, of course, to double-check. There had been no phone call from Ruby, but would she have said if she'd found something? And to her mother, of all people? No one was more protective of Jessica than her daughter.

"Saul," she called. He was in the conservatory, at a large Victorian oak-topped potting table they had in there, and she was in the adjoining kitchen, making coffee. "I'm heading over to Mum's today, okay? Bag up a few more things for charity."

"Sure," he said. "You okay to go on your own?"

"Of course. I'll be home around five, I should imagine. No later."

"Me too. I'll pick up something for our dinner on the way back."

"Something bland?" she teased, leaving the coffeepot and closing the gap between them, her arms snaking around his waist.

"Something other than seafood, certainly," he said, raising a hand to tuck a few strands of hair behind Jessica's ear. Such a luxuriant brown once, it was now threaded with grey, although recently she'd begun dying it again. Some vanities never waned.

To her surprise and delight, Saul pulled her further forward until their lips met. Whenever he held her like this, it was as though she melted into him; not separate anymore, they became one being. They might have shared a chequered past, but all that mattered now was their future. He was her soul mate, and she was his,

Jessica suspecting that whatever happened beyond this life, they would remain entwined. Which was why – uncharacteristically – she cut the kiss short, stepping out of the circle of his arms. Guilt rose within her. He was fragile, they both were, and yet what she was about to do, would it blow that fragility to the wind?

"I have to go," she said, ignoring the slight look of surprise on his face, pretending a breeziness instead. *I'm just going to check, that's all. Just…check.*

The journey from Bexhill to Hastings wasn't far. Within half an hour she was in another house, one that oozed with personal history. Before entering, she had to take a deep breath, something she knew Ruby did as well. She tended to avoid the kitchen too, the very spot where Sarah had died, thankful that Ruby had taken it upon herself to clear the cupboards there, that she understood why her mother found it so difficult.

Still striving to keep her breath from trembling, she turned left and into the living room, raising an eyebrow as she did. She was impressed. Ruby had worked hard this weekend, bagged and boxed up so much. Various local charities were coming to collect it at various stages, items that were in good repair, that would hopefully be treasured by someone else, just as this house would be – beautifully located as it was in the heart of the Old Town. How would the new owners decorate it? What furniture would they choose? Modern or traditional? She eyed the fireplace with its oak surround. So many times she would sit by it, the grate not cold like now but alive with flames. For hours she'd sit there, staring into the fire, lost in her thoughts, and then Sarah had given her a jigsaw puzzle to do, something she hoped would absorb her. She had told her to at least try to piece the shapes back together again, to lose herself in that instead of the memories that tortured her.

And eventually she'd obeyed. She'd lifted her hands, leant forward, plucked a piece from the box, then another and another. And Sarah was right – it *had* absorbed her, something so simple, a game, really, but a harmless one with no consequences, nothing like the game she'd played with Saul that had then backfired on them both. Following the successful completion of that jigsaw, Sarah had given her another and another until Jessica had begun to crave them, entering a different world entirely as she silently completed each one. And sometimes Ruby would sit beside her rather than staying with Gran in the kitchen, her small hand also reaching into the box, plucking out a piece just as Jessica's hand had, equally immersed in the desire and determination to complete it.

It was a memory she both smiled at and felt saddened by, that for so many years she'd only connected with her daughter via the medium of a jigsaw. In all other respects she'd remained distant, helpless, a victim of her own stupidity. *It's all been rectified!* Although she told herself that, it wasn't strictly true. There'd been too much time lost, years in which her child had needed her. All the pieces of their lives…scattered.

Ah, but before she'd done that, they'd been extraordinarily close. She loved her child, and her child loved her. Jessica had to admit, she'd been like a child herself with Ruby, playmates rather than mother and daughter, the pair of them teasing each other, chasing each other in the park, playing on the swings together, the slide and the roundabout. Always laughing. And then she'd met Saul, both her slayer and her soulmate. A man she'd put high on a pedestal. She was ashamed to admit it now, but higher than Ruby.

Enough!

The mind could be such a terrible thing, continuing to punish you long after others you'd hurt had forgiven you. Was she really healed from everything that had befallen her, all that she'd propagated? Now was she really the woman she wanted to be? More than that, was Sarah the woman she'd been portrayed as? Not always so strong, had she fallen prey too, like Jessica had done with Ruby's father, to the very worst of men? Just who was Edward Middleton? Why was his name in her head so much lately? Could she not fully become who she was unless she knew something more of him? Would it be a relief to know? Sarah Davis had been a gifted woman, full of light. She'd been Jessica and Ruby's rock, the foundation on which they had built their lives. Surely, she wouldn't have made the same mistakes Jessica had made. But Jessica had got her reckless streak from somewhere.

Jigsaws. How she'd loved them. And Sarah had known she would, known the way her daughter's mind worked – that Jessica would take more than solace from what she was doing, but inspiration too. That slowly she'd see the bigger picture and all it contained. That was the genius of Sarah, but it was also dangerous. Dangerous because the bigger picture was still lost to Jessica, and inside was still a craving to complete it.

A look, that's all it would be, a peek in the box. In case it held the missing piece.

Her sigh as ragged as it had been when she'd been sitting in front of the window in Bexhill, Jessica swapped the living room for the hallway and climbed the stairs.

Chapter Twelve

IF you've found this, then fate has decided. Which one of you is it, I wonder? Jessica? Ruby? Of the two, who couldn't resist?

Before anything else, I want to say how proud I am of you both.

If it's you, Jessica, reading these words, don't shake your head. I am proud of you. There are not many that can look darkness in the face and survive. You're stronger than you know.

Ruby, if it's you, you're stronger still. Remember what I'd say to you often as you were growing up, that you're the best of us. I meant it. There is so much light in you. You burn so bright. But I won't deny it, there is an element of darkness too, which I have fought to temper since the day you were born. I refused to let it get a hold and have you repeat the mistakes of your father or your mother. Or mine.

If you are reading this, then I am dead, and I promise I will not linger. I will allow my spirit to soar, to tackle the worlds beyond this one. But this is your world still, your domain. You know so much of it already, both materially and spiritually, but you want to know something more. Your full heritage.

Jessica, it's you, isn't it? As I sit here at the bureau in my bedroom, writing and unburdening myself, I can almost see your face hovering in front of me, the look in your eyes, no longer terrified, no longer trying to hide but eager again like you used to be. Eager for knowledge. It's you because I trained Ruby well, and there's a reticence in her. There was never any such reticence in you. Until you were broken, you were always wilder and more reckless. Characteristics that never disappear, not entirely.

Oh, Jessica, darling, I'll tell you what you want to know. I won't argue with fate. Not anymore. I have to believe in the grand scheme of things, not continue to rail against it, and trust that it has led you here for a reason. I'll tell you about Edward Middleton, and it isn't all bad. On the contrary... but it did become bad. Very bad indeed.

I pray that with knowledge will come solace. History cannot be denied or erased, no matter how hard we try. And so the truth must be told. All of it. Would I erase it if I could? Once I would have done, for certain, but now... now I find I'm not so sure.

Brace yourself, darling, before reading on, and, as always, draw on the light. Even now as I scribe, I'm infusing these words, this paper and my intent with light, hoping it will help to soften the blow. Although I am gone, my prayers remain with you. My love too. Forever.

Wide-eyed since she'd found the notebook in the box – the only thing that the box contained – Jessica's heart was also pumping. Her instinct had proven right, as had Sarah's instinct that fate would lead her daughter to liberate what was in the darkness.

Jessica closed her eyes, had to close the notebook too. She couldn't read further, not just yet. Instead, her mind returned to their final argument, when she'd accused

Sarah of being just like her, *worse* than her. Had she meant it? In that moment, yes, she had. She'd truly believed it. She'd called Sarah a hypocrite and a liar, someone who hadn't protected her daughter and granddaughter at all, who'd instead made them vulnerable by withholding truths, having done so for selfish rather than altruistic reasons.

And yet…what would she do when she left Lazuli Cottage today? Would she phone Ruby and share this development? Would she even tell Saul? She shook her head. No. Not yet. At least not until she'd read further. She'd withhold too. *Who's the hypocrite, then?*

No longer in the attic but in the bedroom that she used to occupy, perched on the bed there, so much still to bag up around her, she continued her inner conflict. *You're repeating the same mistakes! Over and over.* Maybe, but it was too early to share this information. Her mother knew it would be her that would find the notebook. Perhaps there was a reason for that in the grand scheme of things, as Sarah had described it. Whatever. Her mind was made up. Stubbornness should also be added to her list of qualities alongside wild and reckless, a trait that had indeed been passed on, this time from Rosamund to Sarah to Jessica to Ruby. All were stubborn. Would Hendrix be stubborn too, or was it different for boys? Only time would tell.

With the notebook in hand, leather-bound and tan in colour, she rose from the bed, intending to make her way downstairs to the living room, where her coat and bag were.

Having reached the hallway, she stopped, sure she'd heard a noise, a bump or…a scrape, was that it? Coming from upstairs. She inclined her head and listened, tiny goose bumps rising on her arms. There was nothing, no further sound. Imagination, that's all it was, probably because she was rattled and slightly spooked by the discovery. White light. That was a psychic's armour and what she needed to employ right now.

She continued into the living room, duly visualising white light, drawing it straight from source the way that her mother had taught her. After shrugging on her coat, she picked up her bag and stowed the notebook inside it, telling herself she was all right, that she'd be fine, absolutely fine. She'd be out of there soon and on her way home.

The room, however, seemed to splinter, to disintegrate. Right before her eyes.

What the hell?

Her hand immediately reached out, searching for support, the back of a chair, anything. Unfortunately, it met with nothing, causing her to sway, to stagger, to almost lose her footing. What was this? What was happening? Earlier, she'd been remembering how she'd sat by the fire, working the puzzle in front of her, Ruby by her side sometimes, but it was only that: a remembrance, nothing more, seen in her mind's eye. A snapshot. Now, though, it was as if she'd travelled through a corridor in time. The room was exactly the way it used to be, walls no longer bare but adorned with pictures, a rug on the floor that hadn't yet been rolled up, a fire that glowed in the grate. She could see it all, crystal clear, and could smell, too, the aroma of freshly baked cookies in the air, but with something else underlying it, something…less sweet. And there she was, like she used to be, in that chair by the fire, hunched over, her hands working, working, working. Manic in their intensity.

But that wasn't right; she'd never been manic like that, as though not completing a jigsaw but creating a spell of some sort, her whole demeanour desperate.

A flashback. That's what she was experiencing. No need to panic despite the slight distortion of events. Although rare, they did sometimes occur. When she'd been with Saul, she'd taken drugs just as he had, her reasoning being that it would help her to see further, opening up the pathways in her mind, doors that remained previously shut. Alcohol was dangerous for a psychic, but drugs even more so. They *did* help you to see, but nothing that existed on higher planes, only what squirmed in the depths. They could also produce flashbacks, even years later, happening quite suddenly, out of the blue like this one and leaving you so shaken afterwards, cold to the core.

Just a flashback. All she had to do was keep calm, regulate her breathing and visualise white light. Wrap it around herself. A blanket. Impenetrable.

No need to panic at all…

"You!"

The woman that was her, in the chair, had lifted her head and craned her neck forward, way too far, unnatural, as was this whole scenario.

In response, Jessica turned her head to the side, forcing herself to focus only on her breathing. Whatever this was would vanish as quickly as it had appeared. She wouldn't be stuck in its grip for long.

"You, at last!" the figure continued, scratchy words

produced through an arid throat and full of terrible wonder. "Look at me, girl. I said look at me!"

Just a misfire in a brain bruised by abuse, no matter how distant that abuse might be. It would all be over soon. *Please, please, let it be over!*

Although she remained staring resolutely to the side, she couldn't help but catch movement from the corner of the eye. What was the figure doing? Rising?

Her breath hitched despite her efforts. Her hands, clutching at the bag, felt slippery, slick with sweat, as if they might drop the bag and spill its contents. *Don't panic.* Panic would make this whole experience so much worse; it would *lengthen* it, and that was one thing she didn't want, for any of this to last a second longer than it had to.

Why a flashback now, after so long? It had been years since the last one – two, three, maybe more. Saul experienced them more regularly than she did, and night terrors too, but for both of them it was becoming fewer and fewer as they continued to heal and grow.

This was a hallucination fuelled by trauma, by opening the box and finding the notebook. The past being dragged into the light in more ways than one.

Pandora's box – something regarded as a source of great and unexpected troubles. If Ruby had found it, she hadn't opened it. Why, oh why had Jessica?

"Reckless! That's what you are." The figure was speaking again – no, not speaking, *hissing* at her. A cackle then escaping it. "So wonderfully, deliciously reckless."

As she'd feared, the figure had indeed risen and was inching its way towards her. Even with her head turned,

127

she could tell there was something wrong with its movements. There was no flow to them, no real cohesion. Instead, it jerked and flickered from side to side, like something released from an old silent movie, born not of the light, though, but darkness.

Her own breathing was ragged. She could hear it, loud as thunder in her ears, impossible to regain control of now it had broken the reins of constraint. *This is not real!*

With the figure drawing ever closer, Jessica tried to remember all she knew about flashbacks, if only to distract her mind and where it was leading her. They were sudden, she'd established that, triggered by something familiar – the house, maybe, or Sarah's writing, not the words but the actual letters, the loops and the swirls. Flashbacks could be more vivid than real life, often involving disturbing images of animals or people. Unbidden images, which forced themselves into the psyche to become lifelike and threatening. Images sometimes described as having 'a will of their own'.

This figure certainly fulfilled the criteria.

She had to move, take a step back. And then another.

Her plan was to back out of the room, steadily, slowly, somehow reach the front door and open it, inhale fresh air, great gulps of it, return to the real world, not stay in this…hell.

She had to stick to that plan, keep telling herself she was safe, feel the ground beneath her feet and get her damned breathing under control.

The figure rushed at her. From moving so awkwardly before, it had galvanised itself. Jessica couldn't help it – her scream was bloodcurdling.

It had hold of her, fingernails like talons digging into her flesh, its breath fetid.

A scream might have left Jessica's mouth, but nothing else. She would *not* converse with this creature, make it any more real.

But the creature, as she thought of it, had no such hesitation.

"I want you to look at me! I want you to see what you really are!"

No way Jessica would comply. Instead, she squeezed her eyes shut. And then only seconds later opened them. There was no comforting darkness to be had by such an action, no oblivion. What she saw with eyes wide open lay beyond her eyes too.

"There's no escape," the figure continued, such mockery in its voice, such loathing, the latter causing Jessica to finally speak.

"I don't hate who I am. I am not a bad person."

Laughter rang from the rooftops, reverberated, then rushed at her as the creature had.

"You are bad! You're the worst. And I am what you will become. Look at me, little Jessica, look at me. Curious child, aren't you? Such a curious child. Little Jessica, sweet Jessica, look at me, come on, one look and then I'll go. It'll all be over. I promise."

Cajoling her, that's what the figure was doing, its voice once again changing, becoming more and more familiar, not her own but reminding her of Sarah's. *Little Jessica. Sweet Jessica.* Those were words that her mother used to say to her when she was young, and also when she was not so young, when she was ill. She'd cajole her too, try to bring her back to reality, a reality

Jessica had so desperately wanted. But this? She didn't want this!

"Look at me!"

The figure, the creature, whatever it was, repeated its demand. Still Jessica refused, clutching the bag with the notebook even tighter between her hands.

"Darling, look at me."

Sarah's voice. It was!

"It's okay, sweetheart. It's really okay."

"Mum?"

Maybe the flashback was changing, some safety mechanism in her head kicking in the way that it did in dreams, able to change the course of them entirely, flipping them. Even the grip on her arms had lessened, become gentler.

"Jessie."

One look and it would all be over. The figure had said as much. It would then disappear in a puff of smoke.

She started to obey, turning her head in fractions, her chest heaving and pulse racing.

Soon she'd see; she'd solve the puzzle. Was this the creature or her mother?

DON'T DO IT!

A voice in her head screamed at her, not her own, nothing to do with her, something external that had entered her brain, demanding of her.

Do not look into its face! Not again.

What should I do? Jessica fired the thought back.

Run!

Before the grip on her could retighten, Jessica shook it off and spun around, not treading slowly now but lunging forwards, grabbing at the door handle that seemed to shimmer and shift beneath her hands. "Fucking open, will you!" It did. Somehow. The hallway was fragile with reality too, shimmering, vivid one minute, so dark the next.

Not many steps between the living room door to the front door – Jessica had lived there all her life; she knew how many, not even six. Release was just a heartbeat away. A heart that felt like it would soon explode, a bloodied mess, a raw and livid thing.

She flung open the front door. Freedom! And light streaming in. Blessed light.

And then it was gone, replaced by nothing. A void. An emptiness.

Her legs buckled beneath her, and she sank down, still on the hallway side of the threshold, having not escaped at all.

Chapter Thirteen

"THERE, there, love, get that down you. A nice cup of tea solves everything, eh?"

"Um…yes…yes, thank you, Mrs Richards. It's so kind of you."

"Feeling any better?"

"Much better."

"Don't want me to call an ambulance or your doctor? You know, just to make sure."

"No, there's really no need. It was just…a funny turn."

"Okay, all right, well, you sit there and drink your tea. There's no hurry. I've been out, done my shopping. I'm not going anywhere else now today."

Jessica thanked Mrs Richards again, picking up the cup and drinking from it.

A funny turn… That was one way of describing it, she supposed. She could hardly have told the old woman before her – one of Sarah's neighbours – what it really was, a drug-related flashback, coupled with post-traumatic stress. Some things really were better kept to yourself. Thank God, though, she'd had the presence of mind to fling open the front door even if she hadn't managed to step over the threshold; that was how Mrs Richards, who'd been passing, had spotted her and come rushing up the garden path. If she hadn't, Jessica would still be in Lazuli Cottage, trapped there…

"Oh God!"

Jessica hadn't realised she'd said those words aloud until Mrs Richards started to fuss over her again.

"You do look very pale," she was saying. "Very wan. Forgive me if I'm speaking out of turn here, but I gathered you suffered from an illness for a long time, didn't you? And that your dear old mum looked after you. Oh, she was a lovely woman, was Sarah, such a kind face, I used to think. So elegant. You must miss her dreadfully."

At the mention of her mother, Jessica burst into tears. Shocked at the force of them, she immediately apologised, but Mrs Richards waved it away. "You've nothing to be sorry for," she insisted.

Closing what gap there was between them, she then enfolded Jessica in her arms, Jessica clinging to her just like she used to cling to her mother, this woman who was only slightly younger than Sarah, in her mid-seventies or so, who had a kind face too.

What had just happened in the house she'd grown up in? Was it truly a flashback? Because it had seemed so real. Flashbacks could be, though, she reminded herself, very real, every damned detail perfect. It had been like being…dead, she supposed, being able to see herself like that, as if she'd become detached. And what remained tethered to the material world – the creature – was the true her, the Jessica that wasn't in recovery or trying to make amends and embrace the light but whose heart was rotten through and through.

That's not who I am!

Rather than abate, her tears flowed faster. She had to get herself under control. Poor Mrs Richards' jumper would be soaked otherwise.

Eventually, she pulled away. "Memories," she said in an effort to explain, glancing at the bag beside her feet that contained a notebook of yet more memories.

Mrs Richards returned to her chair and sat down, her own cup of tea in front of her.

"You know," she said, "although I had no clue what was wrong with you, and Sarah…well, she could be cagey whenever I asked, I always tend to remember you before you got ill, as a young girl, a teenager. My! I'd only just got married, and my Liam was already on his way. You were so…full of life back then. You had a kind of wonder about you, as if being here was just about the most exciting thing ever. Admired it, I did, that kind of spirit. Wanted my own kids to look that way too once they were grown. But life's a funny old thing, isn't it? It can take a few twists and turns."

Jessica nodded, dabbing at her eyes with a piece of kitchen roll that Mrs Richards had pushed towards her. "It can," she agreed.

"Some knocks we avoid, but others? We don't see 'em coming. You're selling the house, I see?"

"That's right. Due to exchange soon."

"Hope they're a nice bunch taking over. We like a peaceful existence around here."

"I'm sure they are. They're a young family."

"Ah, that'll be nice. They got a baby, have they?"

"I think so, yes."

"Lovely. How's that daughter of yours, Ruby?"

"She's good, thank you. Lives in Lewes, has a baby

too."

"Saw her the other day when she came round. Saturday, was it? She didn't see me. I was sitting in my living room, staring out the window, watching life go by as I do. I saw her go in the house and leave a little bit later."

"She was packing stuff, just like I was."

"Ah, I see. I hope your mum wasn't like me, a bit of a hoarder! My kids have got themselves a task when I finally hang my boots up." She laughed, but there was a glimmer of sadness in her eyes too. Facing your own mortality was never easy.

"You've got years left in you," Jessica replied, not knowing what else to say.

"D'ya think so? Really? I hope so, but I'm not so sure. With every year that passes, you just feel...frailer. And now that I've lost Graeme—" she pointed to a framed photograph on a Welsh dresser close to them "—that's my husband, by the way. Not sure you remember him? But now that I've lost him, I don't worry about it so much. He was much older than me, mind, reached the ripe old age of eighty-eight before he called it a day."

As Mrs Richards rambled on, talking about Graeme and how she'd met him at a factory in Hastings that was no longer in existence, and about the children they'd had, three in total, Jessica felt herself relax at last, enjoying the reminiscences alongside her. Mrs Richards might have remembered her when she was a teenager, but the young Jessica tended to take no notice of anyone but herself. She would glide out of Lazuli Cottage, down the pathway and all the way into town to meet her friends. Even she smiled at the memory of that. Wild, yes, but as Mrs Richards had said, she'd also been so enthusiastic. A good way to be, usually, if that enthusiasm was channelled correctly.

Their tea drained, it was finally time to leave, go home – Saul would be worried if she didn't show up soon. In fact, she should check her phone. Although always switched on, she usually kept it on silent – sudden noises were not good for her. As soon as she was outside the old woman's cottage, she'd retrieve it from her bag and check.

With that plan in mind, Jessica made to rise. "Thank you so much, Mrs Richards, for all you've done for me. I really am feeling so much better now. I should head off."

"Of course, of course." Mrs Richards also rose. "Do you live in Lewes too?"

Jessica shook her head. "Bexhill."

"I see. And is there a special someone you live with?"

"Yes, there is."

Mrs Richards laughed. "As cagey as your mother sometimes."

"Oh, I'm sorry—"

"No! Stop with the apologies. I appreciate the need to remain private. It's just me. I'm a sharer, you know, one of those that are completely transparent."

Jessica smiled. There was no way Mrs Richards would want her to be completely transparent, but she envied her that she could be, that she felt she had nothing to hide.

Her hand closed around the bag, shaking slightly as it did, at what it concealed. She'd read more, she had to, but not today; she needed to bolster herself further. Recover. Take it step by step, like everything else in her life.

As she walked down the hallway towards the front door, the layout identical to Sarah's cottage, Mrs Richards followed her. She stepped aside so the old woman could open the door and again thanked her.

"It's been lovely seeing you, dear, but make sure, if you have any more episodes, to see a doctor, won't you?"

Jessica assured her she would. Before departing, though, Mrs Richards spoke again.

"As I said, I saw your Ruby the other day. She looks so much like you, doesn't she? Well, a cross between you and Sarah. I remember her when she was little too, such a sweet child, always smiling. Can't believe she's got a baby of her own now. Girl or boy?"

"Boy," Jessica told her. "Hendrix."

Mrs Richards' eyebrows shot up. "Hendrix? That's...um...unusual."

"You get used to it. It suits him."

"Lovely, really lovely. She didn't have her baby with her when she came to the house."

"No, likely his father was looking after him. Cash."

"Cash?" Mrs Richards' eyebrows went higher still. "So, it wasn't him with her, then."

It was Jessica's turn to pull a face. "She was on her own, or at least she said she was."

"No, there was someone with her, although I only caught a glimpse of them, really."

"Oh?"

"Yeah, following her out of the house, right at her heel, I'd say. Although..."

137

When Mrs Richards faltered, Jessica prompted her. "Although what?"

"It's just…Ruby didn't seem to acknowledge him. In fact, she had her head down and was hurrying, as if trying to get away."

From having eased, Jessica's heart raced again. "This man, what did he look like? Can you describe him?"

Throughout their encounter, Mrs Richards' expression had been bright and clear. Now confusion seemed to blight it.

"Funnily enough, I can't, no. He was just…tall. That's the only thing I can say, really. He was someone who was tall."

* * *

Saul had indeed been worried about Jessica.

When she finally left Mrs Richards' house, hurrying to her car, barely even glancing at Lazuli Cottage as she passed it, she also checked her phone. He'd called five times. Not because he was clingy, she knew that. He'd be anxious, though, wanting to know she was okay, and she would answer him, tell him that, yes, she was fine. What she wouldn't do was tell him about the 'funny turn' and what had caused it.

She could, of course, dispose of the notebook, stand on the seashore and consign it to the waves, there to disintegrate on the ocean bed – but for one thing: what Sarah had said about fate. That if one of them was meant to find it, they would. Also, Sarah would never put them in harm's way – not without a damned good reason. Truth could be painful, but it could also free you. *Am I not free, then?* She asked herself the question as she left Hastings and drove back to Bexhill. She'd thought she was, finally. But there was still so much about herself and her heritage that remained a mystery. Could you ever be free if that was the case? Probably only if you really didn't care. But she did.

And there was another reason she had to find out what Sarah had to say: the shadow that Mrs Richards had seen following Ruby as she'd left the cottage. What was it? *Who* was it? An echo from the past, the demon that Jessica had once conjured? Had it returned? More to the point, had it ever left? Was knowing the truth about what had gone before the key to expunging it entirely? The light was supreme, against it the darkness could hold no sway. All psychics knew that: Jessica, Sarah, Ruby and Rosamund too, who had written so extensively of her experiences with both forces. But the darkness was also sly, insidious. It was a patient thing, used to biding its time, waiting, waiting, waiting for the perfect opportunity, for circumstances to change so it could crawl out from its hiding place and strike again.

And circumstances have changed. It was the end of an era, their childhood home about to be handed over to another family, another history waiting to be carved out there. A *better* history, she hoped. For it could hardly be any worse.

She'd resolved to tell no one about it, not yet, but should Ruby be the exception? Was this a journey they should embark on together?

Still, she was reluctant. Just until she knew better what it was that they would indeed be dealing with. Her daughter had only recently had a baby and was struggling slightly; the last thing Jessica wanted was to stress her further. A day or two was all she needed, time in which to gather more knowledge, more armour and more strength. That was vital too. She couldn't risk falling like she had before into a deep, deep pit filled with not one demon but many and most, if not all, of her own making. Should any climb out of the pit, like the parody of herself she'd already encountered, they had to be vanquished. Or, if that wasn't possible, at least kept at bay behind a wall of light impossible to scale.

What did you start all those years ago, Jessica? She berated herself, but perhaps she should cut herself some slack, just a modicum. Because perhaps it wasn't her who had set in motion the chain of events that had affected them all so badly, but someone else entirely.

Chapter Fourteen

I remember the first time I met Edward Middleton. It was during the late 1950s, a riotous time, and I was young, nineteen, and, like all people my age, busy embracing every minute of my youth. We were a breed apart, a new invention! Thanks to the likes of Bill Haley and His Comets and Elvis Presley. My parents, Rosamund and Stephen, didn't begrudge my happiness; they would smile to see it.

I was the youngest of six children, and the only girl. I grew up in London in a beautiful house on Prince's Square, in the hub of it all. At nineteen, I'd just finished secretarial college and was yet to start work, and I'd been invited to a party, one being held by Clementine Nichols.

Clementine and I had been at school together, and, if I'm honest, I'd always been in awe of her. The school where we'd received our education – Crawley Manor in North London – was a private school for young ladies. We were comfortably off, but the Nichols family were far wealthier. Something every young lady at Crawley Manor knew.

We boarded there, but during term breaks, Clementine's father's chauffer would pick her up in the family Bentley to transport her home, not to a townhouse but a mansion in the Surrey hills near Brockham. It was my mother who would pick me up, via far more modest transport, a Vauxhall Velox, dark green and much loved by my mother, who cut a dashing figure at the wheel, often wearing a paisley-patterned scarf around her neck, winged sunglasses and a dash of coral lipstick. An older mother than most – she'd had me late in life, there being a significant gap between the youngest brother and me – I couldn't have been prouder of her, and I knew from sneaking glances at my fellow students as I hurried across the gravel driveway to where she waited that she dazzled them.

That was the thing, you see. Rosamund had such an air about her. An unusual woman for her time – a psychic investigator and co-founder of the London Psychical Society (not that my friends knew that; she kept her profession very private) – she had a magnetism, a belief in herself, and this despite all she'd experienced in childhood at the hands of a sadistic father. So, although I might not have matched Clementine in material wealth, I, by extension of my mother, perhaps, had clearly intrigued her every bit as she intrigued me.

That she should invite me to her party, described as a summer ball, came as both a shock and a delightful surprise. We had finished school two years earlier, and although I had gone to secretarial college, what Clementine had done since we'd last met, I had no idea. Several of us had exchanged addresses before going our separate ways, including Clementine and me, although I'm not sure we truly intended to stay in touch. A new chapter in our lives was about to begin, and at that age the excitement of it all can consume you.

I so enjoyed secretarial school, seeking to be as independent as my mother. Certainly, she and my father were happily married, and I don't think I ever witnessed a cross word said between them, but she had her work, and Father had his, an arrangement they were both content with. Indeed, they were absorbed in their work, Mother particularly. Father wasn't psychic and neither were my brothers, but I was showing the telltale signs of being so, although…this wasn't what I wanted. Not wholly, at any rate. I wanted to have fun, normal fun, with normal people. Mother knew that; she respected that. She showed me how to tune in but also how to tune out, to force a barrier between myself and the numerous spirits that sought my attention. To pull the shutters down, as she called it. I grew quite adept at it. Having fun was my priority, and now here I was, set to have the most fun time of all at the grandest event I'd ever attended, invited by a friend who apparently hadn't forgotten me, who'd said she'd stay in touch and had fulfilled that promise.

The party was in two weeks' time, short notice, really, as there was so much to prepare for. Like all girls my age, I loved the fashions of the day, the brightly coloured patterned dresses, tight around my slim waist, or wide skirts and fitted blouses. Often, I would curl my hair, which was a pale shade of brown, letting it fall in waves below my shoulders. Or I'd tie it back in a ponytail. I had a dozen outfits, two dozen, but for this party, none of them would do. On the invitation, gold embossed, it specified formal dress. This was a masked summer ball, adding to the thrill of it all.

A shopping trip was required. Most likely several. Who else would be there? Lucinda, perhaps? She was thick with Clementine at one stage, also Diana and Betty. I'd love it if they were there too, to talk about how our lives had changed over the short time we'd been apart. Or perhaps I'd been singled out, more special than I'd realised.

I told Mother about the invitation, and she smiled whilst

asking me to hand it over. As she read, her smile faded.

"Why a masked ball, I wonder?" she said.

I shrugged my shoulders. "Because it's more fun. It's…" I paused, trying to find the right word. "Mysterious."

It wasn't an answer that appeased her. "I'm not sure, Sarah." She looked again at the square card, frowning now. "Perhaps it would be best to decline."

My outburst was immediate, taking even me by surprise. "I can't! I won't. I'm not a child anymore. I'm nineteen and capable of making my own decisions."

How indignant I was! But in part it was true. I was the only child left at home. My brothers had long since moved out into homes of their own; some had married, some remained single. I loved my parents dearly, but I wanted my own life to begin in earnest too. I'd find a job, my own home, never have to ask for permission to do anything again.

Jessica, if it's you reading this, do you see? I wasn't so unlike you after all.

In fairness, Mother wanted those things for me too, but as independent as she was, as feisty, as kind and as loving, she was also wary.

Mother had dealt with not just tyranny as a child and young woman at the hands of her father, William Howard, but insanity too. He had been an ambitious man, and it was that ambition that had pushed him into the everwelcoming arms of madness, a desire to get what he wanted at any cost. As for Rosamund's mother, Anna Sarah Claremont, after whom I was named, she was confined to an asylum when Rosamund was very young, by the very man who'd professed to love her, who'd married her. Aware that she had a psychic talent, he had attempted to bend it to suit his own will and perverted desires. When Anna resisted, he had looked for signs of a similar talent in his daughter instead. On deducing it was so, Anna was disposed of, incarcerated, his word against hers the only proof needed in those days. Consequently, mother and daughter were wrenched apart. How Rosamund missed her! She lived in fear of the man she'd been left with, who tried to break her too. But fate is kind in its intervention, on occasion. He died whilst Rosamund was still young, although I don't know the full details regarding how. She met Stephen, moved to London, and seized life instead of dreading every waking hour, oozing love and happiness instead of becoming embroiled in bitterness. But she remained wary. There were just some things she didn't trust. An invite to a masked ball being one of them.

After my outburst, we stared at each other for the longest time. A silent battle of wills.

And then she relented. "I will drop you off and pick you up. I will be on standby."

It was a compromise I was willing to make.

The two weeks prior to the party flew by, mostly in a blur. As I'd promised myself, I embarked on several shopping trips, tried on so many outfits, dismissing every one of them. But then something miraculous happened. I found the right dress! One that made me feel and, I hoped, look not like a princess but a movie star.

It was black, a very daring colour but sophisticated too. As well as a flattering portrait neckline and a dart-fitted bodice, it had a full skirt with a clover-shaped hem. I would team it with pearls, long black gloves, a heeled shoe and, of course, a bejewelled mask.

Mother didn't approve of it being black. "Why not

something bright, Sarah? Something more…lively? Emerald green, perhaps. That would suit you. Compliment your eyes."

I shook my head. "This is the dress I've chosen, Mother. I adore it. It makes me look…older, don't you think?"

"It drains you," she said with a sigh, turning away and coughing into a hankie.

Immediately, I was all concern. "Are you quite all right?" I asked.

"I'm fine," she said. "Nothing to worry about. Your mind is made up about the dress?"

"Yes," I said, standing my ground. She simply nodded, let me have my way, although there was sadness in her voice when she spoke again.

"Don't rush to grow up, darling," she said. "You're perfect just the way you are."

As there were to be no more objections, the countdown to the party could begin. Only two more days to go, each hour that passed dragging its heels. Finally, though, it arrived, the morning of the big day. A day I intended to devote to beautifying myself. Yes, it was a masked ball, but at some point masks would be removed, and when they were, I wanted to make my mark.

The cough that Mother had dismissed, however, had developed. She was ill, quite ill, describing it as a summer cold, although it seemed more serious than that.

Confined to bed, she couldn't drop me off or pick me up. Couldn't give me that final word of warning.

Chapter Fifteen

THE man yelping beside her tugged Jessica from the deep reaches of sleep to full wakefulness. Saul suffered from night terrors, but for months and months now, for the best part of a year, they hadn't beset him. So, why now? That was the question. Like her own flashback, was the timing mere coincidence?

She knew better than to wake him, although that's exactly what she wanted to do, hating to see him suffer. Likely, though, he wouldn't remember the nightmare that right now held him in the thick of it. If she did wake him, he'd be disorientated, confused, taking perhaps a long time to settle. The advice for someone experiencing a night terror was to let them ride it out, if possible, to hope it would pass sooner rather than later.

Yelping, that's all he was doing for now. Soon, though, he might thrash around, arms and legs flailing. She should get out of bed, sit in the easy chair in the corner of the room, stay close but not so close that she could be hurt, even if inadvertently.

She shivered as she threw back the duvet cover. It was cold in the room, as cold as you'd expect for a night in January. This was a large house, and the radiators, although plentiful, were sometimes not enough to combat the chill. No matter, there was a woollen blanket on the armchair. She could wrap that around herself, keep warm until this episode passed, and then she could return to bed, hold him gently as his breathing eased.

In the dark corner of the room, she tried to dispel from her mind what she was reminding herself of – something that squatted in the shadows, always there, always observing. She blinked hard, not once but several times, determined to shake such a comparison off, but imagination could be a curse, and hers had always been vivid.

Before Saul had woken her, she'd been dreaming too, not about something terrible but something nice that warmed her through and through. She'd continue to think about that while she waited. About a girl, someone she knew but at the same time had no clue about. The woman her mother had been in her youth and the party she'd gone to, the masked ball. Although Rosamund had been described as wary about it in Sarah's telling of the event, Sarah had been ecstatic to go. It had felt like such a privilege to be asked. That's what the dream had been about, Sarah experiencing such happiness, such excitement, a dream in which her identity had been interchangeable with Jessica's own. Sarah had been looking in the mirror, checking her appearance. One second it *was* Sarah, the next it was Jessica, then back to Sarah and then Jessica again, confused, jumbled, as dreams often were. Whatever had happened at the party – and Jessica would find out soon – was still a way off. It was a memory she'd been enjoying, even if someone else's, that again she relaxed into, her eyes still on Saul, who was still occasionally yelping, his head now turned to the side as if something were in front of him and he was trying to avoid it. Whether he'd get worse or better, she couldn't predict.

There'd also been a song in her dream, one that she now began humming. A familiar song, although not from her era.

Her mouth opened, sang the words.

"Each night I ask
The stars up above
Why must I be
A teenager in love?"

A song from the fifties, familiar because it had become a classic, was still sometimes played today on low-budget local radio. She couldn't recall the artist, but right now that hardly mattered. Just the sentiment.

She understood it. Most girls would. And boys too. In teenage years particularly, the heart held dominion over the head, and the world was a passionate place.

Lapsing into silence, something else came to mind, not lyrics this time from a song that was both frivolous and heartfelt, but a quote from a play – Shakespeare's *Much Ado About Nothing* – one that suddenly seemed loaded with meaning: 'Speak low if you speak love.' Because love, as she knew, could lead you towards trouble. It could trap you...

The party, was that where Sarah Davis had met Edward Middleton? And yet, she'd been nineteen. It would be many more years before she had Jessica. So she'd met him, and then what? Sarah and Edward had never married; she'd left him during her pregnancy and moved from London to Hastings. Not long after Jessica was born, Rosamund had died, Stephen too, leaving

Sarah quite alone with a baby. But that was all to come. For now, her mother had been an excitable young girl. It was sweet to think that. Excitable, not...reckless. *I wasn't so unlike you after all.*

Damn love and lust for being able to corrupt a situation so readily.

Her head drooped, most likely because she was tired. It had been a long day, Jessica reading the first chapters in the notebook after Saul had retired to bed. Little wonder she'd dreamt about it too. One hand rising to rub at her eyes, she caught movement, her gaze rapidly lifting and her shoulders straightening.

Saul was sitting up, his shoulders as rigid as hers.

"Saul?" she said, rising from the chair.

He didn't answer. Instead, he swung his body to the left, his feet on the carpet now, his hands pushing himself up into a standing position.

"Saul, are you awake?"

There was no answer, Jessica realising that he was sleepwalking, and her breath catching in her throat because of it. What he was doing could occur whilst experiencing night terrors, but as far as she knew, he'd never done this before. And nor had he ever mentioned he had. This was something new. Something...disturbing.

The way he moved, not fluidly as you did whilst awake, both body and brain fully engaged, his actions were jerky instead. It was another reminder she didn't want of the woman in the cottage, the...*aberration.*

She shouldn't wake him. She mustn't. All the advice went against that. You had to let what was happening exhaust itself, which it would, she told herself. It would.

Despite her determination to keep a rational mind, she was shaking more than before, shivers making her jerk too. What if what was happening with Saul triggered something in her? Another flashback? They'd both be helpless, at the mercy of past horrors.

Oh, Saul!

Were those tears on her face? She reached up and felt her cheeks. Yes, they were.

Such a nice dream she'd been having before being torn from it, getting to know further a woman who'd been so close to her, who had been her saviour in so many ways. How she wished Sarah were here now, that she could talk to her instead of just reading about her, that she could listen to sound advice that would keep her from sinking into an abyss too deep to emerge from.

Such a nice dream… She resented that it had ended, resented Saul, a man she loved, had *always* loved from so young, but right now she experienced a flash of hatred.

He had come to a halt, was still, but now his head snapped upwards, towards her. As if…as if he'd heard her wretched, traitorous thoughts.

You hate me, do you? YOU hate ME?

She was unable to breathe as those words ricocheted in her head, not transferred by Saul, surely; her own imagination must be planting them there. Nonetheless, he was on the move again, lurching towards her with stiff limbs, as if it was agony to move them, his eyes remaining stubbornly closed.

What was happening? What was he doing?

She had to wake him; she had no choice. His expression was menacing.

"Saul!" she called. "Saul, snap out of this. Wake up."

When young, he'd been tall and strapping, athletic in build, so striking. Age and trauma had shrunk him. He was a little stooped now but still strong, still able to inflict damage with his fists if he wanted to. Not that Saul would want to – he was gentle in every way, but this Saul she didn't recognise. There was menace in his expression, as if he indeed wanted to hurt her. As if he was *alive* with that prospect, his lids still closed but such rapid movement behind them.

His gait might be tortured, but quickly he closed the gap between them, cornering her. Unless she pushed past him, there was nowhere to go. The chair was against the wall, and she was against the chair, the backs of her bare legs pressing against the wood.

What kind of nightmare was he living? Who or what did he think he was?

"You're a good man, Saul. *My* man. Now, wake up. You have to."

His hands were rising, inch by inch. So were hers.

She grabbed hold of his arms.

"Saul!" Even to her own ears, her voice was shrill. "Wake up! Now!"

So easily he flung her off, causing a gasp to escape her, laced with shock.

His hands gripped her instead, his fingers pinching into her flesh, emitting from her the same yelps he'd been guilty of earlier.

"Saul, what are you doing? Wake up. Please."

With barely a few inches between their faces, she continued to plead with him, noticing too that his eyelids were opening, slowly, cruelly, as if the terror he was inflicting was to be relished.

If his eyelids were opening, he was waking. Wasn't he?

Now his eyelids snapped open. Just as quickly, she turned her head away, knowing she wouldn't see Saul. Saul was gone, had been swallowed whole.

"Look at me." The creature's voice was guttural.

"No," she whispered. "I will not."

"Look at me!" it repeated. "See who I am. *What* I am."

Violently, she shook her head.

"See what you are too. The same as me."

She wasn't. She was nothing like it. Not now.

Things had changed. *She* had. Saul had changed too.

Her voice was pitiful, a mere whimper at first, but she injected strength into it. "Saul, this isn't you. Fight back. Expel it. Wake up." Everything would all be all right if he just woke up.

As the man who was not Saul grew closer still, the smell of decay on his breath, she forgot all about light, all about armour, could only scream three words.

"SAUL, WAKE UP!"

Chapter Sixteen

"JESSICA, wake up. Come on. You're all right, I've got you. You're okay. You're safe."

Wake up? What did Saul mean? It wasn't her that was asleep. It was him. He was...sleepwalking. That was it. But beginning to wake...

"No, don't do that, stop fighting. Jessica, believe me, please. You're all right. I've got you. I won't let anything bad happen to you."

Her eyes snapped open, saw not a demon in front of her, just Saul, his tired blue eyes so striking even in the gloom, and full of kindness. So much so that she wept to see it, confused still, relief not quite able to wash away the fear.

Without another word he held her close, and for a while Jessica clung to him, as pitiful, as fragile as she'd ever been. And then her heart gradually settled, skipped to a more normal beat rather than hammering away. She turned her head slightly to where she thought she'd been sitting, watching Saul in the grip of night terrors. It hadn't been him dreaming; it had been her, and yet the dream had seemed so real, as vivid as any flashback, every detail in place except the most important one, Saul himself, who'd become something other than human, a creature from the charnel house.

She'd been the one afflicted with the night terrors, and yet – mercifully – it wasn't something she'd suffered from before. So what had changed? Because something had. It was to do with finding Sarah's notebook but also something else – something bigger than that.

At last she found the strength to pull away from Saul, wiping at her tears with the back of her hand and turning the tables by checking how he was.

"Me?" he answered. "I'm fine."

"I woke you, then? You were…fast asleep?"

He nodded. "Yes. Yes, I was. But you had a nightmare?"

"It happens sometimes, I suppose." She smiled ruefully as she said it.

He reached out again, gently caressed her shoulder. "You're okay?"

She loved him so much. Everything about him. They'd endured nothing less than horror together but had finally found a way through. Had been parted for so many years but reunited. It was the demon that had torn them apart and which, ironically, brought them back together. It had done so because Jessica had gone in search of Saul, needing to face what had hounded them with him by her side. They had raised it, and they – with the help of Sarah, Ruby and her team – needed to vanquish it.

Was the demon ever real?

The jury was out on that one and perhaps always would be.

Her belief, such as it was, was that heaven and hell existed within a person, was something internal, and it was up to the individual which one you gave dominance to. But whether you chose good or bad, somewhere down the line, and for all sorts of reasons, you could change. The years of suffering with remorse and guilt had changed Jessica, just as it had with Saul, for the anguish they'd caused those that loved them. They were trying to make amends for so much damage done. Good could lead to evil, and evil could lead to good. They had found each other, had endured, were enduring still, right here, right now, in this big old house in Bexhill. Love had resurfaced, every bit as intense as before, as deep, but with one difference – it was tender. Beautifully tender. Despite what was happening to her, the flashbacks, the night terrors, what she'd recently discovered and what she sensed – that change of some sort was on the way – she felt lucky, *determinedly* lucky. From being so frightened, she now felt…invincible because of that tender love. So invincible it was almost frightening in itself.

In answer to his question whether she was okay, she kissed him, felt his grip on her immediately tighten. They lay back down. Whatever hour it was, it was still too early to rise, but perhaps they wouldn't sleep. They could fill the time in other ways.

As she continued to kiss him, as he continued to caress her, her mind strayed only a fraction – to the notebook, of course. After the usual day's activities, she would settle somewhere quiet with it again, alone, whilst Saul pottered in the conservatory, perhaps, or elsewhere in the house. But she would not approach it with as much trepidation as she had done before. That had been her mistake. She would trust in her mother, in the story that she perhaps hadn't wanted to tell, for reasons known only to her, but which she knew would come to light at some point. Because fate decreed it. Because nothing stayed the same. Too much was fluid. Except resolve, and love, and light, and good intent. As she arched her back in the grip of ecstasy rather than terror, she felt that about love especially.

* * *

The Nichol family estate was nothing less than astonishing!

In a semirural setting, it was both secluded and exclusive, perfectly manicured lawns giving way to the plethora of trees that surrounded it. My father dropped me right outside the house, first travelling up a gravelled lane, one car in a procession of many, various men and women alighting, being directed by ushers deep inside its hallowed portals.

I couldn't say a word, sure that if I opened my mouth, there'd be only a squeal. Instead, I strained my neck to see if I could recognise anyone. With all masks in place, however, it was impossible, but, as my father had already informed me and I'd suspected, at the end of the ball on the stroke of midnight, it was custom for masks to be removed, for the full identity of the people you'd been mingling with all evening to be revealed.

He was frowning, though, as he said it. Like my mother, he didn't see the need for masks. Of course I asked why.

"Your mother and I value transparency in all things. This goes against the grain."

"It's just a bit of fun! A novel idea."

"Novel?" he repeated, one eyebrow raised as he

continued to drive us. "No, darling, it's rather...a traditional idea."

"I was afraid Mother wouldn't let me attend."

He turned to me then. Despite nearing seventy, Father was still a handsome man, the grey in his hair giving him a distinguished look. He was a happy man, still very much in love with the woman he'd married, something that shows, I think, that can make a person shine. He wasn't shining now, though; his inner flame seemed dulled.

"Father, I'll be all right," I insisted.

"Sarah, you're a grown woman. A woman as special as your mother. As gifted. We have to trust you. If you want to attend this party, then do. Just...use your intuition. If you're talking to someone and you feel uncomfortable, move away and talk to someone else. You've never been to an event like this before; they can be a little overwhelming. Darling, I don't have to leave the grounds, you know that. I can wait right here."

I was appalled by his offer, especially as when we drew closer, I could see cars were dropping people off and then moving swiftly on. If Father stayed, he'd be the only one! Of course, it was too far to return to our London home just to begin the return journey again a few hours later, so he would wait for me at a nearby pub, where he would have dinner during the wait to fetch me. An old friend was due to meet him there. They'd dine together.

"Just be careful," he continued without me having to say another word. "We trust you, your mother and I, and in turn you must trust your instinct."

At last, it was my turn to alight from the car, one of the ushers rushing forwards, not dressed in the fashion of the day but suited and booted and...masked. The fifties *invented the teenager; it was an age that sought to free young people from the restriction of formalities, but here at the Nichols' house, formality was embraced, if just for tonight.*

"Your mask!" Father called as I opened the door.

"Of course," I replied, laughing. He and Mother might not like the idea of masks, but I was glad of it, fitting it across the top half of my face before fastening it. I liked the idea because behind the mask I could be whoever I wanted to be. Not just Sarah Davis, who'd never been to a party in a house like this before in the countryside. Something this grand. I could be anyone! A bohemian artist, a singer, an actress! It gave me a confidence I might otherwise have lacked. My parents might have valued transparency in all things, and my brothers and I had been brought up to value it too, but tonight, mingling with strangers that I considered exotic, exposure was the last thing I wanted. Secrecy all part of the thrill.

If the house was impressive outside, a country residence fit for royalty – parts of it dating back centuries, I'd bet – it was even more so on the inside, the grand entrance hall heaving with people, waiters weaving between them on nimble feet, holding gilt trays high in the air, filled with either champagne glasses or plates of hors d'oeuvres.

I didn't know a soul. No school friends, no Clementine, although of course they must be here, Clementine, certainly. Masked as they were, everyone was a stranger to me, sipping from wide-rimmed glasses, delicately nibbling on food or simply waving a cigarette holder around as they chatted to one another, as they laughed, sometimes uproariously, heads thrown right back.

I stood and observed all of this, totally entranced, totally captivated. And that's what astounds me now when I think back on it, my total lack of nerves, of fear of any kind. Father had said trust your instinct, and instinct was telling me, it was urging me, to have the best of times. And I would. The ball was to end at midnight, and Father would pick me up shortly afterwards. I'd been dropped off at seven o' clock. Five hours to enjoy this wonderful extravaganza. Not nearly enough time; the minutes were already disappearing.

There was music, not the popular songs of the day but classical music, drifting on the air from a room to the left of me. As though it had a magnetic pull, people gravitated towards that room, the swell of the crowd pulling me along with it.

Another breathtaking sight awaited – possibly the grandest room I'd ever seen or even imagined. Certainly, it was the largest, a musical ensemble at the far end producing such a beautiful, whispery sound. My head buzzed as though I'd drunk a thousand glasses of champagne already, although not one had yet passed my lips. People began to dance, not jiving as I would with friends but gliding gracefully along the floor, women like butterflies, the men all so noble, and everyone masked.

I could have stood there forever, immersed in this scene. When eventually the night was over and I told my friends about it, they would never believe me! I could hardly believe it myself. Why had Clementine asked me? Although I was grateful that she had.

A voice startled me. Female. Familiar.

"Sarah! You're here!"

It was Clementine's voice, as though thinking of her had been enough to conjure her. She was standing before me, resplendent in a dress that made my creation look less glamorous. There was so much beadwork upon it, and jewels that sparkled. Her mask was just as elaborate, curving upwards at the edges and edged in yet more jewels.

"Oh, Clementine!" I enthused. "Thank you so much for inviting me. This is…" How could I even begin to describe it? "Tremendous!"

She waved a hand in the air as if dismissing my comments. "It's just a party," she said. "But at Far Acres we do tend to do things in style. My father's preference, not mine." She shrugged, still nonchalant. "I'd have been happy with something a little less…formal. Anyway, there it is. Come on! Come and dance with me!"

Before I could object, tell her I didn't know how to dance to classical music, the music abruptly changed. Here was a tune I recognised, one I loved, Bill Haley's 'Rock Around the Clock'! Such a contrast to what had gone before! The crowd around me that had been dancing so elegantly in pairs, their arms entwined, had now parted, had lifted skirts, loosened ties and were dancing still but wildly, with such abandon, arms and legs flailing.

Although dragged onto the dance floor, I stood there at first, simply too stunned by the sudden change of tempo to do anything else. But then Clementine grabbed my arms and forced me to dance. And just as suddenly, I complied. This music, this…vibe. Here was something I knew, that I didn't have to stand and observe but could join in with.

The music played on, the dancing continued, Clementine and I laughing as if we'd been best friends rather than only acquaintances.

"Thank you," she yelled over the music, "for coming."
"Are there others from school?" I asked.

"Yes! Yes, of course. They're here. Somewhere…" Her voice trailed off as she looked around her, something in her eyes, a frisson of something. Fear?

"Clementine, are you all right?"

She returned her gaze. "What? Yes, fine!"

More tunes played, 'Rockin' Robin', 'Rave On', 'Let's Have a Party', and we danced to them all. Eventually, I was exhausted, couldn't take another step. I was parched too. I needed something to drink. I was about to tell Clementine this when someone loomed up behind her, turned her around and swept her away. Just like that, she vanished.

No matter. I was sure I'd find her later. I needed a drink, and so I left the dance floor, spotted a waiter in the distance, noticed too how different everyone looked. Like lords and ladies previously, now they were sweaty and unkempt, dresses having slid off shoulders, ties well and truly discarded, and jackets too.

I raised my hand, signalled to the waiter, stood there beaming as he approached.

But it wasn't the waiter who handed me a drink; it was someone else. Someone who, like the man on the dance floor had swooped in and taken Clementine, swooped in too from nowhere, taking the glass from the waiter's tray and handing it to me in one swift gesture.

A man. Tall. Slim. He was dressed in a more modern take on the usual evening wear, the jacket he wore shorter and more fitted, and his narrow trousers were cuffless. His tie too, if indeed he'd worn one, had been discarded, and three buttons remained unfastened at the neck. But that was the only similarity between him and those others surrounding me. This wasn't a man pink-cheeked or breathless from dancing; this was a man — from what I could see of his masked face — who looked as if he'd never break a sweat. Cool as the proverbial cucumber, as every teenaged girl dreamed her man would be.

Chapter Seventeen

JESSICA inhaled deeply.

Edward Middleton. Sarah Davis had met him. At the Nichols' family ball, aged nineteen. A tall man, dashing, enrapturing her mother despite his mask.

She could hardly wait to read on, but she could hear Saul approaching. It had been hard to find some quiet time today. Because of what had happened during the night, he'd felt even more protective towards her than normal, hovering close. Eventually, she'd feigned tiredness, told him she needed a nap and had returned to the bedroom, collecting the notebook en route, kept beneath the mattress in a spare bedroom. Before lying down, she glanced only briefly at the chair she'd sat in hours before, then opened the notebook and lost herself once more in her mother's world.

Sarah and Edward had met, and, as desperate as Jessica was to read on, she had to close the notebook, secrete it away, this time beneath the pillow she was lying on.

Saul entered the room, a cup of coffee for her in his hand.

"Thought you might like this," he said.

"Thanks," Jessica replied, yawning and stretching her limbs, keeping up the pretence.

"You get some sleep?"

"About half an hour, just enough to keep me ticking over."

Saul reached out a hand to graze against her cheek. "You look pale."

"I'm fine."

"You'd say if there was anything troubling you?"

As curious and excited as she was about her mother and father's history, not feeling that she could be open and honest about the notebook was a burden. In a sense, she too was hiding behind a mask, her expression kept carefully neutral. She *would* tell him, she reminded herself, and soon, but this was her history, personal to her. At last she was meeting a man she'd always been so curious about. Sarah was finally talking about Jessica's father, just as Jessica herself had had to finally talk about Ruby's, letting her daughter know the truth of who he was. Certain truths wouldn't – *shouldn't* – stay buried.

Despite this, she didn't have the heart to blindside Saul anymore. It was clear he didn't want to let her out of his sight today, and so she'd have to wait until later to read more. Return to it tonight. Better to read than sleep, keep the nightmares at bay.

Having drunk her coffee and further reassured Saul she was fine, Jessica rose from bed, declaring she'd like a walk along the beach.

Half an hour later and they were wrapped up in coats, hats and scarves, making their way towards Bexhill's iconic modernist building, the De La Warr Pavilion, which was hosting an art exhibition.

Saul suggested they go inside and check it out.

"You just want to escape the biting wind," Jessica

teased.

"That too," he confessed. "We could get a cup of tea afterwards."

The exhibition comprised a series of photographs taken by a local artist, Yoko Shakti. There was a small entrance fee, which Saul duly paid, Jessica admiring the spiral staircase that led up to one of the building's cafés whilst he did.

"Here we go," he said, recapturing her gaze. "Prepare to be amazed."

In truth, neither had any idea what to expect from this artist, unknown to them, but it was with surprise that they entered not a light and airy exhibition area but one shrouded in darkness, black-and-white photographs on the wall highlighted with carefully hidden spotlights, the light they imparted as stark as the artwork itself.

"Interesting," mused Saul, wandering over to the nearest photograph.

It was of a hut on stilts over an expanse of sea, with a boardwalk leading out from it.

"What was the name of this exhibition again?" asked Jessica.

"*Intro Spective*," replied Saul. "The guy on the door gave me a leaflet. Here."

She took it from him, noted how the word had been spelt, split in two. Without her glasses, however, and in this darkness, she couldn't read the artist's biography; the print was too small. No matter. She could read it later if she still wanted to. Right now, there were more photographs to see, interesting photographs, she had to admit, the atmosphere as quiet as the grave, with only the two of them in there.

More photographs of lonely places, seascapes used a lot but also vast plains that stretched on and on, stepping-stones peppering one such vista. But stepping-stones to what?

"I think," said Saul, his head to the side as he studied the photograph with the stepping-stones, "these photographs are a representation of the artist himself, his inner feelings. He's...lonely...confused...feels isolated. He's on a journey, but where it's taking him, he has no idea. Yet it's not one he fears. He just...keeps going."

Jessica smiled. When he was a young man, Saul had been interested in so many things, not just occult matters but subjects such as art and literature. In his later years, those interests were emerging again, and she agreed with him, his take on it, studying once more the leaflet Saul had handed her, on which was a snapshot of the artist, who seemed very young, likely in his early to mid-twenties. No wonder he was on a journey still. It could take a lifetime to find out who you were – several, even.

The main hall led into a smaller room with more photographs for them to admire.

"They're getting eerier," Saul noted, glancing at Jessica. The worry and concern in his expression caused her to reach out and pat his arm.

"I'm fine. Are you?"

He nodded. "I'm enjoying his art."

She'd stuck close to Saul's side so far. Now, though, she drifted away, another photograph having captured her attention, that of a staircase rising out of the sea. She stared at it for what felt like an age, like Saul, trying to read its message.

A staircase…rising out of the sea…no one on it, no one emerging from watery depths. Not yet. Would they? Was something currently beneath the waves, waiting to break the surface? What sort of creature would it be? Not a creature at all, perhaps, but a person, having finally fought their way to the light, reaching out, wanting it to infuse them, tired of murky darkness and all it contained. Yes, yes, that was it. It would be a stronger person emerging. One who was…healed. Not partially, rather their entire soul.

This explanation, this knowledge, this *certainty* emboldened Jessica, fired her with the impetus to explore the photograph next to it, which was part of a series.

In the first, a shrouded figure, just the top half of it, was holding a branch, the figure looking away to the left and behind them another expanse of sea, the horizon indistinguishable from the grey sky. A haunting figure, lonely, one that many could identify with, and the branch, bereft of any buds, signalling despair.

Before continuing to the next photograph, Jessica turned, feeling the weight of Saul's stare. She was right – he was looking at her, his gaze still uneasy.

"I'm all right," she insisted.

"It's just…these photos…they're disturbing, some of them."

"You think so?"

"Don't you?"

Jessica thought for a moment. She understood what Saul meant; in this dark, silent room of only black-and-white photographs pinned to a wall, it was certainly what the photographer intended it to be: an intense experience. One that gave you almost too much of an insight into the person behind the lens, that crossed boundaries every bit as much as psychic ability could. This was Yoko Shakti laying his soul bare. She wasn't feeling disturbed by it, but something else: privileged.

"I love it," she answered eventually. "I think his artwork is exquisite. I'm so glad you suggested we visit."

Relief replaced unease as Saul turned away.

The shrouded figure, what happened to it in the next photograph? And the next, and the next? There looked to be about ten in the series.

She stepped further to the side. In the second photograph, the change was oh so subtle. The head of the figure had moved slightly, more towards the camera. As far as she could discern, that was the only change. She went to the third, the figure's head still moving in increments. In the fourth, something else was visible, although Jessica had to squint to make sure. There was a bud on one of the limbs of the branch being held, emerging, as though from slumber. The shroud too was beginning to slip.

Her breath caught in her throat at the sight for reasons she couldn't quite fathom, not yet. Instead, she peered at the next in the series and the next, wanting to rush the experience, as she was impatient for the outcome, but also trying to savour each shot and the way in which it spoke to her. What kind of man was this that had taken them? A young man but wise beyond his age, profound. Not only was he revealing his soul to the viewer, it was as though he looked into the viewer's soul too. As though he was speaking directly to Jessica, no one else in the room but her now, not even Saul.

Each subsequent figure was different to the last, and although you had to look for that change at first, it was becoming more and more obvious.

She came to the last in the series. It was everything she wanted it to be. The figure – who was the artist – was now completely de-shrouded, buds on the branch blooming fully, and in the sea beyond, tinges of blue were evident. He'd done it, he'd triumphed, cast off all that had blighted him and snatched victory from the jaws of defeat.

"YES!" The word emerged from her mouth to punctuate the silence. Her fists, held up in front of her, were tight balls of glee. Here was someone she'd never heard of before she'd stepped foot into the exhibition hall but who was nonetheless a kindred spirit. Their experiences might be different, but the end goal was the same. Not to run or hide anymore but to face up to the past, for it was that which defined you. If you could do it, if you were brave enough, the future was yours. Entirely.

As he stared out of the photograph, Shakti's gaze was steady and direct, no smugness in it, only relief and a pride he'd come this far, that he'd managed to.

It was a sign, she realized. Almost God-given. What she was doing, reading Sarah's journal, was not only right but also timely.

Saul, drawn perhaps by the cry she'd emitted, came to stand by her side, although his eyes were not on her but on the photographs in front of him, as if he too was mesmerised.

"Brilliant," he breathed. "They're just…brilliant."

She threaded her arm through his.

They were more than that, in her opinion.

They were the Fates, encouraging her to go further.

Chapter Eighteen

TRUST *your instinct, and that's what I did, standing there in front of this man, holding the champagne glass he had given me.*

He intrigued me. How assured he was, his confidence. He'd handed me a drink, and he'd disappear soon – why on earth would a man like him hang around a girl like me? And so I wanted to soak up every second of his company that I was graced with.

Would he say something? Speak to me? Should I perhaps seize my chance?

"Thank you." The words fell from my mouth. "For the champagne." Although hardly groundbreaking, it was a start, at least.

He smiled but said nothing. And then he turned, fulfilling my worst fears.

There were so many people ahead of us, a horde. What if I lost sight of him, lost him completely? I didn't know what the time was, only that it continued to slip away.

I couldn't lose him! I wouldn't! I was nineteen, and no man had ever made such an impact on me. No one had come close.

"Wait! Wait," I demanded, pushing through the crowds and hurrying after him.

It was such a bold thing for me to do! So…out of

character. I was never this forthright.

"WAIT!"

Thank goodness my voice managed to somehow penetrate the wail of the music. He stopped and turned, slowly, his eyes, what I could see of them — bright blue — locking with mine. I inhaled. All courage left me. What was I going to say next? I had no clue, but I prayed he wouldn't just turn and leave me stranded once more.

He didn't.

Instead, he inclined his head, as if curious.

I came to a standstill before him, my smile shy, silently cursing because of it. This wasn't a man who'd warm to a shy smile.

Oh, there was so much music in the air, so much chatter, but in that moment it all seemed to fade to silence as, again, he waited for me to speak.

Confident. Assured. I've already said those were qualities he oozed, qualities I'd been taught too by a mother who was also that way inclined. Time to make use of them, to believe in myself, because as Mother liked to say, belief was everything.

As my mouth opened, I could feel myself grow in stature, becoming taller somehow, less naïve and more dazzling. Like him, someone who was something to behold.

"You gave me a drink," I said. "I'd like a cigarette too. Do you have one?"

* * *

We talked. Endlessly. We laughed. Endlessly.

Edward Middleton, a friend of Clementine's older brother, was twenty-five, and although not from London but further south, he now lived there too, not far from me, only a short bus ride away. His flat was on top of his place of work: an antiquarian bookshop. It was a job he loved, spending all his time in between customers immersed in those books — ancient texts, he called them, and so beguiling.

I hung on to every word he uttered, determined to commit them to memory, just in case, after tonight, they were all I was left with.

We drank more champagne, smoked more cigarettes, my heart racing all the while. It was nearing midnight, and the crowds around us were becoming more frenzied. Since discovering Edward, I had taken no notice of anyone else in the room, had forgotten all about them, and Clementine too, although their numbers had multiplied dramatically, pairs becoming groups, huddled together, their laughter not the same as ours but raucous.

Midnight. The time when masks were due to be ripped away, revealing who you'd been cavorting with all evening. There was a desperation in the air, and that, at least, I could understand, for I was feeling quite desperate myself.

His eyes, his mouth, were perfect. Would I still think so when the mask was removed?

I cried out as someone from behind shoved into me. I'd been standing close to Edward, but because of their actions, I was closer still.

"Sorry," I said, brushing at his jacket. I'd splashed champagne upon it.

"Don't worry," he said, enclosing my hand in his, not a light grasp; rather, I could feel the strength that pulsated through him. "Look, shall we go outside? Get some fresh air?"

He was right. It was hot inside, the atmosphere stifling with so many heaving bodies in such close proximity. I too longed for a reprieve so nodded in agreement. Still with my hand in his, he pushed himself away from the wall he'd been leaning against and led me through the crowd, cutting a swathe through it; that's what it seemed like, people stepping aside to let us pass. From all I'd gleaned so far, he wasn't from particularly wealthy stock, but his intelligence – fierce, I'd describe it as – was obvious. It gave him an air of command, the type usually only afforded to people of wealth. And that's why people moved aside, because consciously or subconsciously, they reacted to it.

Outside, the cool air was delicious. Others had come to take advantage of it too, and so he guided me further from them, away from the terrace, as greedy as I was for privacy. At last we reached an area of trees and bushes and hid in amongst them.

"It's almost midnight," I said, not wanting to return inside, even for the grand unveiling.

"I couldn't care less."

"Really?"

"Really," he insisted. "Tell me more about you. Your plans, your dreams. Sarah," he said, and I loved the way my name sounded on his lips, "what is it you're best at?"

Nineteen. That's all I was. I'd done well at school and at college, but saying so beneath the moonlight, the sound of the music now thankfully distant, didn't seem interesting enough. Here was a man who worked in a bookshop, but not just any bookshop, one stuffed with antiquated gems, which he read avidly. Earlier, he'd described the books he'd been reading, those to do with ancient religions and races, the Babylonians and their descendants, the Mesopotamians. Sometimes it was like he spoke in a foreign language as I realised that, although I'd received a fine education, there was so much I remained ignorant of. My pride flared. To tell him I wanted to work as a secretary wasn't going to cut it. Besides, it wasn't what I was best at. "You talk about ancient religions, ancient races, ancient wonders too," I said. "And I feel...thirsty, not for champagne but for you to continue talking, to teach me. I want to know everything that you know. I'm inspired too. I feel naïve next to you."

"You're not naïve—"

I raised a hand. "It's no bad thing. Really, it isn't. You've awakened something in me that's been dormant ever since leaving college. I've been drifting a little, and now I realise there's no time to waste, not even a minute, not when there's so much to learn. I want to be more like my mother. She's an avid scholar too, a founding member of—" I paused, wanting this to sink in "—the London Psychical Society."

There was a moment of silence between us as I held my breath, as the world around me seemed to be doing so also, nothing moving, not even the branches of the trees.

"The Psychical Society?" he repeated. "Do you mean...? Is she...?"

"She is," I said. "And so am I." I'd never played this card before, not at school or through college. If I saw a spirit wandering the corridors – and I had, I'd seen several – I would deal with it in my own way, in my own time, reach out, try to connect, to send them to the light as Mother had taught me. Sometimes I was successful, sometimes I wasn't. But never, never had I told anyone outside of my family, and never had I used it to impress.

But impress it did.

His eyes widened, and his mouth fell open slightly; I heard the rushing of his breath as he inhaled. This wasn't a man who'd be frightened of what I was, who'd back away as if I were not gifted but suffering from a disease, that of the mind rather than the body, a madness that was somehow infectious. Only the ignorant would react in such a way, and he was far from that.

Instead, he reached up and began to remove his mask.

"Midnight's still a few minutes away!" I protested.

"I couldn't care less," he said, repeating his words of earlier, and now it was me who held my breath.

Devastatingly handsome. That was the only way to describe him. A man more beautiful than any I'd seen. His nose perfectly sculptured, his pale skin flawless.

Having removed his mask, he reached towards me and peeled away mine. It was only our masks being removed, but it was as intimate as if we were shedding clothes.

His hands cupping my face, he brought me closer and closer until his lips hovered just before mine, teasing me again so artfully. Making me want him more than life itself.

When our lips finally met, an enormous cheer erupted, enveloping us and the night.

The clock had struck twelve.

Chapter Nineteen

JESSICA hugged the notebook to her. She could see in her mind's eye the evening her mother had described, every detail: the country mansion, the sheer grandeur of it, Sarah's expression as she met the enigmatic Edward, who stole her breath, who made her throw her head back with laughter. An impressive man that she had also sought to impress.

Of course, Jessica knew there were further memories recorded in the notebook, those filled with despair, but she would cross that bridge when she came to it. For now, all she wanted was to embrace something good, just lose herself in the moment when two people had gazed at each other in open wonder, their lips touching.

Such joy. At least on Sarah's part. Such…hope.

She would read more, but she needed coffee.

The kitchen clock showed midnight. Just gone. It was almost as if she were reliving Sarah's memories in real time.

She smiled at this. Not quite. As lovely as the kitchen was in their Bexhill home, it could hardly compare to Far Acres.

The kettle came to a boil, and a second cup of coffee was made, the fuel to keep her going for a little longer. Saul had made his way upstairs an hour ago. He'd be asleep by now, and she'd join him in due course, praying for a more restful night. Returning to the table, she set the coffee mug down, reached across to the notebook but found herself hesitating.

Perhaps it was right to leave it there. To end on something good would keep the nightmares at bay, the night *terrors*. Or would her mind fill in the gaps regardless?

She'd continue reading, for a while longer, anyway. An hour or so. When would she tell Ruby? she wondered. At what point? This was her history too, and her son's. As Jessica opened the page, focused once more, it was *what* she'd tell her that was more the issue.

* * *

Inseparable. That's what we became. Every minute that we could spend in each other's company, we did.

Not openly, not at first. It took a while for me to broach the subject of Edward Middleton with my parents. I couldn't help but remember Mother's concern at my attending the party, concern that I wondered about, whether I'd meet a man, perhaps? Mother was, like most mothers, protective of me and concerned also that any potential suitor would have to contend with my gift, would have to at least try to understand it. Edward understood. He was fascinated by it. But there was a doubt in my mind. Not concerning him, only Mother and whether she'd be dubious about such curiosity.

Oh, I was so in love! Hopelessly and completely. A teenager still, a dreamer.

I would visit him. Sit with him in the shop he managed,

Atterley's Antiquarian Books.

"Who is Atterley?" I asked him. "The owner?"

He nodded, golden hair flopping over his eyes, which he pushed away. "He is, although I've never met him. I was appointed by letter."

"You've never met him?" I was surprised. "You'd think he'd come in from time to time."

"From the correspondence we've had since, he's often abroad, searching for books to add to the shop and also his private collection. No matter. It suits me. With no one here looking over my shoulder, I can read as much as I like. No need to stand to attention."

"And the flat above? It came with the job?"

His smile was seductive. "Absolutely. Handy, don't you think?"

It was in that flat, above that dusty bookstore, which itself was situated down one of central London's dark, dark lanes, that we consummated our relationship. His hands on me, my hands on him, falling deeper and deeper.

In those early days, Edward Middleton loved me just as much as I loved him.

We would lie in bed, and he would read to me from those pages he'd told me of when we'd first met, my mind like a sponge, soaking it all up, wonders that had been forgotten.

When it was my turn to speak, I'd tell him of my gift and all that I'd experienced, spirits like wraiths, lost between the passage of here and there, and yearning for help.

He would close his eyes and sigh.

"We've forgotten, haven't we, in this hedonistic modern world, that the spiritual world exists right alongside us. Past *civilisations knew that, didn't ignore it. They respected it."*

"They did!" I'd agree. "And they had no fear of it, not like we do now. The prospect of dying terrifies most people, and yet, in life, it is the only certainty."

"Do you think hell exists?"

"I think there are lower realms, in which there are baser entities clawing to escape. That's what Mother's taught me, but she's also taught not to focus on that aspect of the spiritual unless I have to. To focus on higher realms and the light, which is also home."

"Your mother sounds like a fascinating woman."

I pretended at annoyance. "More fascinating than me?"

He grabbed me by the waist, pulled me close. "No one is more fascinating than you!"

Of course he had to meet my parents; he wanted to. It took a while because I was reluctant, as I just wanted him all to myself. Not because he was a secret but because I craved him like he was a drug and I the addict.

I was twenty when I brought him home. By that time, I had a job as a secretary in a law firm. I wasn't enjoying it one bit. I hated too how it restricted my time with Edward, but work I must; it was the modern way. I couldn't sneak off like I used to in the middle of the day to spend time with him either at his flat or in the shop, wondering in the latter whether the bell might ring, a curious customer entering. They rarely did, thankfully, as often we couldn't help ourselves, our lovemaking not confined to the flat upstairs but to a room at the back of the shop too, one that in passionate haste we would forget to lock! The young really are so reckless. Our arrangement had to become more formal and, consequently, more serious, more intense. Each moment no longer snatched but planned.

Rosamund met him, and she frowned upon meeting him. Why, I couldn't fathom. Never had he looked so presentable, more handsome. We were at our house, afternoon tea duly served, and she wasn't her usual self but austere, formidable, even, quizzing him about where he worked, whom for, what type of books he liked and why. All the things that I had quizzed him about myself, but with Mother, it was as though she were searching for fault.

Of course, after he'd left, I refused to stay quiet. I challenged her.

"You made him feel uncomfortable with all your…prying."

"Prying?" she repeated, as though incredulous. "I'm just trying to protect you!"

"I don't need protection, not from Edward! Mother, he is…intelligent, he is fascinating, the most fascinating man I know. He truly cares for me. He tells me over and over. The miracle is that he should. That I deserve his care and love."

"Darling, you are young—"

I wasn't. Soon enough I'd be twenty-one.

"He knows you don't approve," I insisted.

"Nonsense—"

"It isn't nonsense! He's a very sensitive man. He's as aware as I am of how frosty you were towards him. And Father was no better. He sat there and hardly said a word, just…appraised him. It was rude, Mother. I was mortified."

"You're my daughter! My youngest child. I have to keep you safe."

"I am safe!"

"*You hardly know him.*"

"*I've known him a year!*"

"*A year?*"

I nodded furiously.

"*Where did you meet him?*" *she asked, and then it was as though something clicked in her head.* "*The party, the masked ball, that was where you met him.*"

The party Father had dropped me off at, then had to wait over an hour after our agreed time post-party before I turned up at the car. Dear Father, he had stayed inside his car and waited, a patient man, a man who hadn't wished to embarrass me by searching for me, calling my name out over and over. Mother would have searched for me, though, found Edward and me kissing in that quiet spot we'd found. She would have torn me from him, hurried me home, refused to let me see him again. I loved my mother, she was an amazing woman, one I was proud of, but heaven help me, I saw her as something else in that moment. Unreasonable. Old-fashioned. When I told her that I'd met him at the party, something sparked in her eyes, the same anger that was in mine.

"*He knows about your gift, doesn't he?*"

"*Yes,*" *I replied, seething with indignation.* "*I told him.*"

"*When? When did you tell him?*"

"*At the party.*"

"*Sarah! We've agreed your gift is not something you need to hide, but, even so, you must be careful whom you share this with. You don't tell strangers.*"

"*He knows, and he is fascinated by it, not repelled. He treats me with respect. With reverence. I've seen him almost every day since for a year. He's not a stranger to me.*"

"*Almost every day?*" *she breathed, her shock increasing.*

She wrung her hands. "This is my fault. I've been remiss, too wrapped up in my own affairs. He does seem like a nice man, granted. But there is something…" She shook her head, clearly exasperated. "What was he doing at the party? Who invited him?"

"I don't know," I said, still defiant and still confused. "He mentioned that he's a friend of Clementine's older brother. It must have been him."

"Vague, too vague," she muttered.

"Mother, I don't understand—"

"For goodness' sake, Sarah, you are psychic and therefore sensitive, not just to spirits but to all things. Don't you feel as I do right now?"

"How? How do you feel?"

"Uneasy. He makes me feel uneasy. There it is, I've said it. Yes, he is charming, I can see how your head has been turned by him, but…he is all too vague. Have you truly not noticed? That whenever you ask a question, he avoids giving a full answer? For instance, the man he works for, who owns the bookstore, he hasn't met him. It's convenient, you see, all of it. Did you approach him at the party or he you?"

"He approached me, but then I went after him, insisted he talk to me. Mother, we hit it off straightaway. I didn't feel uneasy at all."

"And now? Now that I've brought it to your attention?"

"Brought what to my attention?" My voice had risen.

"That you should feel uneasy, girl! Because something isn't right. I can't pinpoint exactly what, but… You've become inseparable, you say? How long did it take?"

"Straightaway. It happened straightaway. Mother, he loves me, and I love him."

"Darling, no, please, you must stop seeing him."

"What?" I was stunned. "I'm a grown woman. That's for me to decide."

"It's for your own good."

"He hasn't harmed me in any way! What are you talking about?"

How stricken she looked, but also as confused as I was. "Dig deep, Sarah, become objective, not subjective, and trust your instinct. What does it tell you?"

It was madness what she was asking me to do, and yet...there was a glimmer of something deep inside. Our love affair had grown so intense so quickly, this man I considered glorious always willing to see me, to teach me. To have me teach him...

'Could I be psychic too?' he'd asked, not once but several times. 'Can you...train me?'

And I had, to the best of my ability. I'd sat on the bed with him, telling him to focus on white light, to open his mind, to sit in the 'power', as it is sometimes called, and stare into the void, the space that exists all around us but isn't empty at all. To begin to see, to communicate, to let whomever lingered know that you were aware of them, watch as they turned towards you, slowly, so slowly, confused eyes seeking you out too...

"Did he know you were psychic before you told him?" Mother asked. "Did anyone at the party?"

"No, he didn't know I was psychic," I said. "Clementine, who invited me, didn't know either."

"Are you sure Clementine didn't? Think, child, think. You saw spirits whilst at boarding school, you told me. You spoke to them. Did you ever speak out loud?"

I denied it. "No! I was careful." But then I had to retract

185

that. *"Well, maybe. Once or twice."*

"And could Clementine have been anywhere near when you did?"

"I…I don't know. Why, Mother? Why are you asking this?"

"Because if she was and she told someone else, her brother, and her brother told someone else too, his friend…and word got out…"

"I was targeted. Is that what you're trying to say? Edward…targeted me?"

"Never trust people willing to hide behind masks. Even when you think they've taken the mask away."

"Mother!" I almost screamed the word at her. *"I was not targeted. Many of my school friends were invited that night."*

"Were they? Did you see or speak to any of them?"

"No, but…Clementine told me she'd invited them."

"Are you in touch with any of them? Can you get proof?"

Damn it, I couldn't. We'd all just grown apart, even more so since I'd met Edward. I'd been too wrapped up in him to bother with anyone else.

My heart, having been so full of joy for so long, sank.

"Mother, everything in me screams Edward is true. He is loyal, loving and good."

She held my gaze, her eyes still blazing. *"And everything in me screams he won't stay that way. He'll change. And when he does, he'll try to drag you down with him."*

Chapter Twenty

THERE'D be no more sleep tonight. Even if she stopped reading and hauled herself up the stairs to bed, Jessica doubted she would sleep. Rosamund had been wary, and she'd been so right from the beginning when Sarah had told her she was attending a masked ball, sensing something untoward in a way that not only a psychic would but a mother as well. Of course Jessica was no fool; she knew why the party had made her grandmother nervous – because of what she'd associated with it.

All organisations that sided with the darkness, be it the Illuminati or the Ku Klux Klan, had a penchant for wearing masks at any event they hosted. It not only concealed their identities but was a way to dehumanise people as well, something their beliefs alone should have managed. It seemed to Jessica that the people at Clementine's ball wore Venetian-type masks, but at least they'd been discarded at midnight, a time when perhaps anyone was too drunk to care anymore. But she agreed with Rosamund – why the need for them in the first place? Was this a theme of all parties held by the Nichols family? And if so, was there indeed a dark reason behind it? A wealthy family with a family seat in the Surrey countryside, they'd certainly have ancestral involvement with an organisation such as the Illuminati, people of power and status being the backbone of such self-serving establishments.

And if this theory was correct, had Edward also been connected to whichever society it was? Clementine herself, had she been just a pawn who'd realised Sarah had a gift and felt the need to inform her family about that? They'd insisted she be invited to the party, there for Edward to corner her, the spider and the fly. Jessica remembered well Sarah's words about being with Clementine on the dance floor and how someone had swooped in to commandeer her, the girl's look of fear before that. A pawn, as she'd just thought of her, in a sinister and elaborate game, and Sarah, a mere teenager, such easy prey.

Conjecture. Just a hunch. Something that Rosamund must have struggled with too prior to the party. No proof. No evidence. And a daughter whom she'd wanted to soar high rather than have her wings clipped.

But what if she'd been right…

Jessica glanced again at the notebook, then at her laptop, which was also on the kitchen table. Moving closer to it, she brought it to life and then typed *Illuminati Ball, 1972* into the search bar.

As pages flashed onto screen, she couldn't help but marvel. It was so easy to find out information today. With a simple flick of a button, the world was yours to discover. There it was, an article with photographs of another masked ball, hosted by Marie-Hélène de Rothschild, a member of another elite family, at Chateau de Ferrières, one of the biggest and most luxurious chateaus in France. In Jessica's day, this kind of information was so difficult to find, you had to dig and dig or form connections, usually of the wrong kind, to get any insight whatsoever. As dark as the internet could be, it also had a way of dragging things into the light, ensuring there was little place to hide.

The photographs were truly disturbing, Mrs Rothschild herself in a white gown and wearing a stag's head with diamond tears. An image Jessica baulked at. A man beside her, unnamed, wore a mask with four faces, one of them the enigmatic Mona Lisa. Not just the elite families had made the guest list but the famous too – actors, actresses, artists and fashion designers. Dismembered baby dolls were placed onto dining tables, perhaps meant to indicate human sacrifice, and the exterior of the chateau was lit in blazing red, no doubt representing the supposed satanic rituals held inside. Even the invitations were written backwards, forcing the guests to use a mirror to read them.

Jessica continued to scan various images – of plates covered in fur, of food served on a mannequin corpse on a bed of roses, of servants and footmen dressed as cats that pawed at each other, of 'Sir Loin' on the menu, and 'extra lucid' soup. Whimsical on the face of it, inventive, perhaps genius, but a genius that intended to mess with your head and steal your soul. No wonder Rosamund had held such a distaste for masquerades. Not so the attendees, some of whom, it was reported, had threatened suicide if not invited to the next Rothschild party.

This somewhat iconic ball later inspired a series of others, those offered to smaller, more ordinary groups of people who wanted to get a taste of the 'high life'. Raising an eyebrow, Jessica read about these too, held all over the world for those willing to subject themselves to a series of tests, a key feature of these parties. Guests had to identify themselves as either a pig, monkey, mouse, cow or chicken, each animal representing their various personality traits. Such ostentatiousness – there were fire-eaters, trapeze artists and opera singers, all held against the backdrop of a country mansion, walls an homage to erotic art and taxidermy. Wine and champagne flowed, and the drama unfolded, the host wanting to create a kind of immersive play. Even now Jessica was fascinated by the concept, even when she knew how dark it could get, how out of hand. Ultimately, these weren't games, although much effort had gone into making it appear that way; they were tests, a way of sorting the wheat from the chaff, of detecting who was most likely to fall and fall all the way, to become drawn to evil and succumb to it.

Of course, the Nichols' party had been nowhere near as overt, but sometimes these organisations could be subtle, more on the hunt for those who would benefit them rather than simply throwing a jolly for established members.

Now deleting what was in the search bar, she typed the name *Clementine Nichols* instead. All that came up was a Clem Nicholson, an actress, too young to be the aforementioned, unless, of course, Jessica mused, the former had drunk the blood of a thousand virgins to ensure perpetual youth. As bleak as she was beginning to feel – the joy of what she'd read earlier, prior to Sarah and Rosamund's conversation, now on the wane – she couldn't help but smile. That smile faltered, however, when she again cleared the search bar and typed in *Edward Middleton*. Just how infamous was he?

Not an unusual name, many Edward Middletons appeared on-screen, one a senior policy advisor to 10 Downing Street, another an English architect of the nineteenth century, and there was an Edward Middleton of the South Carolina Middleton family, a US Navy rear admiral who'd defended the United States' Pacific borders.

So, he was neither famous nor infamous, no rival for Aleister Crowley. That, or he'd worked far more covertly than him, kept below the radar rather than courted the spotlight.

Sarah had been nineteen when she'd met Edward; he was older, twenty-five. It was during the late fifties, around 1958, Jessica surmised. And yet, she hadn't been conceived until 1970, when Sarah was in her very early thirties. And Edward was definitely the father. An older man, as she'd described him once to Jessica, someone she hadn't loved, which was why she'd left him during that pregnancy, left London too for Hastings. The former was true; he had been older, but not as much as she'd made out. The latter, that she hadn't loved him, was *not* true. Sarah had been a girl besotted, as the song declared, one that even now Jessica could hear playing in her head – a teenager in love. And she had grown into a woman in love. Had she defied her mother and her wishes? Had she run off with Edward, thus tearing her family apart? The answers were all there in the notebook.

Jessica shut down the laptop and reached towards the

book again, its tan leather so luxurious. As she opened it, she heard the slightest of noises, a creak on the stair. Was that it?

Immediately her heart began to hammer.

"Saul?" she called. "Is that you?"

Although no reply, there was another creak, as if someone was indeed approaching.

As she rose from her chair, the scraping of its wooden legs against wooden floorboards delivering an abrasive sound that made her shudder, she glanced at the clock and gasped. So much time had passed! Time that she hadn't been aware of, lost as she was in Sarah's story, reading…imagining… Even so, how could it possibly be three a.m.?

She glanced too at the coffee she'd made earlier, which she'd barely drunk. Picking it up, she could tell without tasting it that it was stone-cold, a congealed film covering the surface, making her feel queasy in the pit of her stomach to even look at it.

A third creak.

"Saul," she repeated but knew it wasn't him. He wouldn't do this, creep silently around the house.

She'd placed the mug back on the table, but she needed to hold on to something else, something that would ground her, prevent another flashback. A crystal would be ideal, one of many she had dotted around. On the kitchen windowsill was a chunk of black volcanic glass Ruby had bought her as a present – obsidian, one of the chief protection stones. Hurrying over to it, she picked it up and held it tight within her hand, bringing her other hand over to cling tighter. Although cold to the touch, it was comforting.

White light. She envisaged that too. Nothing negative would get to her, not even her own mind, which she refused to allow carte blanche. Houses made various noises at night as they settled, especially a big old Victorian like this. Steps creaked, pipes rattled, moans and sighs that sounded so human were actually the product of shifting temperatures. She'd leave the kitchen, enter the hallway and face the stairwell. No more reading, not tonight. As much as she might want to continue, depriving herself of sleep was not a good idea, because it was then that a tired, overwrought brain could start playing the trickster. Yes, it was late already, but no matter; she could lie in during the morning, catch up then.

If only her heart would stop beating so furiously. A thing apart, it was as if it betrayed her.

Just as Sarah's heart betrayed her.

The thought – which had formed so suddenly – took her by surprise.

It *was* her own thought, wasn't it?

Another creak, sounding closer this time.

The kitchen door to the hallway was closed. What lay beyond, a mystery.

But mysteries could do the most damage. She knew that and felt not frightened but buoyed by the knowledge. By the memory of something else too, the photographs Yoko Shakti had taken, his bravery, his transparency, his willingness to expose what lay inside.

No more creeping around, not by Jessica or whatever was on the other side of the door. The demons in her head had been purged. Time now to purge this one.

She strode across the floor, opened the door and

entered the hallway, all the while brandishing the crystal like a weapon.

There was something there, something shadowy, caught whilst still on the stairs but fleeting. Something that had *meant* to be seen before vanishing, to tease.

Something tall. Edward, perhaps?

For he had been a tease too.

Chapter Twenty-One

SAUL clearly sensed there'd been a change in circumstances too. As soon as they both woke on Wednesday morning, Jessica having finally climbed the stairs and eased herself into bed beside him, he was even more attentive than usual.

Had he been awake when she'd entered the bedroom earlier? If so, why hadn't he said something then? Let her know. It wasn't as if he was saying anything now, as the morning sun brightened the room. But he was looking at her in a curious way, a certain suspicion in his gaze. Later, when they moved from the bedroom to the kitchen, he remained close to her, not pottering around as he usually did.

They were both aware that their mental health was delicate and that each day was about controlling it. And yet Jessica had never felt better despite becoming increasingly aware that, however it had ended between her parents, it hadn't been on the best of terms, that Sarah had fled from Edward with good reason – for the sake of her sanity, perhaps?

The truth, it was so compelling. Despite having to steel herself before she read further, protect herself to the maximum, keeping the chunk of obsidian she'd grabbed from the kitchen close by at all times, she was still convinced the truth would somehow set her free, which was what her mother had intended. That *fate* would. And so, she'd continue.

Saul, though, wouldn't give her that chance. Not during the day, anyway.

After breakfast, he declared they needed food and so they went to the supermarket to stock up. Coming home and unpacking the bags, he then suggested another seafront walk.

"Saul," she answered, "it's freezing out there. Why don't we just…stay here?"

He refused. "The fresh air will do us good, and we'll be okay if we wrap up." He pinched some nonexistent fat around his belly. "Needs must."

If only he were weightier; she'd prefer it. How skinny he was sometimes worried her. He was adamant they needed to walk, though, and so they did, Jessica first dashing off a text to Ruby, asking if she was okay. Why she was suddenly concerned about her she didn't know. Obviously, all that she was finding out affected Ruby too, and Jessica would tell her in the fullness of time, but right now she just felt a need to check in.

Ruby returned Jessica's text swiftly.

Everything's good, Mum, thanks. Hope you're okay too. We'll catch up soon. Perhaps at the weekend? Let me know. Got an interesting case on the go. I'll tell you about it then.

As usual, her daughter signed off with three kisses.

Intrigued by the case and looking forward to seeing her, Jessica then joined Saul for their walk and, with a good five miles covered, returned home to drink hot mugs of tea beside a freshly stoked fire in the living room.

The day passed with Jessica trying not to watch the clock. Evening came, and they had dinner together, Saul helping her in the kitchen, chopping vegetables and washing pots and pans, suggesting that after dinner they watch a film.

Finally, *finally*, it was time for bed, not a single one of the stairs creaking as they ascended.

They both read for a while, Jessica sensing that Saul's eyelids were drooping. Hers were too, and she had to fight to stay awake, surreptitiously pinching the skin on the back of her hand or having to blink rapidly on occasion.

She looked over at Saul, who'd turned onto his side and was breathing deeply.

For a while she simply stayed put, waiting for him to fall deeper into slumber. As she switched off the bedside light, he was gently snoring. It was late, later than usual for Saul, as if he'd been resisting sleep too.

Now, though, he'd succumbed, and it was time for Jessica to head downstairs again.

* * *

He'd gone. Vanished. Just like that.

The day after my argument with Mother, her words like a knife cutting right through me, I fled from our house. 'He'll change. And when he does, he'll try to drag you down with him.' That's what she'd said. Why? What could she see in him that I couldn't? Or should the question be, why couldn't she see what I could? A man so different to others, full of a desire to learn, to better himself through knowledge. It was this that made him so attractive to me, his gentle understanding of my own gift too. Yes, he'd asked me to teach him about it, to help him explore his own psychic ability, which we'd agreed was something all people possessed to varying degrees, that could be brought to the fore, teased out, kindled. That was our experiment. Sit in the power. He liked that phrase. And he'd do so, fascinated by the prospect of what he might see. I'd watch him as he meditated, as he sat not with eyes closed but wide open, staring into the space before him. I'm not fooling myself; there was no madness in his eyes, none.

Not then.

I loved him. He loved me. We were going to be together despite my mother's misgivings. Of that I was determined.

And so, I hurried from the house, through the streets of London. It was a cold, grey day in winter, and it was raining, clouds low in the sky. At last, the bookstore was in sight, and I gasped with relief to see it, my heart feeling like it would burst for a thousand different reasons.

Mother hadn't said I couldn't see Edward. I think she knew better than to demand that, but if she did, if she wouldn't relent, I'd ask him if I could move in with him, into the flat above the bookshop. Surely, he'd want that, fearing being parted as much as me?

On reaching the bookshop, I burst through the door, the bell that rang whenever a customer entered loud in my ears.

"Edward, Edward," I said, "I have to speak to you. Urgently. Edward, where are you?"

It was not Edward who stepped out from one of the shop's corridors of books but a woman, far older than me, her hair swept into a bun, spectacles perched on her nose.

"Who are you?" I said, my voice full of surprise. "Is...Edward here?"

"*Edward Middleton?*"

"*Yes!*" How impatient I sounded. Rude, even. "*Of course!*"

"*I'm his replacement.*"

My head spun. "*His replacement? What do you mean?*" Looking from side to side, I searched for him. Was this some kind of joke? And he'd emerge too from one of the tome-lined corridors that seemed darker than ever, dustier? "*I have to see Edward.*"

"*I'm not sure who you are—*"

I was incensed. "*I'm his…*" I began but then stopped. I was his what? His girlfriend? Yes, I supposed so, although in that moment such a term seemed trite. "*Please tell me what you mean when you say you're his replacement.*"

"*He's gone. Quite suddenly, I have to say. It was only yesterday he informed us of his plans. Yesterday evening, in fact.*"

"*Us? Who's us?*" I further demanded.

"*My uncle owns the shop, my father's brother. And so, yes, it was us,*" she continued, injecting such a simple word with a punch of superiority. "*Hence why I'm here today, keeping the shop open because someone has to.*"

My gaze flew upwards. "*If he's not here, is he upstairs, in the flat?*"

Not even waiting for an answer, I turned to go, retracing my footsteps out of the shop, intending to head to the door by the side of it, one that would lead up to the rooms where we'd spent so much of our time together, living, laughing, learning.

"*He's gone.*" The finality of that statement stopped me in my tracks. "*Don't you understand? He's not here, in the shop nor in the flat. He's left that too. I'm sorry if it*" *inconveniences you. Certainly, it's been inconvenient for us. But there you have it."*

Eventually her words sank in, made sense in one way and in another none at all.

Edward had gone. Left without a word.

After the visit to my home, after meeting my mother.

Chapter Twenty-Two

I'D run all the way to the bookshop, and now I wandered through the streets slowly, without thought or direction, like a ghost, a wraith. The streets of London are full of ghosts, did you know that? They look just like you and me, just…trudging along, heads down and hands in pockets, with no direction either. Lost souls. Entirely lost.

I have no idea what time I arrived back home, but it was much later in the day, both my parents waiting for me, Mother most anxious in particular. She rushed over, threw her arms around me and declared how worried she'd been. I couldn't hug her back. It simply wasn't in me. Instead, when she released me, I made my way upstairs to my bedroom, which I'd occupied all my life, overlooking a long, narrow stretch of garden and the backs of other houses, often ghosts at their windows too, the shades of residents past.

Oh, I could have taught him so much! That's what I lamented. We'd only just got started. And he would have loved me more and more, which was all I wanted from him, just the sight of him, his touch, the look in his eyes when I spoke, full of awe.

Mother continued to fuss around me as I took to my bed, acting like a mother should. We both knew what was wrong with me, the malady I was suffering from – heartbreak, of course – but we spoke no more about it. I couldn't, not to her. And she knew that, refused to torture me any further with her opinions, her thoughts, her insights.

She had triumphed, or so she thought. But that triumph brought her no joy, not when it had broken me like it had.

The days passed, the months, the years. I got on with life. I had to, securing a job in another office just as dull as the first one. Time passed, and all of it so empty.

I went out with friends, met other men, men who expressed an interest in me, and sometimes I dated them, just to see. They were boys, though, whereas Edward was a man. They seemed so consumed with themselves, most of them. With how they looked, with fashion, all the things I now thought tedious and unimportant.

I saved and I saved until I was able to rent a flat of my own. I needed that, some independence. I still hadn't forgiven Mother, you see. I held her responsible for my pain. She hadn't liked Edward from the start, had been suspicious of him, and he'd sensed it, been driven away by it. Spectacularly. As though she'd clicked her fingers and vaporised him.

Now, of course, with the benefit of hindsight, it hurts to think of how I was towards Rosamund. How I wasted our last years together. If she acted at all, it was only in my interests. And she was right, of course; that was the thing. Perhaps even in the midst of my heartbreak, I knew that deep down. But if I did, it hardly mattered. I still resented her.

Best to put space between us, that's what I thought, visiting home but less and less often. Just pursuing the course of my own life and praying that a broken heart could mend, that I would wake one day to find the agony had ended. Because if it was permanent, I couldn't bear it.

I'd met my soul mate, and then I'd lost him.

My soul mate! A term I don't use lightly. Even now. Because he was.

Being without him only reinforced that fact.

The day I met him again started like any other.

After the usual seven hours' sleep, I rose and readied myself for work. I left the flat I occupied, a small space in a building that was tired, the people that occupied the other flats sometimes looking equally as tired when I passed them on the stairs.

Another grey winter's day, the rain pelting down. It was weather that suited my mood as I traipsed along the streets, taking my usual route past restaurants and cafés and shops preparing for the new day. My eyes were downcast, my hands were in my pockets, the hood of my rain jacket up. I was thirty but felt old beyond my years, scarred by life.

On my usual route, but still lost.

Someone stepped out in front of me. With my eyes still downcast, I simply moved to the side to avoid them. A hand shot out, however, and grabbed my arm. A bolt of fear coursing through me, I opened my mouth to scream as I lifted my eyes.

And there he was – Edward Middleton – more distinguished than I ever remembered him, a smile on his face and something in his eyes too. Excitement?

"Edward!" I breathed but could say no more. All I could do was stare, his once floppy blond hair now short and neat and glistening with raindrops.

"I'm sorry," he said. "I never meant—"

I didn't want to hear it, not another word. All I wanted was to feel his mouth on mine. I wrenched back my hood and threw myself at him. So readily his arms came around *me, his lips returning the pressure, my emotions breaking free of the restraints I'd kept them under and finding themselves more than matched.*

Afterwards, he took my hand, and we ran through shiny, wet streets. I didn't know where we were going, and I didn't care. Not about work or anything. I just wanted to be with him. We arrived at another flat, one not nearly as comfortable as his last, more down at heel. Again, who cared? Words, explanations, could all come later.

The room, though, it really was squalid, not befitting him at all, the bed wholly unkempt. Still, I didn't hesitate. Not for one second. We fell on the bed, reunited in body as well as soul, that union more exquisite than ever, something curious happening to me afterwards, a tingling. A sensation even sweeter than those experienced just minutes before.

I didn't know it then, but I had now conceived a child.

I didn't realise it until it was far too late.

* * *

I refused to admit it at the time, but during those years that we'd been apart, so many of them, he'd changed in more than looks. Although how, I couldn't quite pinpoint.

Of course I asked him why he'd left and so suddenly, and the reason was as I had suspected.

"Your mother didn't like me. I didn't want…to cause trouble."

"But you broke my heart, leaving like you did without a word!"

"My heart was broken too."

"It was the not knowing!" I continued as we lay in his room on that messy bed. "Thinking something might have

happened to you, worrying about you. Also, that I'd been wrong all along and maybe you didn't love me after all, that you felt nothing for me."

He shook his head. *"Not true. I did. I do."*

"Then why didn't you stay with me and have the courage of your convictions? We could have faced my mother together. Something we'll have to do now, at any rate."

"No. I'm sorry. I'm…" He swallowed hard before continuing. *"I'm going away."* He gestured around him. *"I can't stay here. This was just a stopgap. I'm here for a week or two, if I can bear it that long."*

I was dumbstruck but forced myself to speak. *"Where? Where are you going?"*

"There's a house in the Sussex countryside, cheap rent but grand, apparently. It belongs to a friend of a friend, so I'm going there."

Tears sprang to my eyes. *"What about me?"*

"I—"

Rather than let him speak, I asked another question. *"How did you find me, Edward?"*

He gave a rueful smile. *"Not because of my psychic abilities, sadly. Through another friend of a friend, someone who works for the same firm as you. He just happened to be talking about you one day, was rather taken with you, mentioned your name."*

"Who?" I was incredulous.

"Ronnie White."

"Ronnie White?"

"Do you like him too?"

From gazing downwards, I lifted my eyes. *"No! Of course not."*

"Has there…been anyone else?"

"No." Fervently I shook my head. "Only you. And you?" I challenged.

"No one who's meant as much."

"Fate," I said, marvelling at it. "Fate has thrown us together again."

"Come with me."

"What?"

"Come with me to this house in the country. You're a grown woman, fully independent. You don't need the say-so of your parents, not anymore."

"Mother's ill," I said. "Father's becoming frailer."

"Please. I beg you. I can't lose you again."

"But…" Neither could I lose him. Once had been bad enough. As for Mother and Father, it didn't mean I had to lose touch with them. Sussex wasn't far away, and trains ran to London every day. I could have them all, combine both worlds. The only obstacle was my job.

"Do you love what you do?" he said when I voiced that concern.

I didn't. I hated it, spending day after day typing letters and answering the phone, but what I did enjoy was the money I earnt. Although I came from a well-off family, I didn't take an allowance; none of my siblings did. Our parents wanted us to be self-sufficient, and we wanted that for ourselves too, the inheritance due to us being a double-edged sword, as it would only come about because of tragedy – the loss of them. How would I live if I didn't earn money?

As though Edward read the conflict in my eyes, he grabbed me by the arms and forced me to look deep into the blue of his.

"I will look after you," he declared. "In all ways."

"Edward—"

"Please, listen to me. I have money. In the years we've been apart, I've had work, I've saved. And as I've already said, the rent at this house, despite its size, is very, very reasonable. Please let me look after you. Sarah, I want to marry you!"

Words I'd been longing to hear, that I'd dreamt of all those lonely nights that had seemed to stretch into infinity. At last they were being said and with such passion.

My love wanted to marry me.

And so, I agreed to leave my job, to move away with him, to begin our life together with no one casting doubt over us. I didn't even ask him what he'd been doing to save enough money to support us both. I just didn't care. I wanted to forget the years without him.

When I told Mother of my plans, I admit I was trembling. But she simply sighed, told me to remember all I'd been taught and that the door was open for my return, day and night.

I left London for Sussex, the pair of us travelling in his car, the hood down and the wind in our hair. I was happy. I felt so free, so alive, young again, twenty-one instead of nearly a decade older, the span of time that had passed rendered meaningless suddenly.

As much as I loved him, though, as I've already said, there was something about him that had changed. He smiled just as much as he used to, was as attentive, as loving, every bit as thrilling. And yet…for the first time, I understood my sick mother's fears. Was he thrilling because he was dangerous? And if so, in what way?

How could he possibly be a danger to me?

The house, when we arrived, stole my breath but for all

the wrong reasons. It was grand, certainly, but it was also...wrong somehow. A mismatch of styles. Nothing about it gelled. Edward saw something quite different, though. He saw a palace.

And that's when I realised how little I knew of him. How much I saw only what I wanted.

He'd changed, but in that house, situated as it was down a lane as dark as any London mews, seemingly in the middle of nowhere – because that's what it felt like, removed from the world, from civilisation – he changed further. Bit by bit, his humanity was drained.

This was a bad house – even now I cannot utter its name; I don't want to – full of darkness, of those that played games, that taunted me with their presence then hid from me, both distressed and evil. Why I stayed, I'll never know. I was just so in love. I clung to hope, and, slowly, gradually, I realised I was pregnant.

As I've said, there was evil in that house, and also those in the most terrible distress. I tried to tune in to the latter, to help them, seeking somehow to rectify the balance there, to infuse it with light, but Edward tuned in to something quite different.

And I began to suspect that, via the friend of a friend, he'd known exactly what this place was, what it held, and that was why he'd come here, why he wanted me by his side.

"Tell me, Sarah," he would say, "what can you sense? What can you see? Teach me again, help me to sit in the power, to reach out."

"What for?" I'd ask, trying to hide the tremor in my voice.

"So I can help, of course! Like you're trying to help." But then he'd slip up. "I want the power so much." And in his

eyes, there it was, that first glimmer of madness.

I told him then how evil could fool you, that it promised you everything but delivered nothing but debt. That we had to leave, get in the car and put as much distance between us and the house as possible, flee to the far end of the country if we had to.

He wouldn't listen; he refused to, succumbing more and more to the darkness, believing it to be something beautiful, something benevolent, when it was exactly the opposite.

And so it was that I decided to leave, finally. That first time, though, he stopped me. And the second. And the time after that. "Don't leave me here," he begged. "I need you."

But what he needed from me I no longer knew.

When I tried a fourth time, that's when he became violent, when he hit me.

"You cannot leave, Sarah! We're in this together! Now help me to sit in the power, to communicate. It will profit us both if you do. We have to learn to deal with what's here and make use of it. You cannot leave. I simply won't let you."

The first stirrings of madness, the real Edward receding. He was doing exactly as my mother had feared, a narcissism in him that the house had found and nurtured. His fascination with the dark side had been there all along, as far back as Clementine's party, when he had mixed with those that he considered above him, seeking now not to emulate but outrank them. Sell your soul and you can rule the world. Therein lies the myth.

I had to leave. I could take no more beatings, not with his child growing inside me, something he wasn't aware of, that I was keeping to myself.

"Edward, stop, please! You have to!"

And he would stop, and he'd blink, so confused. He'd remove himself from me, lock himself in a room in the house. I would creep up to that room, press my ear against the door and listen. Not to his voice, though, but another's. "You're one of us. We'll look after you. You belong here." Sometimes Edward would laugh, would agree. "Yes! Yes, I do! I belong at last." But sometimes he'd cry, a heartbreaking sound, a sound that told me my Edward still remained but was buried deep.

It was during one of these episodes that I seized my chance and left. This time succeeding. I'd already planted the car keys near the door, in my coat pocket. Whilst he was deep in whatever trauma he now romanced, I grabbed the coat and ran out the door, hearing behind me so much laughter, frenzied clapping too. And a voice, the one I would hear conversing with him in the locked room, that of a boy, not speaking out loud but in the confines of my head. An image of his eyes appeared, as black as ink.

"Run as fast as you like," he said, his voice dripping with equal amounts of amusement and mockery. "And as far as you can. Just like Edward, you'll never escape. You're mine – you, your daughter and your daughter's daughter too. You all belong to me."

Chapter Twenty-Three

FOR the longest time Jessica stared at the page. Edward hadn't known Sarah was pregnant, but the boy, the spirit, whatever it was, did. It knew Sarah was having a girl and that, in turn, Jessica would have a girl too. And he'd laid claim to all of them?

No! Absolutely not! No way! This was *exactly* how evil worked. It wormed its way into your soul, preyed upon your mind and your fears, then devoured you, bit by bit. Evil had no claim on the Davis women. Not anymore.

Edward, though, had fallen easily, willingly, into its clutches. And that was what was key here, what Sarah was trying to tell her, that he'd *become* corrupted, believing evil's lies.

Who was the friend of a friend who'd directed him to this terrible house? Had they done so because they could see a potential for wickedness in him? Turning fierce intelligence and curiosity into something perverted, forever seeking out people they could use. And had that potential been spotted a long time previously in Edward, before he'd attended Clementine's ball, a whisper in his ear about a girl who talked to ghosts, an idea carefully planted? *She could help you, Edward. She could help us.* A woman able to bridge the material and spiritual worlds, who could take him on the journey he longed to go on, that journey taking a dark turn as the demonic lay in waiting.

A plan. A devious one. And yet Sarah had loved him, and she'd loved him because she'd seen something else in him, another potential – for good. And then there was Rosamund, who'd recognised his weakness even from a distance, who could see it as plain as day. An intuitive man, it had riled him, and he'd fled. To protect Sarah, as he'd claimed, or himself? Sarah, whom he couldn't resist, whom he'd tracked down again, years later.

The tears that he'd cried in the locked room, were they for a man who'd chosen the wrong path and now couldn't find a way back?

Was Edward both good *and* evil?

Her breath was still heavy as she continued to scan the pages, desperate for her mother to provide answers. *What happened, Mum? What happened?*

I drove his car, all the way back to the outskirts of London, me who'd only ever driven recreationally before, my foot heavy on the pedal. I then abandoned the car and caught the train into London's Victoria Station, and walked from there all the way home.

As ill as Mother was – she had cancer – she was waiting at the door to greet me, her arms wide open. She held me as I sobbed, as I cried not for myself, although once again my heart was broken, but for Edward too, for the fact my love alone couldn't save him.

Mother insisted I was to leave London in case he came looking for me, to draw on my inheritance now, when I needed it most. I was going to have a child, and, thanks to the money, I could live in a small town, near the sea, perhaps. Raise that child in a house filled with love.

Upon arriving in Hastings, I stayed in a boarding house until I bought Lazuli Cottage, our home. For Jessica and then Ruby too.

But I couldn't forget him, couldn't rid myself either of the guilt I felt in abandoning him. What if he'd come to his senses? If he was trying to find me?

I wrote once, not to that house in Sussex but to the bookshop, to tell him I was carrying his child and that I loved him. I had to put it down in words. The letter was returned to me in due course, as I knew it would be, 'No longer at this address' scrawled across it.

Jessica was born. Such a beautiful, fierce, intelligent thing, a perfect mix of us both.

Since then, there has never been another man for me, only ever Edward. Did I abandon him too soon, however? Succumbing to something too, my own fear of him?

I think not, but either way, I cannot change it.

I held him in my thoughts, sent him love and light, every day of my life. Prayed he hadn't done dreadful things, hurt people, exploited them. Prayers that were sadly in vain.

Edward Middleton was, once, a good man, the best; he was ahead of his time. He might have been manipulated and our meeting engineered, but what those puppeteers hadn't foreseen was that we would fall in love, so quickly and so deeply, on the very night of Clementine's ball. And even as I write this, an old lady now, nearing the end of this glorious and troubled life as Sarah Davis, I still love him. We connected; our souls fused. And that's how I knew my prayers were in vain, because every time he courted evil, *every time he carried out its will, I felt the keen sting of his pain. But that pain was becoming less, becoming merely a wisp.*

He is angry. He will lash out, and he will call on all the agents of hell to help him.

Watch out, Jessica and Ruby, tread carefully.

Despite him not knowing about you, in reading this, in simply being his offspring, a connection could form. Somehow, someway, he will sense someone close is reading this account. Close in blood, that is.

If so, he will try to hurt you in whichever way he can.

He's still alive, at least at the time of writing this. Instinct tells me so.

Find him, Jessica and Ruby. Do what I couldn't and help him to see, truly see, before it's too late. Ironically, helping him may be the only way that you can now help yourselves. Somehow, it's Ruby I fear for the most because, if a connection is formed, she is one step removed, not solely our flesh and blood.

In reading this, everything has changed. There is no going back.

The only solace I have is what I've said all along. Fate intends this.

PART THREE

Ruby

Chapter Twenty-Four

LEA Monaghan was verging on hysteria.

"What in God's name have I done inviting you here?" she screamed, her voice so high that it cut right through Ruby. "What have we unleashed?"

"Corinna…" Ruby managed. Still reeling from the second attack that had taken place in the spare bedroom of Lea's house, she could say no more. Corinna heard the appeal in her colleague's voice and continued trying to pacify Lea. They weren't in the spare bedroom anymore but the kitchen, having staggered downstairs.

The attacks, not one but two of them, had come out of nowhere, wholly unexpected. When Ruby and Corinna had entered the house, Ruby had sensed something, although whether it was residual or intelligent, she hadn't known – but whatever it was, it was gentle.

Lea had previously described a sadness in that room, and she was right, there was; it drenched the atmosphere, made it different to that of the other rooms in the house, where the energy was high rather than low, as you'd expect from a busy family home. Ruby and Corinna had gone straight to the source of it, the spare bedroom, and expected to do the usual: tune in, make contact if the spirit was intelligent and try to send it to the light. A straightforward enough procedure. A lot of cleansings were.

Yet although she always expected the unexpected, what had just happened was beyond reason. Two forces, vengeful, that sought only to hurt and frighten, that had struck out of nowhere, that didn't belong there, she was certain of it. That were external to the house. The second one...worse than the first, though the first had been bad enough. Thankfully, she'd summoned a degree of light to protect herself by that time. If not... She dreaded to think, one hand reaching up towards her neck and rubbing at the skin there.

Corinna had already told her about the copious messages on her phone, from Theo, Ness, Carrie-Ann and...her mother? As desperate as she was to find out the reasons behind the barrage, it would have to wait. She and Corinna had Lea to deal with first.

"I thought you were going to die up there!" Lea continued, tears streaming down her face. "And us too!"

Corinna was assuring her that no one had been in such danger, although even Ruby could hear the lack of conviction in that statement. Ruby might have been the one to suffer the physical attack, but Corinna was equally in shock.

From leaning against the kitchen table, Ruby now had to sit, pulling out a chair, hoping that Lea wouldn't object, because she needed a minute to compose herself.

216

Eventually, she spoke. "Lea, what just happened to me, it was…highly unusual. And I don't think central to this house."

"What do you mean?" Lea was still standing. "That you've brought something in with you? Some sort of…devil. Oh my God! My good God!"

Funny how people called on God for help when terrified, Ruby thought. Lea was suddenly very religious, and yet when they'd spoken before, there'd been no hint of that.

"We can't stay here," Lea continued to insist. "We're in danger. We'll have to pack our bags and leave. If this house was haunted before, it was at least tolerable. What you've done has made it worse!"

"You don't have to leave," Ruby told her. "I don't know what happened to me upstairs yet, but I'll find out – *we* will," she said, nodding towards Corinna, "the whole Psychic Surveys team. We'll make it our priority. But please listen when I say that what happened, the attacks, were focused on me, *just* me. I think…like I've said, they're external to this house; they have nothing to do with it whatsoever. So, yes, in a sense, I have brought something in with me, but when I leave, it will leave with me too."

Lea's eyes, already on stalks, would pop from her head if she forced her lids to open any wider. "If that's the case, and I'm not saying I believe it is, then you have to go, get out of my house. Right now, and never come back."

Whilst Ruby faltered, due to exhaustion more than anything – a psychic attack such as the one she'd just experienced could leave you drained for days – Corinna stepped in.

"Mrs Monaghan," she said, dispensing with any informalities, "we apologise about what happened. It wasn't what we expected, and it was astonishing to see, I agree, as well as extremely unsettling. But as Ruby says, and I suspect that this is true too, it has nothing to do with this house or the alleged presence in the spare room. This is something—" she swallowed as she said it, faltered too, but for less than a second "—personal to Ruby. And, as she's also said, we will find out what it is, issuing you with a full explanation. But for now, in our professional opinion, you are safe to stay in your own home."

Perhaps it was the way Corinna had spoken, so calmly, so *persuasively*, her shoulders straight and her head held high – adopting the glamour, as Theo called it, literally brimming with confidence and authority – that Lea breathed easier.

She too pulled out a chair and sat, Corinna doing the same, all three of them taking a moment now to calm down further, Lea's shivering becoming less visible. Ruby had no idea what kind of woman Lea was, but she prayed for a reasonable one, who'd be open to giving them a chance to prove her house was safe, that the only presence there was a gentle one. A big ask, but she had to emulate Corinna, act with authority and confidence despite feeling bruised, battered and utterly baffled.

"Lea," she said, "time is all we need to sort out what happened. A few days. If I thought you were in danger here, I would say. But you're not. Staying here will prove it. You're safe, but if you are worried, you can call on us at any time. We'll be here for you."

"What about my husband and kids, though? What do I tell them?"

"Honestly? If you give us time to work out what happened, then perhaps there's no need to tell them anything. Fear breeds fear. If you choose to tell them, however, which is completely your decision, then it's likely they're going to start imagining all sorts of things. That's the thing, Lea. Imagination is responsible for so much."

"I wasn't imagining what happened to you!"

"No. That was real enough." She had the bruises to show for it. "All I'm asking for is time. Please, Lea, we need to rectify this situation, not make it worse."

Lea continued to sit there, staring at the floor and chewing at the inside of her mouth. Eventually she raised her head. "If my mother were alive, it might be a different story. We'd stay with her. Not set foot back in here until the matter was sorted, but…"

"But?" Corinna prompted when Lea stalled.

Lea shrugged, gave a rueful smile. "I can't bear my mother-in-law. There you go, that's another secret between us. My husband would be mortified if he knew. The thought of having to move in with her, of suffering her silent disapproval – I doubt there's a woman alive good enough for her only son – I can't bear the thought of it." She turned her head towards the kitchen door as though expecting their invisible foe to come rushing in, Ruby half fearing it too. "Think I might take my chances here rather than with her." Her gaze back on Ruby, she added, "But only for a few days, okay? And only if nothing more happens. If it does…"

If it did, she could do a number of things that might

make life difficult for Psychic Surveys – go to the press, for example, something Ruby always feared. Although, of course, it would be her word against theirs. There was no proof of what had just happened, Ruby being pinned to a wall, her feet off the ground and arms flailing. And already, in Lea's mind, Ruby hoped she'd be trying to apply logic to such dramatic events, wondering if she could trust the evidence of her eyes, beginning to doubt it. But it *had* happened, in all its strange glory, and Ruby would feel bad pretending otherwise.

The only thing to do was get all hands on deck and meet the deadline.

With the situation tempered, for now, at least, Ruby and Corinna rose to leave, Lea leading them back down the hallway.

"So, if anything happens, anything at all, I can call you?"

"Anything you're uncomfortable with," Ruby said, praying she wouldn't be on the phone every five minutes for the sake of a creaky floorboard or other benign noises.

"Okay, okay," Lea replied, nodding her head. "I hope you're right, though, that what happened, the nasty bit, *is* just to do with you, that the rest of us are safe, at least."

* * *

A psychic attack could leave you drained, and certainly Ruby felt depleted, like she'd undergone ten rounds with Tyson Fury. But there was no time to indulge that feeling, not just because of the deadline regarding Lea, or the fact she had Hendrix to care for, but because her mind was striving to process what had just happened.

On leaving the Monaghan house and hurrying to her car, Ruby and Corinna had climbed inside and sat there, the pair of them staring straight ahead, still stunned.

"The phone calls," Corinna said, handing Ruby's mobile back over to her.

Ruby's eyes widened as she read the screen. "Theo, Ness, Carrie-Ann and Mum. Plus, there're texts from all of them to call back. Cash too – shit, the baby must be kicking off again. Oh, Corinna, I'm not sure I can cope with all this. All I want to do is sleep."

"Ruby, you are okay, though?"

"Technically."

"Then, I'm sorry…"

"I know, I know. No time for sleep. Can you call Theo and Ness for me? I'll speak to Carrie-Ann and Mum, try to sort out what's got everyone worked up."

"And Cash?"

"Cash will have to wait." Sadly, so would Hendrix, which tore at her heart.

A few minutes later, Ruby and Corinna were still sitting in the car, even more stunned. What colleagues, client and family had to say boggling their minds further.

"We need a meeting," Ruby had declared whilst she was on the phone with Carrie-Ann and Corinna was speaking to Theo. "At mine. All of you. Now."

Her mother too, whom Ruby had spoken to before Carrie-Ann, who'd previously phoned because she'd feared something had happened to Ruby, an attack of some sort. She *knew*. Regarding how, Jessica hadn't wanted to say over the phone.

"Crazy!" Ruby said when all phone calls had ended.

"You think?" Corinna said, her voice edged with sarcasm.

Ruby shook her head in dismay. "And it's about to get crazier still. Poor Cash."

Corinna looked further perplexed. "Why 'poor Cash'?"

"Because whether Hendrix is kicking off or not, he's going to have to step into the breach regarding childcare. A few days, Corinna, that's all we've got to solve what's happening. We have to find Dave Lane, aka Leon Vasilescu, and find out what's upsetting my mother too. She didn't say much, but she didn't have to, I can feel well enough whatever it is, it's big."

Chapter Twenty-Five

THE look on Cash's face as person after person traipsed through the doorway of his home in Sun Street was a picture.

"Um…Ruby," he said as she also entered, the last of them to do so. "Any chance of letting me know what's going on here?"

The baby was in his arms, Cash rocking him to keep him placated and failing dismally. Hendrix continued to fidget, his face becoming redder, his mouth opening wide in a threatening manner.

Carrie-Ann backtracked. "Here, let me," she said, holding her arms out for Cash to hand the baby over. An awkward moment followed as he hesitated. Ruby had told him about Carrie-Ann, of course, and perhaps that was what caused him to stall. Also, that she looked frail, to Ruby frailer than ever, her expression really quite drawn. What he didn't know, however, was how brilliantly Hendrix responded to her.

"Cash, it's all right," she told him. "Carrie-Ann has the magic touch."

Still seeming reluctant but trusting Ruby's word, he handed over the precious cargo, the bellow that left the baby's mouth during that process immediately dying down once Carrie-Ann's arms were wrapped around him.

"Blimey," he said. "What are you? A witch or something?"

"Cash!" Ruby admonished, but Carrie-Ann only laughed.

"No, I don't think so, although what I've *become* is open to debate. I just love babies, that's all. It's that simple."

So do we, thought Ruby as she watched the transformation from fretful baby to a contented one. *We love him*. And yet they didn't have this effect. *She* didn't, his mother.

"Ruby," Theo called from halfway up the stairs to the attic, Ness behind her and, behind Ness, Jessica and Saul. "We need to crack on."

Ruby nodded, aware that Theo, whilst on the stairs, had read her mind, that in her words was a gentle reprimand: *Now's not the time to question your parenting skills*. "Cash, I know you're busy, but could you—"

"He's asleep," Carrie-Ann said. "Let's take him with us. I'll just…continue to hold him."

Cash was relieved but also perplexed. "Should I be in on this meeting too?"

"Or I could fill you in later?" Ruby said.

"Okay, let's do that, then I can work." He looked at the crowd in front of him, then at Ruby again. "I want every last detail."

"You'll have it," Ruby promised, ushering Carrie-Ann and Hendrix up the stairs too.

A few minutes later and they were all in Ruby's office, Ruby grabbing some folding chairs so that everybody had a place to sit. Jed also appeared, looking as surprised as Cash to see them all, giving a bark and a chase of his tail before settling.

Behind her desk, Ruby made the introductions. "I'll fetch teas and coffees later," she continued. "Right now, let's try to make sense of this and hear what everyone's got to say, taking it in turns. Carrie-Ann, you okay to go first?"

Carrie-Ann glanced down at the baby in her arms before nodding.

"I saw him," she said. "Leon Vasilescu."

"Dave Lane?" Theo corrected.

She nodded. "Yes, that's right."

"When?" asked Ruby.

"It was last night, about seven. I was restless, so much going on in my head. I thought I'd go for a walk, that it'd help me to think clearer. I was on the prom, and it was cold and blowy. Even so, I wanted to see the sea. I had this urge." Noting Ruby's concerned look, she gave a smile. "I wasn't planning on doing anything stupid, don't worry. Return to the sea, so to speak. Way too corny. I just see it a bit differently now, that's all. I...respect it." She shook her head as if trying to reset what was in there. "Anyway, I walked and walked, and then I thought I'd better turn back, return home, via the town route this time. So I turned right, up one of those grand streets in Hove, shoulders hunched and head down, as it was getting colder. I reached the top of the road, Southbourne Villas, and took a right onto Church Road, hurrying, feeling tired. Really tired, in fact. Drained."

Ruby identified with that, as far as she was able to, anyway.

"And there he was, coming towards me. Leon…Dave…whatever. His head down, also hurrying. Looking not like Leon Vasilescu, the clairvoyant, but…a hobo."

"What did you do?" asked Corinna as Jed sat to attention.

"I shouted out. I said, 'Hey, do you remember me?' He lifted his head, looked confused, but only at first. Then came recognition. I saw it, plain as day. And fear too, just like the first time we met. He stepped to the side, tried to get past me, but I wasn't having it. This man knows about me. Somehow. Thankfully, the streets were quiet or I might have been in trouble with the way I acted. I demanded he stop and look me in the eye, tell me what he saw that day. That he help me, basically."

If Carrie-Ann had a calming effect on the baby, the baby also seemed to calm her. Now, though, recalling what had happened, she grew agitated. Ruby was about to rise, ready to take Hendrix from her, when Jessica reached out a hand and laid it on the woman's arm.

"I don't know your full story," Jessica said, "not yet. All I know is that if he won't help you, these people here will. They've got your back. Every step of the way."

Carrie-Ann calmed again, that motherly touch much needed.

"Suffice to say," she continued, "there was no way he was going to enlighten me, whether for good or for bad. And so…Jessica, is it?"

Jessica nodded.

"What you've just told me, I told him. That if he wouldn't help me understand my situation, then I knew people who would."

Ness stiffened at this. "Did you tell him who exactly? Name names?"

Carrie-Ann swallowed before nodding. "Yes, I did. I told him it was Psychic Surveys." She then elaborated, "Ruby Davis of Psychic Surveys."

"What did he do then?" Ness questioned further.

"He just...he looked terrified. Pushed past me and ran."

"And that was the end of it, was it?" probed Theo.

"No," Carrie-Ann said, something in her voice that hadn't been there before: shame.

"Carrie-Ann," Theo assured her, "we don't sit in judgement. We just need to know facts."

Carrie-Ann hugged the baby close. "I chased after him. I'm sorry. It was a stupid thing to do. I...I shouted, told him that Ruby Davis was the real deal, that she'd help me, and..."

"And?" prompted Ness, her voice perhaps not quite as soothing as Theo's.

"And that she'd go after him too, demand to know what he meant by what he'd said to me, get the truth from him. Punish him if he didn't."

"Punish him?" Ruby was astonished. "You actually said I'd punish him?"

A tear from Carrie-Ann's eye splashed onto the baby's cheek. "I'm sorry. It was so stupid. *I* was stupid. God, even in death I don't learn."

As baffled as Saul appeared by that last statement – Jessica not so much, perhaps beginning to suspect what was unusual about her – Ruby didn't elaborate, not then. What she did tell Saul, though, and her mother too, was about what she'd suffered whilst at the Monaghan house, the reverberations of which Ness and Theo had felt, such was the connection between them and the reason each had called her.

"Not one but two attacks," she told them. "Different energies."

"So, what is it you're saying?" asked Corinna. "Who's the first? Dave Lane?"

"Think about it," said Ruby, trying to piece it all together. "Lane now knows my name. He knows the type of business I run and that I'm apparently the real deal. He can look our website up on the internet, where there's also a photograph of me. He can hold that image in his mind, reach out and somehow, someway, form a connection even though we've never met. He can do all that because his psychic ability is very, very advanced, because he's in no way a fake. He certainly *is* the real deal."

"Shit!" Carrie-Ann exclaimed. "I'm so sorry. I had no idea. Is that really possible?"

"It's not usual, but, yes, it seems it is entirely possible."

Theo shifted in her chair. "And you're sure, absolutely sure, that the attack has no link to what's in the Monaghan house?"

"None," confirmed Ruby. "It's a gentle energy there...wistful. Wouldn't you say, Corinna?"

Corinna nodded.

"How was Lea after what happened?" asked Ness.

"She wants answers," Corinna said, "and she's entitled to them, being as this all took place in her house. But, with a bit of persuasion, she's given us a few days to get those answers before she starts kicking off."

"Fabulous," declared Theo, her manner wry. "I love a bit of pressure."

"Theo," Ruby said, immediately concerned. "Last thing I want is for you to stress—"

"Stress, girl? What are you talking about? I thrive on stress! It keeps this old heart of mine beating." She gave an indulgent smile and shrugged. "Sorry. I'm being facetious. I'm fine, honestly, perfectly capable of helping you to deal with this, as you say, somewhat unusual development. The new medication I'm on is working well, and my blood pressure, my heart rate and even my cholesterol levels are all heading south, along with everything else about me. I've even lost a few pounds, not that any of you have bothered to comment." Waving away the flurry of apologies that ensued once she'd pointed this out, she carried on. "Enough already. I know no one will notice until at least a good stone has dropped. Oh, who am I kidding? Probably more like two, but, hey, I'm pleased with my success so far. The upshot of all this is that retirement's a way off yet."

Something that came as a massive relief, not just to Ruby but to all of them.

"Carrie-Ann," Ruby said, relieved too that Hendrix was still sleeping peacefully, "you said you chased Dave Lane. Where to, exactly? His home, by any chance?" When Carrie-Ann shook her head, Ruby sighed with frustration. "So where, then? How did he lose you?"

"It was strange, now that I think of it. I felt I could catch him, you see, not drained anymore but full of energy. Full of desperation, I suppose. There wasn't that much of a gap between us, but—" she inclined her head to the side "—it grew so dark, so black. One minute he was there in front of me, the next, it was as though the night had swallowed him whole. Sounds stupid, I know." Immediately, she seemed to try to find logic. "There were a few people in front of us. They'd just got off the bus, and I was distraught. I think…I think I just lost sight of him somehow. He must have turned off the main road and down a side road, maybe jumped over a wall, hid in one of the gardens there."

Whatever had happened, whether or not the night had colluded with Lane, he'd got away, and that was all there was to it. Now they had to find him because, strange as it was to think it, his insight regarding Carrie-Ann might be greater than theirs.

"As most of you know, when Cash and I visited the pier," Ruby said, "they said they had no forwarding address for Lane, but being in Hove at that time of the evening, around eight o'clock by then, would you say, Carrie-Ann?"

"Yes, eight to eight thirty."

"Then maybe Hove is where he lives. We could spend time searching that area, plus…" Ruby looked at Ness. "Lee could help us?"

Ness's partner, Lee, was an officer in the Brighton police force, and whilst Dave Lane might not be on their records, if they gave Lee a detailed enough description of the man they were looking for, police officers patrolling that area could keep an eye out for him.

When she suggested this, Ness nodded. "I'm sure that won't be a problem."

Ruby pushed her luck a little further. "And if he could check the database, just in case."

Smiling this time, Ness said, "He's a busy man, as you know, but, again, I'll ask."

"Great, thank you."

"So, what do we do meanwhile?" asked Carrie-Ann. "Don't get me wrong, I'm not worried about me, but if you've been attacked…"

"Launching those kinds of attacks requires one heck of a lot of effort," Ruby told her. "Afterwards, whoever was responsible would feel depleted, needing to recoup. I'd be very surprised if another attack comes my way anytime soon, at least within the next day or two. More importantly, though, I'll be well prepared for it. We all will, Theo, Ness and Corinna as well as me putting in place the necessary barriers."

"So we have time?"

"We do," Ruby assured her. "Just not a great deal of it."

"So, that was the first attack," Theo interjected, "launched by dear old Dave Lane, but what about the second? The one you describe as more vicious. Who launched that?"

Jessica replied before Ruby did. "I think I might have the answer to that."

Chapter Twenty-Six

IN the attic of Ruby's home in Sun Street, you could have heard a pin drop. Jessica was about to speak, to reveal something, and the air of expectation was intense, Ruby still suspecting that what she had to say would blow what they'd learnt about Dave Lane into the ether.

"I found something," Jessica said at last, clearly having to compose herself. "In the attic of Lazuli Cottage." To Carrie-Ann, she said, "That was our family home, that we shared with Sarah, who was my mother and Ruby's gran. A notebook. One Sarah had written in recently, in fact. Shortly before her death, I believe."

"A notebook?" Ruby breathed. "In the blanket box? The one in the corner of the attic, covered in magazines and jigsaws."

"So you had spotted it?"

Ruby nodded. "Uh-huh, when I was there last week. You couldn't come because you were unwell. I…" She swallowed hard. "Poked my head into the attic to see what was there. Nothing much, just the blanket box and a few other bits. I was going to check it out, but…"

"Something distracted you?" Jessica said.

"That's right. The phone."

Jessica also nodded. "Gran didn't know which one

of us would find the notebook, if indeed we ever would. I think it was meant to be me, though. The notebook concerns my father."

"Edward Middleton?" Again, Ruby was astounded. "It's about him?"

"It's about *them*," Jessica corrected. "Sarah and Edward. It's…a love story."

Hendrix began to wriggle his body. Ruby's eyes, however, barely grazed him as she continued to converse with her mother.

"Gran didn't love him," she pointed out. "That's what she said, remember? Why she left him when she was pregnant with you and moved to Hastings."

"She did love him. In the notebook, she confesses all. She loved him, Ruby, with every ounce of her being, and right until the end of her life."

If there were tears in Jessica's eyes, they were now in Ruby's. What her mother had said was the last thing she'd expected to hear. A handsome man, charming…Edward Middleton was that, all right. She had a picture of him to prove it. But look where it had been taken. Outside Blakemort! And he was smiling. Glad to be there. As if he belonged. How could Gran, a woman who was good through and through, love a man like that?

Jessica must have noticed how her thoughts were exploding. "Ruby, just…listen."

And so Ruby sat there, as did her colleagues, Carrie-Ann, and an astonished Saul, who was clearly hearing all this for the first time too, whilst her mother related what had happened all those years ago, how Sarah had met Edward at a masked ball, of all places, the instant spark between them, how she would subsequently visit him at the antiquarian bookshop where he worked, that she loved his mind as well as his body, an intelligence that she described as fierce, his endless curiosity. They had loved and laughed in the flat above the bookshop, Sarah falling more and more in love and certain that it had been reciprocated. That Edward had loved her too. Just as much.

Ruby also learnt that he had met Rosamund, Sarah's mother, and that Rosamund had disapproved. And he'd known it. The day after the meeting, he was gone, breaking Sarah's heart. Every day, she'd pined for him. Prayed for him to return. Then, one day, her prayers had been answered. Several years later, there he was once again, right in front of her, not at a party this time but on a rain-soaked street in London, declaring his heart had been broken too, that he'd had to leave but since discovered he couldn't live without her.

A love story, every bit of it, tears continuing to form in Ruby's eyes, splashing onto her cheeks. A story she found herself touched by, not least because it was so unexpected.

"Sarah was working as a secretary, but together they left London for a house in Sussex."

"Sussex?" Ruby's spine tingled. "What about Rosamund? You said she didn't approve."

"Every mother knows that she can only guide her child for so long, not enforce her wishes. Sarah was a grown woman by then. And…" Briefly she faltered. "Sometimes you have to give in to fate. A person walks down a certain road for a reason."

"To learn. To evolve," Ruby muttered.

"Or to try and help someone else," Jessica said, her voice lower now as she reached out towards Saul, giving his hand a squeeze, this person whom she had helped bring out of the darkness, after first plunging him into it.

"Mum, you said they went to a house in Sussex. What happened there?" No reason to think it was *the* house, not yet.

"Edward had changed in the years they'd been apart, although he was cagey about what he had done in between. Remember, this was a man who was thirsty for knowledge, who was aware that in life there was much to learn and on so many levels. Also remember she'd met him at a masked ball, which she'd been invited to by Clementine Nichols, a friend at her boarding school. Who knows why Edward had been invited, what circles he mixed in. He wasn't a man of money – Sarah made that clear enough – just ordinary, one who'd had to work for a living. But still he'd been there, amongst the monied. The elite. Despite all of this, he was loveable, Sarah not overly naïve, not with a mother like Rosamund; she saw what was loveable in him. But that all changed at this house in the country, a house that belonged to a friend of a friend."

A friend of a friend? Of course it did. The owner or owners never tracked down, Ruby would bet. She tore her gaze from her mother to look at Theo, Ness and Corinna, saw too that they had developed frowns. In Carrie-Ann's arms, the baby wasn't quite so content, Carrie-Ann having to stand now and jiggle him. Ruby thought that she should also rise, take the baby from her, but she couldn't. Her limbs felt like stone.

"Sarah didn't like the house in Sussex from the minute she set eyes on it. She could sense there were spirits trapped there, too frightened to seek help, and other entities too, those that perhaps kept them trapped and belonged to a much lower realm. Non-spirit but trying to emulate what was spirit, in outward form, at least. Edward, though, seemed to love the house. At first. He knew of Sarah's gift, she'd helped him develop his own ability, and so he knew her fears were founded, yet he refused to leave. Instead, he became…affected by the house. Sarah feared he was tuning in to the lower beings, becoming…fascinated by them. In part."

"In part?" Ruby questioned.

"That's right. They affected his behaviour too. He became violent. Towards Sarah. Whilst she was carrying me."

"Shit!" breathed Corinna.

"That's why she didn't leave, not straightaway. Because of me and also because she loved him. Because…Sarah would always try to help; that was her nature. So she endured that house, the beatings, his slow decline. After attacking her, he'd lock himself away in one of the rooms, laughing but then crying bitterly. And Sarah would cry just listening to him, because that was her Edward, still there, locked not just inside a room but inside himself too.

"But we know how beguiling evil can be, how relentless. She had to leave. If she was to survive. If *I* was. And so, one day, whilst he was in that room, caught between laughter and howling like a wounded animal, she took his car and drove back to London, to Rosamund. Together they planned her escape. It broke her heart all over again, and, if it hadn't been for me, she might have returned and, as Rosamund feared, entered the realms of hell alongside him. In a way, I saved her. Incredible to think that. If it hadn't been for me, she'd have fallen. She wouldn't have let him fall alone. *That's* how much she loved him."

There was further silence as those words sank in, even the baby quiet now although still awake, his eyes darting around the room.

Ruby broke the silence.

"Did Gran ever name the house?"

Jessica shook her head. "No. She refused to."

"We can name it, though, can't we?" Ruby said, looking at Theo, at Ness, at Corinna.

Ashen, they all were.

"Yes." Corinna replied.

Jessica looked confused. She knew something of Blakemort, but not everything. Why burden her with a concept such as Blakemort? Yet that house, although reduced to ashes, kept bouncing back, refusing to die. Its history not just entwined with Corinna's family, the house she endured for five years as a child, but with the Davis family too.

"Corinna, I'm so sorry," Ruby whispered.

"Not your fault," Corinna replied before squaring her shoulders. "And it's not coincidence either. Our meeting, our friendship. We – *all* of us – can fight this. Together."

"The grand scheme of things." Jessica's voice was also low.

"What, Mum?" Ruby said, leaning forward slightly.

Jessica's smile was not entirely bleak. "Fate has such

a lot to answer for. The name of this house, it's Blakemort, isn't it?"

Cash appeared at the door, right at the moment Jessica said the house's name. Not curiosity on his face but shock.

Ruby took all this in, then reached into a drawer where she'd recently put the photograph of Edward Middleton standing outside Blakemort. Smiling.

As she placed it on the table, necks craned forward to see who it was.

Him. The man responsible for the second, more vicious attack. She was certain of it.

Another of Blakemort's instruments, one of their Legion.

* * *

Only later did Ruby realise something else.

After all that had been disclosed, they'd moved from the attic down to the kitchen, a stunned Cash being briefed more fully, Jessica also briefed about Blakemort, every bit of it, nothing held back. This was, all had decided, no time to withhold truths or use lies as protection, not anymore. The situation required absolute honesty, no matter how brutal or painful for all involved. As for Carrie-Ann, she'd been assured her case was still a priority, that it sat alongside the case of Edward Middleton, a man who'd also formed a connection – who, like Dave Lane, had focused on Ruby, just like Sarah had feared.

Over teas and coffees, and sandwiches, Hendrix being passed from person to person but only really settling with Carrie-Ann, a plan had formed.

Both men had to be found, Dave Lane and Edward Middleton. As she'd agreed, Ness phoned Lee and asked him to help in trying to trace them. Not a police matter, but, like Cash, he was always willing to do his best to help the woman he loved, believing in the team and the nature of their work, no matter how outlandish.

The team – Carrie-Ann included – would also take it in turns to stalk the part of Hove that Lane had been seen in, lingering in bus stops, shop doorways, looking for any sign of a man who fit the description given to them. But Edward, where was he?

"Care homes," Theo suggested. "How old must Edward be now? Nearing ninety?"

Both Ruby and Jessica confirmed that.

"Then despite how powerful his spirit is – because to attack you the way he did, Ruby, he's certainly learnt over the years a good degree of psychic ability – his body is a vessel that will have weakened, as it does for all of us."

"Sure he's not dead, though?" Cash said in between mouthfuls of ham-and-mayonnaise sandwich. "You know, kinda reaching out from beyond the grave."

"I don't think that's the case," Jessica said, and when Ruby wanted to know why, she added, "Because, like Sarah, I would have felt it."

"Really?"

"Really," Jessica confirmed. "He is my father."

"How come such a strong connection with me, though?"

At that, Jessica took the photograph that Ruby had brought down to the kitchen with her and held it in her hands. Her tears might have dried, but she still looked stricken.

"How hard have you been studying this picture?" she asked.

Theo, who, like Cash, had been tucking into the sandwiches, raised her head, also interested in the answer.

"Very hard," Ruby admitted, glancing at Cash, who looked more perplexed.

"Didn't even know we had it in the house," he muttered.

"Then that's how," Jessica said. "You've been holding him in your mind, just like Dave Lane has been holding you in his."

It was true. She'd held Edward in her mind practically every waking minute, it seemed, since Blakemort had thrust that picture at her, wanting to torment her, to prove yet again how it could destroy people in a thousand different ways. In studying it, a connection had been forged, deepened further by Jessica's discovery of Sarah's notebook.

Eventually, the team and Carrie-Ann prepared to leave. It was getting late, nearing Hendrix's bedtime, Ruby secretly wishing Carrie-Ann could stay and settle him further but knowing she had to take the reins back, try to form the same connection with him.

Connections. They were many and varied and always surprising.

But the biggest surprise came just before her own bedtime.

Cash was already upstairs, the baby not in his cot – having kicked up a stink the minute his body had touched his own mattress – but asleep in his father's arms, the two of them snuffling in tandem. Ruby was downstairs, making fresh bottles of milk for Hendrix for the morning and through the night if need be; the boy's appetite was as ravenous as Cash's. The photograph of Edward Middleton was still on the table, having been liberated, no longer a secret kept in the darkness or at a place as wretched as Blakemort.

She finished with the bottles and placed them in the fridge, about to turn the light off and leave the kitchen, try to get some sleep. Friday was a new day, a busy day, not just for the team but Cash, Lee and Carrie-Ann too. Sleep was vital. So, in Cash's arms Hendrix would have to stay, their best chance of passing a peaceful night.

Just one more look at the photograph, more than curiosity drawing her to it, a kind of magnetism. She picked it up. In doing so, was she testing him or, more likely, herself? Seeking to show not stupidity, not naïvety but defiance. Blakemort and those who'd succumbed to it would not rule her life. She'd already made that decision. Corinna had too.

Nothing happened. All was quiet in the kitchen, all was still.

The photograph was as it had been before. Wasn't it?

She examined it, saw no difference, was placing it back down on the table when she stopped, held it for a few more seconds, then turned it over.

With love, Edward Middleton.

The inscription on the back, the very words that identified the subject, had faded to practically nothing.

Chapter Twenty-Seven

"OH, there he is, the little chubba! I'm going to enjoy looking after you today."

Cassy, Cash's rather flamboyant, Jamaican-born mother, dressed in colours even brighter than those that Theo tended to adopt, did indeed appear truly delighted when her son handed over the wailing baby, his lusty cries not bothering her at all.

"I'm so sorry about this," Ruby said, nowhere near as relaxed but flustered, imagining herself to be red-faced also. "He's probably hungry. There's plenty of bottles in his bag, nappies, wet wipes, you name it. It's all there."

Cassy simply laughed in response, burying her face into Hendrix's neck in an act of pure love, her eyes closed in bliss, Hendrix howling louder.

"Mum," Cash said, clearly as worried as Ruby, "we won't be all day, you know, staking out, just a few hours."

His mother raised her head. "Staking out? What are you up to now?"

"Oh, nothing," Ruby said, shooting Cash a look. "It's just a case we're working on, requires us to case the joint somewhat."

"Same old, same old, then?"

Ruby nodded ardently. "Something like that."

Before they could leave, someone else came running down the hallway, that someone causing Jed to materialise. It was Daisy, a brown terrier Cash and Ruby had rescued from a man called Geoffrey Rawlings on the Highdown Hall case. As Ruby was unable to keep the dog, Cassy had stepped into the breach, the pair of them subsequently sharing a very happy home together. Daisy was ecstatic to see them and Jed too, regulars in her life that she adored. Cash bent down, making a fuss of her, the racket she made finally enough to drown out Hendrix.

"Off you go, go on, the pair of you. These two need to settle," Cassy insisted, still with the widest of grins. "Good luck today with your stalking, darlings. And there really is no need to hurry back. It might not look like it, not right now, but Nana's got this!"

As Cash straightened, Ruby grabbed his arm.

"Come on," she said, sure that if they didn't hurry, Cassy would change her mind.

In the car, Ruby in the driver's seat and Cash beside her, both sat for a while, needing to recover from the raucousness of the handover.

"Your mum's amazing," Ruby said at last. "Hendrix doesn't faze her at all."

"Nothing really does. Remember when I first introduced you to her, and you told her what you did for a living? She didn't bat an eyelid."

"Unlike you," Ruby said, smiling at the memory. "Your jaw practically hit the floor."

"It hit the floor because of you, Ruby, not your profession."

"Yeah, yeah, yeah."

"It's true," he insisted, his hand covering hers and squeezing it. "And you still amaze me, in every way."

"Seriously? I'm hardly mother of the year."

Cash frowned. "Why'd you say that?"

Ruby swallowed before replying, surprised to realise how emotional she was. "He just seems…so unhappy, doesn't he? When he's with me, anyway."

"Maybe…maybe…because he's feeding off you, you know? Emotionally, I mean. This is new for you, for *us*. There's no manual. We're learning as we go along, and he realises that, that we're amateurs. It'll be different with our second, our third…our fourth."

Attempting a laugh, she retrieved her hand from his and thumped his arm instead. "I've told you! One is enough. I'm a working mother, not a broodmare."

Cash made a show of rubbing at his arm. "You'll grow to love it, Ruby, and when you do, you'll be begging me for more. Anyway, let's not spend our time off from babies talking about them. What was up with you when you came to bed last night? You were fidgety."

"Fidgety? I was not!"

"You were, tossing and turning and couldn't sleep. You woke me up because of it."

"You never said you were awake."

"I couldn't! Couldn't move an inch either in case Hendrix woke up too. My arm this morning still feels numb."

"Poor you. It's…well, I'll show you what was on my mind. Can you pass me my bag?"

As he reached into the footwell where her bag was, Jed appeared in the back, still excited from his interaction with Daisy.

"Hey there," Ruby said, delighted to see him. "You're joining us today, then?"

Jed wagged his tail and barked, as if to say, 'You betcha!'

"The three of us," Ruby murmured, "just like it used to be."

Cash had also turned around and was busy blowing kisses into the air at Jed, Ruby letting him have his moment with the dog, wishing hard like she always did that he could see him, before taking the bag from him and reaching inside. She retrieved the photo.

"*This* was on my mind," she said. Just like it had been on her mind so many times before. "The house wanted me to know what it had done, how easily it corrupts."

"Not everyone," Cash reminded her. "Only those with a predisposition."

"True," Ruby admitted. "My grandfather being one of them."

Reaching over, he took the photograph from her. "Can't believe you didn't tell me about this beforehand, that it was in our house, and I didn't even know."

"I'm sorry," she said, and she meant it. "I had my reasons, not that any of them make sense now. I was trying to get my head around it. To understand. I was going to tell you, of course I was, in the end. And the team too."

"Either that or you'd have got rid of it."

"Maybe," she confessed. "Set fire to it. The last link."

Cash squinted at the photograph. "And you think that's a figure in the window, possibly Sarah?"

"I have no idea. It could have been one of many

spirits trapped there."

"Who took the photograph?"

"Still no idea. If the figure's not Sarah, then maybe she's the one who took it?"

"Could be." Blakemort was never going to give them all the answers; that wasn't how it worked. It wanted to remain there in your mind, nag, nag, nagging away. The trick was to ignore it. When it forced the issue, however...that was a different matter.

"There was writing on the back, Cash. Did you see it?"

"Yesterday? Yeah, big loopy letters."

"That's right, ostentatious."

"Osten-what?"

"Flashy."

"Oh, right."

"It said *With love, Edward Middleton.* That's how I knew it was him. Turn it over. There's no writing on it anymore."

"Christ, yeah, you're right. Where's it gone?"

Ruby shrugged. "I don't know. It just...vanished."

Cash was still staring at the blank space. "What do you think it means?"

Again, Ruby shrugged. "Mum described what Sarah wrote about Edward as a love story. You know...maybe it was. Maybe—" this was hard for her to say, playing with her mind more than Blakemort ever could "—she did love him right till the end."

"And he loved her?"

"Somewhere, deep inside. But that message disappearing, it's either a call for help or something else entirely."

"A threat?"

"Exactly."

"You are going to read the notebook, I take it?"

"Damn right, but...well, today's not the day. We have other plans."

"Okay, so what's on the agenda? We go to Hove Library and park up outside it?"

"Yep, we take the first couple of hours, then it's Carrie-Ann, then Ness, then Corinna and Presley are taking the evening watch, complete with takeaway pizza and beer, apparently. Meanwhile, we'll all try to dig as deep as possible for any information on either Edward or Dave. Lee will too. Let's hope he can unearth something."

"Not literally, I hope."

"No, Cash, of course not!"

She laughed again. Jed barked. Cash grinned.

Just like the old days indeed.

Chapter Twenty-Eight

A cold day, grey, rain pouring down, those who were out and about in it as sombre as the dark sky, heads down and scowling.

"What a difference the weather makes, eh?" mused Cash. "The sun brings out the best, the rain just the opposite."

"Well, it's the opposite we want," replied Ruby, her eyes scanning the horizon.

"You really think he's bad, this Dave Lane?"

"Cash, he attacked me!"

"Yeah, yeah, I know, but...why? That's what we have to ask."

"I know we do. And why Edward too? Why me? What's changed? Is he—" she found herself really quite stricken by the thought "—dying?"

Inside the car, the atmosphere was as sombre as it was outside.

"What if he is, Ruby?" Cash's voice was gentle. "He's certainly very old."

Ruby exhaled, straightened her shoulders. "If he is, he is. That's just the way of it. We've got to try to find him beforehand, though. See if his soul's worth saving."

"And Theo's ringing round all the care homes, is she?"

"Yep, she's got a list as long as your arm. Ness is also checking the hospitals."

"Maybe they'll come up trumps. Maybe Lee will."

"Maybe." Again, she scanned the street in front of her. "Come on, Dave Lane," she breathed. "Where the hell are you?"

A couple of hours later, Carrie-Ann knocked on the passenger-side window, ready to take her turn. Exiting the car, Ruby greeted her. "Hey there. You okay?"

Carrie-Ann gamely nodded, but, truth was, she didn't look okay or feel it, and both she and Ruby knew it. She was fading. Fast. But she was also hanging on. For something.

Unable to help herself, Ruby closed the gap between them and hugged her.

Here was a woman she liked. They just…got on. But if Carrie-Ann's theory was right, if Dave Lane's was too – that she shouldn't be here – then Ruby would lose her, maybe sooner rather than later. *Not too soon, though. Please.*

If Ruby'd surprised herself by her actions, she'd surprised Carrie-Ann too, but also delighted her.

"Hey, what's this?" she said, returning the hug.

Eventually, Ruby pulled away. "Sorry—"

"No need to be sorry." Carrie-Ann's eyes were glistening. "It was…nice. Thank you. We could have been really good friends, couldn't we? Case aside, I mean."

"We are already," Ruby insisted. "And you know what, we could be wrong about you. Believe me, we've been wrong before."

"We're not wrong."

"Carrie-Ann—"

"Shit!"

"I know. I know it's a shit situation—"

"Shit! Shit! Shit!"

"But we'll try our best—"

"No, Ruby, listen. There he is, over the road. Dave Lane. He's got a bag in his hand. He must have just come out of Tesco's or something. He's coming towards us! He's going to see me!"

Cash chose this very moment to open the car door. "Ruby, I just had a call from Mum. She wanted us to know that everything's fine—"

Before he could say another word, Ruby slammed the passenger door shut, she and Carrie-Ann ducking down behind it. Noting Cash's stunned expression, she pointed with her finger across the road, mouthing, 'It's him!' Cash whirled around, and so did Jed, Cash then sliding down in his seat, although why he was going to such lengths, Ruby couldn't fathom; it wasn't as if Dave Lane would know him.

"What are we going to do?" asked Carrie-Ann.

"Wait till he crosses onto our side of the road and then…follow him."

"But what if he notices us? What if he senses us? He could launch another attack."

It was true; he could. And it was something she had to be wary of. But his energy, it couldn't match that of the second, possibly belonging to Edward, and she was prepared for it this time, her beloved tourmaline necklace, an inheritance from Rosamund, firmly in place, a comfort blanket of sorts. This time, the element of surprise was all theirs.

"We stay well back, and as we've both got hoods on our jackets, we use them. Cash"—she indicated for him to lower the window—"we'll follow Lane, and you follow us, okay? But keep your distance and pull your hood up."

"Understood," he said, nodding. "What about Jed?"

"Jed?" Carrie-Ann asked, frowning.

"I'll explain later," said Ruby. "Jed will do what Jed wants, Cash. Come on. Lane's just a few feet away now. Let's put this plan into action."

They did, hoods duly adjusted. Ruby and Carrie-Ann walked side by side, as discussed, Cash behind them with Jed bounding forward, his nose in the air as if sniffing, getting the measure of the man, Ruby supposed, as they all were.

Not a tall man, he was slightly built, like a young teenager, although Carrie-Ann assured Ruby he was a grown man, somewhere in his thirties, she estimated. His hair was dark, and he wore a dark grey raincoat that had seen better days. In fact, as Carrie-Ann had said, he looked very much down on his luck, defeated, almost. Not quite a hobo but not far off.

So far, so good. Lane gave no hint that he knew he was being followed, Ruby holding the light in her mind at all times. Such a simple technique but so effective.

Lane led them off the main road and down one that led to the seafront.

"This is Southbourne Villas," Carrie-Ann pointed out. "The very road I'd wandered up before I encountered him the first time."

"This could be where he lives," replied Ruby. "Fingers crossed."

Strange, though, because it was a road full of grand Victorian villas, some still in use as houses, others having been turned into flats but extremely large inside, she'd bet, the architect stunting on neither space nor proportion. The kind of place wealthy families and young professionals might live, enjoying close proximity to beach and town. Not someone like Lane, who was still shuffling along, that carrier bag of his bulging.

They were on the left-hand side of the road, he was on the right, and soon they'd be halfway along the length of it. Ruby glanced behind her, saw Cash still there, keeping a steady distance. As for Jed up ahead, he'd slowed; she and Carrie-Ann would catch him up soon.

What is it, boy?

Was he growing warier? She had to admit, she was too, having to focus on the light in her mind more than ever, keep it burning bright.

Now over halfway down the road, Jed was definitely lagging. Ruby's legs also felt heavier, as if she had to force them to keep going, putting one boot-clad foot in front of the other, determined to solve at least one of the mysteries currently facing them. They'd promised Carrie-Ann, and Psychic Surveys didn't renege on promises. That was not how they'd built their reputation, a reputation Lea Monaghan might bring into dispute should they fail to provide her not just with answers but also a reassurance that what had happened in her spare bedroom would not reoccur.

Craning her neck, Ruby peered through the rain at their quarry, almost jumping out of her skin when a hand landed on her arm. Carrie-Ann's.

"Look, that house, he's going in there!"

Over the road, the house was larger than any they'd passed so far, a double-fronted villa with a paved, walled area in front of it. It was flats, definitely flats, judging by the number of buzzers beside a glass-panelled door, the door itself sitting right in the middle of the house. There was also a variety of curtains and nets at the windows, some pulled shut despite it being daytime, others only half open.

"Bingo!" breathed Ruby from their standpoint, watching as Lane came to a halt and, with his free hand, began digging around in his pocket.

He extracted a key, Ruby's heart beating faster as he inserted it into the lock. Now that they knew where he lived, that was half the problem solved. They could then work out how best to confront him, get him to talk to them about Carrie-Ann and about whether it was indeed him who'd launched an attack on Ruby, the reasons behind that too.

Cash had also come to a standstill a few feet away. As for Jed…he was growling.

Ruby tore her gaze from Lane to look at the dog instead. He was baring his teeth, his hackles raised. Why? What was going on?

A split second later and her attention was back on Lane, a man who'd only half entered the house, who had now turned around and was staring across the road, right at her. The carrier bag he held dropped to the floor, something in it smashing.

"Shit, what is it? What's happening?"

As she breathed those words, Carrie-Ann turned towards her, was saying something too. "Ruby? What's the matter? Are you okay?"

Cash had come closer. "Ruby?"

There was a darkness, an energy, rushing right at her. One that only she could see. She *and* Lane, whose hands were now covering his mouth as if trying to stifle a scream.

She didn't have time to contemplate further. The energy was aimed at her, slamming her back against a brick gatepost and pinning her there, just as it had pinned her against the wall at the Monaghan house. Cash rushed to her side, his hands on her, trying desperately to figure out what was happening, Carrie-Ann too, Jed making an almighty racket. Hands, not Cash's, not Carrie-Ann's, were around her neck and squeezing. A weight on her chest that would surely crush the life from her. The light in her mind...surprise followed by panic meant she had let it go, only for a second, no more, but a second was all that this other force needed. She couldn't give in to panic, though; all would be lost if she did. *She* would be lost. She had to retaliate, even though her heart felt like it was going to burst. And she was cold too, the warmth in her body leeched from her.

"Ruby! For fuck's sake, what's happening?"

Panic breeds panic, which was true in Cash's case. His stricken voice in her ear but sounding far, far away. And Carrie-Ann, what was she saying? What was she doing? Yelling, but not at Ruby, at someone else, Dave Lane?

"Stop it! Leave her alone! What are you doing? What the hell are you doing?"

Consciousness was blurring. Ruby felt like she was

drowning. Sinking far below the waves again. Would there be some kind of calm soon enough? Would she hear those same voices? Familiar, loved voices. Gran's voice. Not frightening at all. The light. Where was it? Why had it disappeared? Just…snuffed itself out.

"Ruby! Ruby!"

There was someone calling her name! Cash? *Is it you?*

"Ruby. The light!"

There *was* a light. In the distance. Softly glowing. The one she'd told the grounded about so often. 'Go towards it. It's home,' she'd say.

Was it her turn? Because everybody's turn came at some point.

"Aargh!" The pain in her chest was intensifying, what had hold of her merciless.

"Ruby, come on, fight. You have to!"

The light…it was so far away. Should she simply let go, let the darkness carry her, or…

She could summon the light and make it work for her instead.

"Ruby! Fight back!"

Dave Lane. The little fucker. Just who did he think he was?

Come to me, she said, she *commanded* of the light. *Come to me and help, because I'm not going anywhere. I'm staying this side of the divide today.*

There was a flash of light, one so blinding that she was certain it seared the retinas of her eyes. Warmth returned, rushing into her as her mouth burst open, gasping for air, seeking to draw it in, to fill her lungs.

She collapsed, but into Cash's arms, opening her eyes when they'd been shut, not sure if she was in fact blinded. She wasn't. There was the world, still dull and grey but dazzling too, droplets of rain glistening like pearls, one of them racing down Cash's nose and falling off the end of it.

She threw her arms around him before seeking to reassure him and Carrie-Ann – as well as Jed, who kept nudging her arm – that she was okay.

"What's happened with Lane? Where is he?" she managed to ask.

Cash growled more menacingly than Jed when he replied. "He's gone, fled inside. I'll get you to safety, and then I'll go in there, bang on every door until I find him."

Ruby asked Cash to help her stand and then stared at the building, at the contents of Lane's bag still on the floor, before addressing Carrie-Ann. "Did you see him go inside?"

"Yes," she answered, more bewildered than she'd ever looked. "Although he stood at the door for quite a while, just…staring. Just…I don't know."

"Carrie-Ann," Ruby said, "tell me exactly what you saw, what you felt."

"It doesn't make sense, though."

Ruby shook her head. "It might."

"He…oh God, I hope I've got this right."

"Carrie-Ann, please," Ruby prompted.

"I think he was just as horrified as us at what was happening."

Chapter Twenty-Nine

THE three of them were still standing in the rain with Jed when Ruby's mobile rang.

"Probably Theo or Ness trying to get through," she said, reaching into her jacket pocket to retrieve it. Looking at the screen ID, she saw it wasn't. "It's Lee."

Before Cash could protest, haul her up the street, back to the car, probably insisting he drive her straight to accident and emergency for a checkup, she answered.

"Lee, hi. What have you found?"

There was no point engaging in preliminaries; she had to cut to the chase.

"Hi, Ruby. Something interesting, that's for sure."

"About Dave Lane?"

"No, not him."

"We know where he lives, Lee. We've found that out. Southbourne Villas, Hove. A double-fronted building, quite unlike all the other buildings here."

"Okay, great, you can give me the full address later."

"So this is about Edward Middleton?"

"Nope, can't find a thing out about him. Maybe Theo will have more luck with the care homes. This is about another person Ness gave me the name of."

"Who?"

"Clementine Nichols."

"Clementine Nichols?" Ruby repeated, having to force herself to recall details. "That's right, the woman who held the ball that Sarah attended when she first met Edward."

"Apparently so. Ness said if I had no joy finding the others, then to try her."

"And?"

"She's an old lady now, in her eighties, and in a care home out in the countryside, not too far away, near the village of Ditchling."

"Oh, Lee, that's incredible!"

"Yep, and she's got a list of offences from when she was younger as long as your arm."

"Offences? Really? What kind?"

"Theft and drug trafficking mainly."

"Wow," Ruby replied, gazing at Cash and Carrie-Ann and the curiosity in their eyes. "Do you think we could talk to her?"

"Already phoned the care home and explained that she could assist the police with a bit of gentle questioning about a past event that's come to light, and they've agreed to let us see her. But we have to go easy, Ruby, and only you and I can go in there. They're quite emphatic they don't want her upset in any way."

"No, of course not, that's fine. When can we go?" Time was of the essence, not just because of Lea Monaghan but because Ruby wasn't sure how many more attacks she could withstand. Dave Lane might well have looked horrified by this latest one, but it didn't mean he wasn't responsible. She mustn't assume. Not yet. Both mysteries had to be solved, Lane's and Middleton's. Clementine Nichols could possibly help with the latter, at least, give them a more detailed profile regarding him. They had nothing to lose.

Lee had taken a moment or so to respond to her question, checking his diary, perhaps, but at last he spoke. "Now. We go right now." Echoing the thoughts that had been careering through her head, he added, "Strike whilst the iron's hot and before those at the care home change their mind, and I do too, for that matter. Because this is against protocol, Ruby. This is…off record. I'm sticking my neck out here for you again, okay? And there's only so many times I can do that before I get into trouble too."

* * *

On the way to Silver Springs Care Home near Ditching, with Cash driving this time, Ruby phoned Theo first, then Ness, both once again aware that something had happened to her. As she enlightened Theo as to what, the older woman sighed heavily before telling her she'd had no luck with care homes or hospitals regarding Edward Middleton, stretching the net – so far – as wide as Surrey.

"We'll keep trying, though. Meanwhile, keep the light in your mind at all times, even with Clementine Nichols. Ness and I will hold you at the forefront of our minds, wrapping you in light too, boosting your protection. Keep me posted, okay?"

Ness was also concerned by what had happened to Ruby but excited by the prospect of her meeting with Nichols. "How old must she be by now?"

"If she was at school with Gran, then in her early

eighties," Ruby replied.

"Full marbles?"

"I'll let you know after the visit."

"Okay, but you've got an address for Dave Lane, at least. You've given that to Lee?"

"Uh-huh, he knows."

Reiterating Theo's words, she said, "I'll be sending you white light. Plenty of it."

"Thanks, Ness."

Still en route, she phoned Jessica, wanting to keep her informed.

"My God, Ruby, you've found Clementine! You're not going in alone, though?"

"Lee's with me, Cash will be in the car outside with Carrie-Ann, and Theo and Ness are holding me in the light."

"As will I, darling. You know that."

"I know, Mum. I'm going to phone Corinna too. She also needs to pitch in." She paused briefly before adding, "Mum, you are okay, aren't you?"

There was a moment of silence, Ruby holding her breath. Whatever they were in the grip of, she was glad she was being targeted instead of her mother, as Ruby was stronger and more likely to withstand it, her mother's mental health still of concern to her.

"Ruby, I'm fine. I'm… This sounds odd, even to my own ears, and we know from what's happened to you that there's a fight on our hands regarding my father, but to know that I was conceived in love, there's…comfort in that."

Ruby understood and, in a way, felt envious, for that hadn't been the case when she'd been conceived, although she'd been loved by family and friends ever since, something she reminded herself of whilst quashing that envy.

"Let me know what you find out, as soon as you can," Jessica continued. "And, Ruby, if you do find Edward Middleton, I want to be there."

"If you're sure."

"Oh, I'm sure. I *have* to be."

"This is it, Ruby," Cash told her as she ended the call to Jessica. "The home's at the end of this driveway, apparently. We're here."

Not just any driveway, it was long and sweeping, with manicured lawns gracing either side. Up ahead, the building came into view, an impressive country mansion, early to mid-Victorian, she guessed, a sign outside declaring 'Silver Springs Welcomes You'.

"Silver Springs." Cash sighed. "Such a naff name, isn't it? So...obvious."

"It is what it is," she answered. "There's Lee. Wish me luck."

He was waiting at the foot of stone steps that led up to the doorway. Hurrying towards him, Jed beside her, she coaxed a smile. "Thanks for this, Lee," she said. "I appreciate it."

"Don't know if it'll be much use," Lee replied, shrugging.

"We'll soon find out," Ruby mused, accompanying him as he climbed the steps.

After ringing the bell, a woman in a starched white uniform opened the door.

"You've come about Clem," she said. Not a question, a statement.

Lee nodded, and they were ushered inside, into a large waiting area.

"It was Kerri you spoke to," the woman continued, "the nurse in charge. I'll fetch her, and she can take you to Clem, who, lucky for you, is having one of her more lucid days."

Whilst the nurse hurried off, Ruby took in her surroundings. Pristine. Plush. If you had to enter a care or nursing home, this was the one you'd wish for, the type that only a lot of money could buy. Clementine Nichols was from a rich family, according to what Jessica had said, the type that threw balls rather than parties, masked or not. Regardless of whether the woman had committed criminal acts, she still clearly had access to funds. It must cost thousands per week to stay here. Was the atmosphere happy? Mainly. Ruby could sense some discontent, but, so far, there was no distressed spirit or spirits still lingering, hands wrinkled with age and reaching out, quivering voices begging for help.

She dismissed such dramatic thoughts just as another woman, also in a starched white uniform, not a blemish upon it, approached them.

"Kerri Burrows," she said by way of introduction, reaching out and shaking both their hands. Jed gave a welcoming bark, but as Kerri couldn't see him, she duly ignored it. "I understand you want to talk with Clem, that she may be able to help you with a line of enquiry, and that's fine, as long as I remain present too. At Silver Springs, her well-being comes first. If she shows any signs of distress, I will ask you to leave."

"We understand," Lee replied, his voice suitably

solemn. "Thank you for allowing us to see her. Does she…know?"

"That you're police officers?" she said, including Ruby in that description too, and neither of them disabusing her of that false fact. "No, she thinks you're volunteers. There are various organisations that do the rounds at care homes, visiting those that otherwise have no one. Clem's had her fair share of volunteers in the past. She's used to them."

"Does anyone, apart from volunteers, come to visit her?" Ruby asked.

"I believe there's a daughter kicking around somewhere, but we've neither seen nor heard anything from her."

"How long has Clementine been here?"

"She's one of our stalwarts. Thirteen years now."

"Thirteen?" gasped Ruby. "Wow. And before that?"

"She's always been institutionalised in one way or another," was her enigmatic answer. "Come this way."

Kerri led them towards a lift, indicating for them to go ahead and enter, which they did, Jed first, his tail wagging at the prospect of hitching a ride. Entering too, the nurse pressed a button for the first floor, which they arrived at swiftly and smoothly. From the lift, they took a right turn down a long corridor, fragranced with the heady scent of fresh flowers, courtesy of a huge bunch of roses and lilies placed on an antique sideboard, so different to the smells you'd normally expect in a less salubrious establishment. Ruby would bet the food was of gourmet standard too. Thirteen years in this place, what a fortune that must have amounted to! It could be that Clementine had paid the price of the building twice over, if not more.

Outside a room that had the number nine emblazoned upon the door, Kerri knocked.

"Hello, love," she called out as she opened it, "it's Kerri. You have visitors today. Remember I told you? Their names are Lee and Ruby. That's it, sit yourself up and enjoy a good chat, why don't you? Sally's coming up soon with a nice cup of tea for you all."

She then motioned for Ruby and Lee to come in. Whilst Kerri took up position on a chair at the back of the room, Ruby braced herself for what they were about to discover.

Chapter Thirty

CLEMENTINE Nichols might have been a jailbird when younger, but now she was merely frail, sitting in an armchair in the bay of the window, staring outwards with rheumy eyes.

Ruby couldn't help but compare her with her grandmother. Sarah Davis had been strong of mind and body, always active, looking after both her daughter and granddaughter, baking for them, keeping a clean house, and providing a shoulder to lean on through thick and thin, and arms that would hug you tight whenever you needed them. Even in her early eighties she had looked younger, her hair a bright silver and a shine in her eyes. This woman, however, appeared at least a decade older, the skin on her face and the backs of her hands wizened, her hair, what was left of it, hanging in strands and her back hunched. She looked like she could take care of no one, least of all herself.

With a criminal record Lee had described as 'as long as your arm' for drugs, theft and larceny, she'd wound up in many a prison over the years, and then had come the care home, another prison of sorts, albeit one with far more pleasing décor and amenities.

Clementine lifted her head as Ruby and Lee approached.

"Hello, Clementine," Ruby greeted, adopting a soft smile. Pointing to two chairs, she added, "May we sit?"

"Do as you like." The woman's voice was scratchy, as if she wasn't used to speaking. She then muttered something under her breath. "Bloody do-gooders."

Lee glanced at Ruby and raised an eyebrow as he also sat. An old, frail lady Clementine might be, but beneath it all she was still a tough cookie, a hardness in those red-rimmed eyes and in the set of her jaw too, one reflecting the type of life she'd chosen to live or, perhaps it might be more apt to say, endure.

Fear. That's what Sarah had seen in her eyes at the ball, a flash of it when she and Clementine had been dancing, and then someone had whisked Clementine away. Someone Clementine had been afraid of. All this Jessica had told Ruby the previous day, pointing out the passage in the notebook. She'd also drawn Ruby's attention to Rosamund's theory that Clementine had somehow known Sarah was psychic, and that was why she'd got in touch with her a couple of years after they'd both left school and invited her to the ball. Because there'd have been people in attendance interested in the kind of person Sarah was, in her skills. People who'd sought to exploit. The question was, had Clementine been exploited too? Ruby cleared her throat.

"So, Clementine, this is a lovely room." Ruby gazed around her as she said it, the décor as bright as elsewhere in the building, homely touches with cushions on the expertly made bed and furniture that looked bespoke. "You must be very comfortable here."

Clementine just stared at her.

Lee also attempted to make conversation.

"I see you've got a book of crosswords on the table in front of you. Do you enjoy them?"

Her look of disgust at such a banal question was withering.

"I love a crossword," said Ruby, determined to draw Clementine out so that they could progress to more meaningful talk. "My gran used to say to me, 'Do one every day, Ruby. They keep the brain active.' Can't manage one every day, though, but when I do, I get really stuck in."

"Your grandmother was a wise woman," Clementine said, but with no hint of meaning behind it. Ruby inhaled briefly at her words. *If only you knew.*

Seemingly as desperate as Ruby for another topic to latch on to, Lee pointed to a nearby bookshelf. "What do you like to read? Romance, is it?"

Clementine almost spat at him. "Those are there for show. Nothing more."

"Right," he said. "So…you don't read?"

Behind them, Kerri cleared her throat. A sign for them to crack on with it and stop wasting everyone's time. Difficult to do when she was listening to every word.

"My gran," Ruby continued, "was a wise woman. You're right. We were very close. She'd be around the same age as you, eighty-two. She lived in Sussex, although she was born in London and lived there for much of her youth, went to school there, a private school. She boarded. What…school did you go to, Clementine?"

"What does it matter now?" Clementine said, the same scathing quality in her voice.

"I just wondered, you know, where it was, whether you liked it."

"London. That's where it was, okay? I went to school in London too."

"A boarding school?"

"Yes, a boarding school."

"Crawley Manor in North London?"

Clementine's eyes widened. "Crawley Manor?"

"Yes, near Highgate."

"Highgate," she breathed.

Ruby glanced again at Lee, who gave her an encouraging nod of the head.

"Do you know it?" she asked, her attention back on Clementine.

"Yes! Yes, I went there too."

"Oh, really?" Ruby enthused, hoping she sounded genuine enough. "Then maybe you knew my gran. Her name was Sarah, Sarah Davis."

The door opening distracted them all, Ruby turning around to see who'd entered the room. It was Sally, with a tea trolley laden with a teapot and biscuits.

"Tea's up!" she said, her voice as jolly as she looked, a rounded woman with pink cheeks and shoulder-length curly hair. "I expect you're all gasping."

Although cursing Sally's timing, Ruby forced a smile. "Lovely," she said, hoping she and Clementine could pick up from where they'd left off, her eyes still on Sally as she approached the table that lay in front of the old woman, getting ready to place china cups and saucers upon it.

"Stop!" yelled Clementine, surprising them all. "We don't want tea!"

Sally's face became pinker. "But...but you must. It's...teatime."

Kerri had also risen and was making her way over. "Clementine, as much as I hope you've enjoyed the visit, if you're tired, we can—"

"Get out," Clementine commanded.

Ruby tensed. Who did she mean?

"Get out!" she repeated, her eyes not on Ruby or Lee but Sally and Kerri.

"Now, now, Clementine," Kerri said, both concern and a warning in her voice. "You mustn't upset yourself."

"Who pays your wages?"

Kerri coloured every bit as much as Sally. "What?"

"Who pays your wages? A fortune," she spat. "A small bloody fortune."

"I don't know what you mean," Kerri continued to protest.

"I pay them, that's who," Clementine informed her, "and all the other residents of this infernal place, where you treat us like dolls, you patronise us, day in, day out. I want you out, and take Sally with you, bustling in here as bright as a bloody ray of sunshine, sicklier than the sugar she stirs in my tea. Go on, out. But you, you do-gooders, you stay."

"This is insufferable," Kerri began, one hand on her chest, the other patting at Sally's arm as if to console her. "I think we had *all* better leave. In fact, I insist on it."

"No." Lee spoke this time. "We came here to talk to the lady, and it seems the lady wants to do just that. I'm sure we won't be long."

Not just pink, Kerri's complexion was puce as she

told them in no uncertain terms that they had better not be long and that she would indeed continue to wait, but outside the door rather than on a chair inside. Sally, meanwhile, had grabbed hold of her trolley and was busy wheeling it out of Clementine's room, huffing and puffing in consternation.

At last the door closed behind the pair with something of a slam. There was silence, but only for a moment before Clementine spoke again.

"You're not do-gooders at all, are you?" she said.

"We don't mean any harm," Ruby assured her.

"You're aware that I knew Sarah Davis."

"Yes, we are," Ruby confessed.

"It's her you want to know about?"

"Her *and* Edward Middleton."

* * *

Rosamund had been right in her assumptions. Clementine had known there was something different about Sarah Davis, had spied on her not once during their time at boarding school together but several times as she talked to an unseen presence.

"A ghost," Clementine described it as. "Sarah Davis was psychic."

"The reason for her invitation to the ball?"

"Yes."

"Why?"

Clementine allowed the question to hang in the air between them, a riot of emotions dancing across her face. There was the bitterness Ruby had seen before, totally ingrained, but also regret, she was certain, sorrow

270

and, yes, fear.

"I was always trying to please them," she said at last.

"Who, Clementine?" asked Lee.

"Them," she spat. "My family and their strange ways. Ways I found...abhorrent. But still, they were my family. Were all I had."

"Abhorrent? How do you mean?" Ruby pressed, one hand surreptitiously staying Jed, who'd begun whining, noticing, perhaps, that the room wasn't as bright anymore as Clementine stared again into the space between them whilst dredging up memories.

"I come from a wealthy family. My older brother and I wanted for nothing growing up, but from an early age I realised this about my parents, that whatever they had, it was never enough. Money...*obsessed* them, and the pursuit of it...it ruined them, ruined us all. Many people seek to increase their fortune through hard work. My parents sought to do so through connections. The people that would come to visit us at our house had eyes that terrified me. I would be brought before them, dressed in such finery, and paraded. 'Isn't she pretty?' they would say, 'So adorable,' their hands reaching out and stroking my arm or my cheek and making me shudder. 'Not her,' Father would say. 'Not...family. Families protect their own.' He'd say that, and then he'd turn from the others and back to me. 'Isn't that right, Clementine? You may prove useful one day.'

"I didn't know what he meant, only that I wanted to please him, as my brother did, their acolyte. I wanted to please Mother too because doing so was necessary to keep me safe. I was sent to Crawley Manor to board at a young age and thank God I was. As much as I hated it there, it offered an escape, at least. At school, I was the wealthiest girl by far, and that gave me status, kept me safe there too. Oh, the respect that money commands! How people worship it." She reached up and rubbed at her hollow cheek in an agitated manner.

"Clementine, would you like some water?" Ruby asked.

"Water? Of course not! I don't want tea or water. And if you insist on interrupting me, I'll have you thrown out too. You wanted to know about Edward, so sit there and listen!"

Ruby did as she was told, again staying Jed with her hand, who was growling.

"Sarah Davis was nondescript. Not someone I took notice of, not until one night, anyway. It was hot, stifling, in fact, the middle of summer, and I couldn't sleep. Some girls shared rooms, but not me. I had a room to myself. Throwing back the bed covers, I intended to go over to the window and open it, but I heard a creak in the corridor outside. Curious, I crept over to the door instead and pressed my ear to the wood. There were footsteps. Someone passing by. Who, though, at that hour? As quietly as I could, I opened the door and caught a flash of something white rounding the corner. There were strict rules at our school; we weren't allowed to just wander the corridors at night, but somebody was evidently breaking those rules, and so would I. I followed, of course, again as quietly as I could, praying I'd avoid creaky floorboards unlike the one I was in pursuit of.

"The girl was heading to the library, conveniently leaving the door ajar so that I could peek around it. It was Sarah Davis I saw standing there, in a shaft of moonlight, in her nightdress, talking to someone…someone that only she could see. Trying to…reason with them, placate them, persuade them that they didn't belong there anymore and to leave, to go to the light because it was the light that was now their home."

Clementine's wizened face became almost otherworldly as she recalled this incident, a gleam in her eyes that was both tragic and repellent.

"Suddenly, she turned," Clementine continued, "as if sensing she was being spied on, but I was wily; living with my parents had taught me that much. At home I would spy on them too, at the gatherings and events they held with their friends, witness the kinds of things they would do…" She shivered as if freezing cold. "So, yes, I was adept at making myself as invisible as the person Sarah was addressing. On silent feet, I retraced my footsteps back to my bedroom and closed the door. Later I heard Sarah as she returned, as she paused just a few feet away from me, wondering just for a split second if she'd turn the door handle, if she'd enter… She didn't. She carried on. From thereon in, she became a subject of study, every bit as much as maths and English. And later, much later, knowing better the kind of things that pleased my parents, I told them about her."

"And that's why you threw the ball?" Ruby said, her voice an astounded whisper.

The laughter that greeted that comment was almost raucous.

"In Sarah's honour? Of course not! Don't you get it? My parents mixed with those types of people all the time, people who could *commune*." How she emphasised that last word. "They were curious, but they hadn't marked her or anything. They hadn't singled her out. No, I had no intention of inviting her to the ball. I hadn't seen her for…what was it…two years, perhaps? But my brother had a friend, a friend very interested in the same things my parents were, the occult.

"Daniel was my older brother's name, and he was the darling of my parents' because he delighted in their ways, the *events*. He threw himself into them wholeheartedly. I was rapidly losing favour because I refused to 'become,' as they called it, to join the circle full of the 'right kind of people,' they said, the kind you needed to impress in order to climb higher and higher. Or—" Clementine paused and took a breath "—sink lower. Not just losing favour, they were becoming angry with me. Daniel too was losing patience. Daniel had become quite enamoured of this friend, telling us at dinner several times how charming he was. 'Single, though,' Daniel would say. 'Perhaps we should find someone for him, someone…suitable.' Mother would nod. 'We know plenty of suitable women.' But Daniel shook his head. 'Not those women,' he said. 'Edward, for all his fervour and enthusiasm, is, in relative terms, still quite the innocent. He'd desire someone innocent too, but someone who can school him, who can steer him further into the arts, who can stimulate that passion.'"

Again, Clementine's laughter was loud. "They knew no one innocent, that was for sure." Quickly, though, her laughter faded. "But I did. And I told them so. My way, once again, of trying to curry favour. 'Is she pretty?'

That's the first thing Father asked. I told them she was pretty enough. 'Pretty *and* psychic,' he mused. 'Perhaps we need to keep her for ourselves.' 'No!' I said; I think I dared to shout it at him. That would be too much, like throwing her into a nest of vipers. Father stared at me for the longest time, his eyes boring right into me, making me wish I'd never opened my mouth, never said a word, but then he laughed and shrugged his shoulders. 'Edward's she is, then,' he said. 'But if he doesn't want her…' He never finished that sentence, and it was too late for me not to invite her to the ball, not once I'd mentioned her, and so, after obtaining her address from the school, I went right ahead. Edward *did* want her, though, as you obviously know. And I was relieved because…at that time, perhaps, he was the lesser of two evils.

"After the ball, I decided I had to escape, just take off. Live by my own rules, not my family's. As I've told you, their patience was running out; I'd either have to become fully integrated or be dealt with. You know, the thing is, at school, after finally noticing Sarah, I'd come to like her. She was humble, she was clever, she could be fun." The smile on Clementine's face for a few seconds made her look younger. "I wasn't going to tell my family anything about her, honestly I wasn't. I'd promised myself, but…why is it that a child, no matter how terrible the parent is, always seeks their approval? Why? Why?"

"I don't know," replied Ruby. "Only that it's true. We do."

Clementine lifted her head. "Are you psychic?"

"I am."

"What about Sarah's daughter?"

"She is."

"And you," she said, turning her head to Lee. "Who are you?"

"Really, just think of me as a volunteer," he told her.

Her attention back on Ruby, Clementine's eyes were every bit as piercing as she'd claimed her father's were. "Do you really want me to continue?"

"I do," said Ruby.

"For what reason?"

"Only good. I swear it."

"To help in some way?"

"Yes. It's my grandmother I take after, not my grandfather."

"Ah, Edward, Edward. He came to the house before the party. That's when I first met him. A friend of my brother's but…more intelligent. There was more about him in every way. No need for me to feel bad; I was doing Sarah a favour. Here was a man any girl would be proud to snare – me, for one – but he looked straight through me. Sarah, though…I witnessed the moment they met, how his eyes flashed as he teased her, her determined strides as she followed him, seeking more than the glass of champagne he'd offered. From that moment on they were lost to all but each other. Oh, how that irked Daniel, because Edward had no time for him anymore. Indeed, he pulled away from the circle rather than became further involved in it. But, as we know, their type won't let go for long. As we also know, Sarah taught him, didn't she? She taught him all too well."

Clementine's breathing changed, although subtly at

first. "Daniel bided his time, waited patiently. I never understood his continued fascination with Edward, but then I didn't really want to understand. I'd left home by that stage, run away, although, in all honesty, I never really did get far. They kept tabs on me, just like Daniel kept tabs on Edward. Boarding school had been an escape, and so prison became one too. I'd rather deal with the people in there than with my family any day. Edward, though, there was a time when he split with Sarah. That's when he came back into the fold, although Daniel was never smug about it. Rather, he reeled him in slowly, slowly, would take him away for weekends to a certain place in particular, a house in the country, a house my parents also visited, all their kind did, one that was infested, Daniel said, with all they held dear."

Revulsion rose in Ruby. "Blakemort," she said. "That house was Blakemort." And the photograph of Edward outside it could well have been taken by Daniel. Sarah in the window but not physically, not then; she'd made no mention of visiting Blakemort with anyone other than Edward. The house was simply showing Ruby what would come to pass eventually, inevitably. Because Edward *would* take Sarah there, and he'd do so because he'd been seduced, not by Daniel but by Blakemort itself.

"Daniel, Blakemort, Edward Middleton. Blacker than black, all of them. Even more than my parents, who both lived long, long lives. Not as figures of terror, though, not in the end. In the end they were husks. The darkness just…ate them. Daniel too is dead, as a result of the drugs I secured for him. Sweet justice, I'd say, and good riddance. The family fortune was left to me, and I squandered it. I still do, on this, the most expensive care home I could find, just another damned institution. I don't know about Edward. Not anymore. But I used to know about him. I never wanted to, but snippets of what he was up to always managed to reach my ears."

Not just her breathing becoming laboured, Clementine blinked rapidly too, one hand reaching up to clutch at her chest. Alarmed, Ruby rose from her chair.

"Clementine, it's okay. You don't have to—"

"Boundaries. Everybody has them, even my parents. As bad as they were, as *misguided*, they could have been so much worse. Because there is *always* worse. And Edward was it. He knew no boundaries, not according to all I've heard. He became such a willing agent of the darkness, worshipping at the altar of Satan. Oh God, these people, these terrible people, they're so damned clever too. Able to avoid justice. But can he escape it now, the final justice? Because we don't live forever, no matter what the Dark Lord promises. And there is always a reckoning. For every one of us. Including me. For all the wrongs we've committed. Oh God…oh God…oh Lord."

"Lee! Call the nurse, call Kerri."

Lee leapt to his feet, began hurrying to the door even as it opened, as Kerri appeared, as pale as her uniform, and little wonder if she had copied Clementine all those years before and pressed her ear to the door to listen.

Ruby, meanwhile, had placed her arms around Clementine's bony frame and was holding her. "It's okay, breathe, just breathe. It's okay. You've told us more than enough. Please…just breathe."

Clementine reached up and clutched at Ruby's jumper, Ruby surprised to feel how much strength the woman's grip still had.

"I'm sorry about Sarah, for bringing Edward into her life, into yours too."

"It's okay, it's fine, it doesn't matter."

"It does matter! That's why you're here. Because it matters very much. I'm not psychic, never have been. But I know something."

"What, Clementine? What do you know?"

Ruby was asking the question even as Kerri peeled her hands from the woman, insisting Ruby step back. Better than that, leave the room, just go.

"Clementine, what do you know? Tell me, please."

"The reckoning's here. Finally. If Edward isn't dead already, he soon will be."

Chapter Thirty-One

WHEN Lee and Ruby emerged from the nursing home, Jed racing ahead as if he couldn't wait to get out of there, as if the smell of fresh flowers and money was worse than the stink of carrion, Cash and Carrie-Anne were on the driveway waiting for them.

"There you are!" said Cash, hurrying over. "You were so long!"

"What is it?" a dazed Ruby asked. "Hendrix? Oh God, is he okay?"

"He's fine. Behaving himself for his Nana, but…Ruby, are you okay?"

"Yeah, yeah, we just… Shit, we're running out of time!"

Lee broke into the conversation. "I hate to do this, but I have to get back to work."

Ruby turned to him. "Yeah, yeah, sure. Thank you for helping."

"That Southbourne Villas address, I'll check it out. Let you know if there's anything significant about it."

"Great, thank you, Lee. It's number fifty-eight."

"Fifty-eight, yep, got it."

Now just the three of them stood on the gravel drive, Jed also having disappeared, no doubt trying to clear his head in an Elysium field somewhere.

"Sorry," Ruby said. "For taking so long."

"Can't wait to hear what Clementine said," Cash replied.

"I'll tell you in the car, on the way back to Lewes."

Satisfied with that, Cash strode off towards the Ford, promising he'd give his mum another quick ring to check all really was well.

Ruby and Carrie-Ann lingered, Carrie-Ann more aware of how shocked Ruby was.

"That was really tough, wasn't it?"

Ruby nodded. "It's not easy finding out how depraved your family is."

"I'll bet. I'm sorry for you, but you're not tarnished, not at all. You're the balance."

"Strange, but I was hoping Edward would be."

"What do you mean?"

"My father wasn't exactly the greatest man either. He…" She swallowed. "He's locked away, criminal insanity."

"Shit!" Carrie-Ann's eyes were wide.

"And my great-great-grandfather was dubious too." She pulled a face as she added, "To say the least." Why she was telling Carrie-Ann all this escaped Ruby. Edward was one thing, but she had no obligation to spill the beans on the rest of the men she was related to. And yet…this client, this…friend, she felt she could tell her anything and she wouldn't judge. Something that worked both ways between them. She apologised again. "This isn't stuff you need to know, and, as I've said before, it in no way detracts from your case."

"Hey, one thing at a time, eh?"

Carrie-Ann reached out, pulling Ruby into a hug. As

she did, Ruby tried not to gasp.

Not because she was surprised at Carrie-Ann's gesture. Far from it.

It was because of how cold Carrie-Ann had become, the chill that emanated from her sinking right into Ruby's bones and lodging there.

* * *

In the car, Cash driving again, Ruby told them all that Clementine had told her.

"A reckoning?" Cash repeated. "Bloody hell, that's a bit dramatic, isn't it?"

"A reckoning between who?" Carrie-Ann asked, perhaps a tad more constructively.

"I don't know," Ruby said, reaching across and turning the car's heater to maximum. The chill inside her, courtesy of Carrie-Ann, wouldn't abate.

"Do you think it's between you and Edward?" continued Carrie-Ann, oblivious to how she'd left Ruby feeling. "After all, you're the one he seems to target."

"Maybe," Ruby replied, nodding. The photograph was the connection between them, the one she had in her bag even now, which she was tempted to retrieve to see if anything else about it had changed – just as Carrie-Ann had changed yet again – but also wary of strengthening the connection by giving it attention. "We have to find him." An old man in his late eighties, he was still powerful. What had Sarah taught him, and Blakemort too?

"At least we've made some headway," Cash remarked as if in appeasement, "not with Edward, perhaps, but

Dave Lane. It's not too shabby for a day's work."

"I suppose," said Ruby, although the day was far from over yet.

Frustrated and depleted from the weight of her family's history, as bad as any psychic attack, she leant her head back against the headrest, wondering what she should do next.

Although aware of where Dave Lane lived, they couldn't exactly force their way into the building. Could they? Lee could as a police officer, knocking on every door until they found him, but only if she made an official accusation of assault to the police, which would probably be ridiculed by any rational police officer and then countered by an accusation of stalking.

Was there a way they could act without involving Lee? Lie in wait again for Dave Lane, perhaps. But even if they did, if they cornered him, they couldn't force him to talk, to shed any light on Carrie-Ann's case. Rather, he seemed hellbent on *not* talking or helping in any way, only hindering, attacking her, even, if only the once.

Ruby sat up straighter, one hand reaching up to clutch at her tourmaline necklace.

What if it, in fact, *had* been just the once? What if, up until he'd spotted them following him, he'd thought that was enough?

If Ruby was feeling chilled enough already, now it was as though her blood froze.

She twisted around to face Carrie-Ann in the rear seat, Jed suddenly materialising beside her, having recharged himself like she suspected he sometimes had to do, and now appearing excited, barking at Ruby, encouraging her to ask what was on her mind.

"Carrie-Ann, earlier, when we were in Hove, in Southbourne Villas, you said something, something that…I don't know…maybe because I was in shock at being attacked again, it didn't register, not properly, but it's registering now."

Carrie-Ann was frowning. "Okay. Go on."

"Whilst I was pinned against the post, you were looking at Lane, weren't you?"

Oh, if only Carrie-Ann could see the dog beside her, thought Ruby. He was seemingly urging her on too, continuing to fuss when she also straightened her back. "That's right. I was trying to get him to stop attacking you. I was just…so scared."

Ruby nodded. "I know. Of course you were."

"But…it's like I said, he seemed scared too."

"You used the word *horrified*."

"Did I? But, yes, he was. We all were."

"Ruby," Cash interjected, "what's going on? What are you getting at?"

Before she could answer, her phone rang. "Hang on, Cash. It's Lee. I'll put him on loudspeaker."

"Ruby, hi. Me again."

"Hi, Lee. You back at the station already?"

"Almost. Just got some info from one of my officers on that address you gave me."

"Southbourne Villas? Okay, yeah?"

"It's what you might call a halfway house."

"A halfway house? What's that?"

"Somewhere the social services place people in need, emergency housing, if you like. They could be homeless, for instance, just released from prison or from psychiatric care. It can be a real mishmash of people.

The reason the address is known to the police is because there's often trouble there, punch-ups, rows, domestics, you get the drift."

"Yeah, okay, thanks, Lee," replied Ruby. "That helps. That really helps."

"Good luck with it all. Shout if you need me."

After thanking him a second time, Ruby ended the call and glanced over at Cash.

"So, Dave Lane's in a doss-house," he said.

"Cash! That's not what you call them nowadays."

"Okay, okay, but political correctness aside, that's what it is. So, does knowing that really help? And in what way?"

"Because…because…"

Again, her phone rang, Ruby looking down to see that the caller ID was unknown.

"What the hell?"

Her mind was still whirring as she answered it, wondering if the theory developing in her head was nuts or viable and how she'd be able to put it to the test, get into the building on Southbourne Villas and knock on all the doors…

"Hello? Is that you? Is that Ruby Davis of Psychic Surveys?"

The voice on the other end of the phone – male – was panicked.

"Hello," she responded. "This is Ruby Davis. How can I help?"

"You have to help! You have to!"

"If I can, I will. Look, calm down and tell me what's the matter. I'm listening."

With the phone still on loudspeaker, Cash raised an

eyebrow. "Who is it?"

Ruby held a hand up and mouthed the word *wait*.

"Hello, are you still there?" she asked when the line went silent.

The only response this time was the sound of him crying.

Immediately adopting Theo's soothing tone, Ruby continued to placate him. "I understand that you're frightened. You need to tell me, though, what you're frightened of. Like I said, I'm listening, and I will do my best to help you."

When he didn't respond, Ruby grew increasingly concerned.

"Please speak to me. At least tell me where you are. My team and I will get to you as soon as we can. What's your address?"

At last the man spoke. "My address?"

"Yes, that's correct. What is it?"

"If I tell you, you promise you'll come? You won't...back out?"

"Back out? No. Why would I?"

Another sob escaped him. This man, whoever he was, was in a terrible state. "I don't know what to do anymore. I just don't know what to do."

"But we might," insisted Ruby. "We might know *exactly* what to do."

"I'm sorry. Before...I was scared. Now, though...now I'm *terrified*. I didn't want this. None of it. It's too much...it'll send me mad, it will. I can't cope!"

Ruby did her utmost to inject authority into her voice, the kind that Theo and Ness were so adept at doing. "Tell me where you are. Now."

"Fifty-eight Southbourne Villas," the man answered at last. "Flat six."

Ruby's mouth fell open. "Southbourne Villas?" she repeated.

"That's right, yeah. It's Dave Lane."

Chapter Thirty-Two

"CASH, are you sure your mum's okay with having Hendrix still? It's just—"

"Ruby, one thing we don't have to worry about right now is Hendrix, okay? He's safe in Mum's hands. What I want to know is how safe *you're* going to be."

"I…" She couldn't reply, not when she didn't know the answer.

After Dave Lane's frantic phone call, Ruby had organised a FaceTime call with Theo, Ness and Corinna to tell them about it and to request they meet her there, outside the house in Southbourne Villas. She'd also given them a potted version of what Clementine had told her and Lee, all whilst Cash sped along trying to reach Hove rather than Lewes as quickly as possible before rush-hour traffic could hamper them.

"It's all linked," she'd said. "No matter how bizarrely, it's still linked."

"How?" Ness asked, Cash adding, "Yeah, how? Ruby, come on!"

"It's linked because I think this halfway house is where Edward Middleton lives too."

"What?" Cash breathed.

Ruby indicated over her shoulder to where Carrie-Ann was sitting, an astonished look on her face as well.

"We were there earlier, and, as you also know, I was attacked earlier, psychically. A vicious attack. For a moment I thought I was going to... Anyway, upshot is, Dave Lane was *not* responsible for it, not this time. Carrie-Ann saw him whilst it was happening and how frightened he was. He seemed *transfixed* by horror, eventually dropping his carrier bag of shopping and hurrying inside. Isn't that right, Carrie-Ann?"

"Yes," she confirmed. "It is."

"And yet the source of the attack came from there, that building. I'm positive."

"So, no posh care home for Middleton, then?" Cash said, shaking his head.

"Nope, like many of his kind, like Aleister Crowley himself, Britain's self-professed Great Beast 666, they end up falling on skid row, realising too late the futility of it all."

"That realisation, though," Theo pointed out, "can make a person even more dangerous. If your theory is correct, Ruby, we need to tread very carefully. *You* do."

"I know. It'll be another ten minutes or so before we reach Hove. How about you?"

"Almost there," said Ness, who, alongside Theo, was hitching a lift with Corinna.

"It's metered parking on the road, but there's usually a few spaces," Ruby advised them. "Park where you can, and we'll find you."

The call had ended, and Cash was still fretting. "Ruby, Theo's right when she says it's you that's particularly in danger. We have to consider Hendrix. You're a mother now."

A fury rose in her. "I know what I am, Cash!"

"All I'm saying is—"

"This is my job, this is what I do, what defines me. Not just being a mother. And this is also a family affair. More's the bloody pity."

There was silence before Cash spoke again, his voice somewhat softer.

"Your mum asked to be kept informed. If you've found her father, she'll want to know."

"I know." Ruby also spoke more gently. "I...I'll phone her now." Before she did, though, she turned to Carrie-Ann. "We'll drop you off at home before going to Southbourne Villas."

Carrie-Ann shook her head, as indignant as Ruby had been. "No. No way. This might be a family affair, but it's also to do with me. I'm coming with you. I want to find out what Dave Lane knows about me and why I horrify him too. I need answers. I need..." There was a crack in her voice. "I need to know what it is I have to do next."

Ruby sighed. How could she deny her, beg her to go home and leave them to it? She herself had just refused, and so vehemently, when Cash had suggested she do the same. Carrie-Ann had been present at every stage, her case growing, becoming bigger, becoming intertwined with the other. Heck, it was because of Carrie-Ann that they might find Edward Middleton. Now a disillusioned, disturbed and dangerous old man.

Should she really tell her mother about the latest development? Or leave her in Bexhill, where she was safe? Deal with it themselves, the Psychic Surveys team, *just* them, no police either, not yet – although Ness insisted she was keeping Lee informed. They were entering a building that potentially housed a dangerous man, so he was being put on standby.

Edward was dying, according to Clementine. Ruby's grandfather was almost at the point where he would breathe his last. Beyond life, would he be as much of a threat? Or would he just keep falling down into the depths, where in life he'd longed to be?

Decisions…decisions… If only she also had the gift of foresight.

She jumped as her phone rang yet again.

"Shit, who is it this time?" she said.

Caller ID told her precisely who: Jessica.

Quickly, she answered it. "Mum?"

"Have you got something to tell me, Ruby?"

* * *

Ruby spotted her colleagues as soon as they turned into Southbourne Villas. Cash spotted them too and bagged a space right by them. Whilst he paid for parking on his phone, Ruby and Carrie-Ann rushed over to Theo, Ness and Corinna.

"Mum's already on her way over," she told them. "She knew something was up. I couldn't dissuade her."

"To Hove?" Theo checked.

"Well, yeah. I redirected her."

Theo glanced at Ness and Corinna before adding, "We can't wait for her. Not if Lane's as much of a mess as you said he was."

Ruby agreed. "We've got to get in there."

"Or we could get him to come out," suggested Ness.

"Not sure that will work," Ruby said. "He might be

too scared to move."

"Ruby, you can't go in there." It was Carrie-Ann, clearly fearing a repeat performance of last time, as was Ruby. "Edward will sense you!"

"Not if we all flank you," Corinna's expression was one of grim determination. "Literally, we create a human and psychic barrier around you."

Theo was nodding. "That should work. That should definitely do the trick."

"I'm willing to give it a go," said Ruby. "We have to reach Lane. Once he's calmer or we've got him out of there, well…we can deal with the second issue."

"Can I come in too?" Carrie-Ann asked.

"I'm not sure that's a good idea, sweetheart," Theo said. "We want to calm him down. Seeing you might tip him over the edge."

Seeing how deflated Carrie-Ann was, Ruby also sought to appease her. "But when he's calm, we can ask about his reaction to you, gain more of an insight. Cash will wait with you."

"Huh? What?" Cash said, approaching them. "Wait out here? No way. I'm coming in. You might need brute strength."

Ruby couldn't help but smile. "What we'll need is for you to restrain Mum when she turns up. Just until we've got a handle on the situation inside."

Cash looked as deflated as Carrie-Ann. "Get all the exciting jobs, don't I?"

"It's a valid job," Ruby reminded him. "This situation, it's delicate, okay?"

"Okay," he muttered. "We'll wait in the car, though, where it's warm. If you need us, if you even *think* you need us, call, okay?"

"I promise," said Ruby, turning back to her colleagues. "Shall we?"

They did as Corinna had suggested and flanked Ruby – Theo and Corinna on one side, Ness on the other, Jed joining in too, lending his light, of which there was an abundance.

"The dog's practically shimmering," Ruby told them as they walked towards number fifty-eight.

"Glad to hear it," Theo said.

Ruby turned to her. "And you're okay with this? You know, you're…"

"Capable?" Theo quizzed when Ruby's voice trailed off. "I think you know the answer to that question by now. Besides which, I've told you, I've never felt better."

Despite the reassurance, Ruby was trepidatious when they turned onto the quarry-tiled pathway of the halfway house, imagining bright white light like never before, her colleagues and Jed doing exactly the same. So far, so good.

A set of buzzers presented itself.

"It's flat six," said Ruby, prompting Theo to reach up and press the bell.

No answer, but the door opened, the five of them continuing to march like Roman centurions heading into battle. Ruby remained in the middle even as they climbed the stairs to the second floor, where flat number six seemed to be. There were four floors, Ruby wondering which flat was Middleton's, if her theory was correct. Had they passed it already, or was it on the floor above, the stairway carrying on into gloomy darkness.

"Quick! Quick! You must be quick!"

A voice reached them, full of desperation.

The team hurried towards it. It was coming from flat six. Dave Lane, having summoned an ounce of bravery in opening both the entrance door and the door to his flat, now retreated back inside, leaving the latter ajar.

A terrible smell assailed them as they entered the flat, enough to make your eyes water. It was the smell of old socks and body odour, of rank fear that had oozed from every pore. The flat was tiny, comprising a living room with a kitchenette, a door that led into a bedroom, presumably, and one that led into a bathroom. In the midst of it all was Lane, still a shivering wreck, huddled not on the small sofa there but in the corner of the room, hunkered down and with his arms wrapped tightly around himself.

Ruby broke rank and rushed forwards. "It's okay, we're here. Tell us what's wrong. What is it that's frightening you so much?"

"Is she…is she with you?" His dark eyes glittered.

"Carrie-Ann? No."

"She…she's not right. She should be dead, not…walking around. Evil."

"She is *not* evil," Ruby told him, her voice firm, "but, yes, something strange is happening to her. Something we're trying to understand and help her with."

"Kill her!"

Ruby was stunned. "No! What the hell's wrong with you?"

Sweat drenched his forehead. "Unnatural. All of this. I don't want it. This…insight. This…torture. It's getting worse, not better. It'll destroy me."

All the while they were talking, the team stood close behind her, taking it all in, making observations of their own, but most of all pumping out the white light. Jed had begun agitating, though. Only briefly did Ruby glance at him, noticing he wasn't shimmering quite as brightly. No time to question or comment on it; they had to try to calm Lane and get some sense out of him, a task that was looking increasingly unlikely.

"There's a name for those kinds of things," he continued, wiping at the sweat. "Things like her. That rise from the dead, that will drain you, not of blood, of your life force. *Strigoi.*"

"*Strigoi*?" Ruby queried.

"It's Romanian," Theo informed her. "A term for a sort of vampire."

Having glanced at Theo, Ruby turned back to Lane, noted just how dark his colouring was, a certain swarthiness to his skin. Perhaps there was Romanian blood in him after all.

"Carrie-Ann is not a vampire," she told him. "It's not her that will drain you. Only fear does that."

He shook his head. "I don't want her near me, and I don't want the sight. Not anymore. It's not a game. Something to make money at. Not after her. Not after…"

His voice faltered as he looked around him, eyes flickering from left to right, up and down. Ruby glanced again at her colleagues, noticed their confusion, Ness turning her head as if trying to discover what Lane was looking at, Jed performing a full circle too.

Struggling to keep her own breath under control, Ruby latched on to what he *hadn't* said. "Not after what?" she said. "Why is your…clairvoyance, your…insight, not a game anymore? What changed your mind besides Carrie-Ann? Dave," she persisted when he failed to answer, "don't give in to fear. My whole team is here, and we can protect you, but you have to help us to help yourself. You have to calm down. Get yourself back under control. Fear feeds fear. Did you know that? It *breeds* it. Tell me what, besides Carrie-Ann, you're afraid of, because it's the greater fear, isn't it? By far."

"It's linked," he said at last. "They are."

"They are? Dave, how long have you been living here?"

"Th…three months."

"Shortly after what happened with Carrie-Ann?"

"I didn't want to tell fortunes anymore. I…I had no money. Couldn't pay the rent."

"So you were evicted, were you, made homeless, and you came here?"

He nodded again with such force.

"Have you met someone here?"

"What?" The pupils in his eyes were almost fully dilated.

"A man?"

"I…I don't know what you mean."

"That attack launched on me a few days ago, were you responsible for that?"

"Sorry. Sorry."

"You did it because you were scared, didn't you? Of Carrie-Ann, of me, scared of the gift you've so far just played with."

"I DON'T WANT THIS GIFT, I'VE TOLD

YOU!"

"But were you taught to attack, by this man you've met right here in this very building?"

Lane scratched at his arms as if a thousand insects were crawling over them. "Leave me alone, just leave me alone."

"The second attack, though, the one that took place outside this very house, you had nothing to do with it, did you? You've never seen the result of an attack before, the efforts of your handiwork. Thought it was still something of a game, at least. But it's not, is it? Psychic ability is real, and it's as dangerous in the hands of someone naïve as it is in the hands of the power-mad."

"I don't know why he attacked you. I didn't even know he knew you. He never said. But, yes, he's taught me things, things I didn't want to know, but he's so hard to resist. He's dying, but it makes no difference. He's evil too. All I see now is evil!"

"Who? Who is it that's hard to resist? What's his name? Where is he?"

"Edward Middleton," he breathed almost in wonder, just as a door opened, the one Ruby had presumed led to the bedroom, the creak causing them all to turn towards it. "He's there. Right there. I really am sorry. But if I give him you, he won't want me."

Before she could take in what he was saying or respond, Ruby keeled over – because of a physical attack this time rather than psychic, although she was sure that too would come. Dave Lane had punched her in the side of the head and then shoved her to the side before rising, fleeing past her, past the team, shoving Ness too as she tried to stop him, past Edward Middleton and out of the flat. Spotting his chance to escape the madness and seizing it.

Chapter Thirty-Three

SO, you're a Davis woman, are you? And very talented, it would seem.

Still half lying on the ground, Ruby tried to think, to gather her senses, to place the voice in her head, one that was smooth, was charming, as soothing as Theo's.

Theo! Where was she? Ness and Corinna too. And Jed. She wasn't alone in this squalid room; she'd entered it with the backing of her entire team, and yet…she felt alone, caught in a moment, trapped within the confines of it.

You're not alone, remember? I'm here.

"Edward?"

That's right. Edward Middleton. But you know that. You're very interested in that.

Ruby pushed herself up. What was happening here? Something new, which she'd never experienced before. She looked around her but could see only darkness. Not a complete darkness, though, scratchier than that. The darkness of a dream or a hallucination. Perhaps the blow to her head was harder than she'd thought.

"Theo, Ness, Corinna, where are you?" she called. "Are you okay? Jed, can you see me? Can you reach me? Let me know you're here. Come on, break through this."

Most likely he will. Eventually. Jed's an interesting phenomenon…just like Lane and that girl he would prattle on about. Tell me, how does a gift like that get wasted on someone like Lane? He really is talented, more than you seem to be. Shame he's bogged down by superstition and stupidity. Once I'd planted the idea of a strigoi *in his head…*

On her feet now, Ruby spun around. She'd caught a glimpse of Edward Middleton, a flash of something white a moment before she'd been hit. He'd been hiding in the bedroom of Lane's flat, and yet none of them had sensed he was so close, the man able to cloak himself as well. Not a psychic, not someone with a natural-born talent, so how had he honed his skills to this level? Who besides Sarah had taught him? Was Blakemort really responsible? Blakemort and a thousand places just like it?

Clever. Good thinking. If only we'd met sooner. The fun we could have had.

She threw her arms out before her. "Where are you? Where the hell are you?"

Everywhere. But in your thoughts particularly. I have been for a while.

"Is that how we connected? Because of the photograph?"

Or something else? Blood, maybe?

"What…what are you doing to me?"

Just…playing.

"Don't! Leave me alone!"

I want to see, that's all.

"See what?"

If it's truly possible.

"If what's possible?"

If I can replace you.

Movement caught her eye. There he was at last. Striding out of the darkness, a man, but not a man, a shadow, huge in stature, far taller than her, powerful arms reaching out as hands gripped her neck, as they had done twice before, and squeezed.

Unable to speak, she begged him by thought instead to release her.

Please, you have to.

I just want to see... Hold still, now. If you do, it'll be easier. Come on, now, dear, don't be a bad girl, don't be tiresome.

I can't breathe, Edward, I... Let go.

More shocking than the spectral hands around her neck, their strength not belonging to a man in his late eighties, was the something invading her mind. It felt like a series of tentacles, reaching out, probing, and ice-cold, every one of them, freezing what was there, her thoughts, her memory, her life.

Theo! Ness! Corinna! Oh shit, Cash, where are you?

He must have seen Dave Lane bursting out of the house whilst waiting outside in the car. Wasn't that signal enough that something was wrong? Why hadn't he come rushing up the stairs to find her? And what about her colleagues; why weren't they also trying to help? How come she was stuck here, with Edward, in this strange, strange place?

The in-between. That's what this place is. Terrifyingly lovely, don't you think?

In the in-between, as he'd called it, there was simply no vestige of light, none that she could summon, that she could…remember.

Perhaps he really was taking her over, becoming her, having found a way to live forever that was beyond spirit, that utilised the flesh instead.

Clever man…clever, desperate man…

Cruel laughter resounded in her head.

The two do usually go hand in hand! You know…I didn't expect this to be so easy, although I'm thankful for it. And for Lane, for bringing you to my attention. As I said, a Davis woman, a psychic woman. What a coincidence that is. I knew one just like you once. The light in her was immense, but you…oh, there's darkness in you, quite a bit.

If there was, she'd always fought against it, against all the doubts that had ever reared up about herself, the fear that the madness in her family was, in fact, hereditary. She had to continue fighting, not give up, keep calling on the light that was there somewhere, and on love too, although the memory of love was fading, and the memory of those she loved, their faces, their names…. It was all just…disappearing. In its place was a void, a stark emptiness that would hold her captive long after Edward had drained her – a true *strigoi* – leaving her stranded in the terrible loneliness of the in-between.

If only she could summon more strength…if only she wasn't fading so fast… What would it be like? Not to exist anymore or anywhere. Not just having your heart stolen but your soul too. Would it really be so dreadful? Would you – *could* you – care?

"STOP WHAT YOU'RE DOING! STOP RIGHT NOW!"

A whooshing in her veins, the force of blood again, not frozen but thawing, rushing into every extremity, bringing back life and memories too. Ruby gasped. How could she have forgotten about the light? About love? Who had the power to erase it like that?

Blinking rapidly, she realised she was still in the half-slumped position Dave had left her in, that she hadn't moved an inch, nor had anyone else in the room, that the experience, such as it was, had not only been momentary but cerebral. The only thing that had actually happened was that Jessica had entered the room, yelling at Edward Middleton.

More change: Corinna came rushing over to her at last, dropping to her knees and cradling Ruby. Cash appeared, also rushing over, Carrie-Ann standing in the doorway along with Saul, both bewildered, whilst Theo, Ness and Jed stood stock-still.

"I'm fine, I'm fine," Ruby told Corinna and Cash. "Wait. Just wait."

Now that Middleton's grip on her had been released, she could study him fully.

She was almost afraid to do so, remembering the creature she'd recently encountered that had stalked towards her with so much confidence, so much power and so much arrogance – a devil of a man if ever there was one. What did he look like in the flesh?

She gasped. An old man, as expected, he wasn't tall or powerful; that was simply the image he'd projected of himself. In a sleeveless vest – the flash of white she'd seen – pyjama bottoms and ragged brown slippers, he was more wizened than Clementine, frailer, and not standing before them either but confined to a wheelchair with a single oxygen cylinder attached to its side that ran to the nasal cannula he wore.

A man whose body was rapidly failing but whose mind was still more than capable.

"Mum, be careful. Mum…?"

Having had time to study Edward, she now focused on Jessica. What was she wearing? Clothes she'd never seen her in before, that was for sure. Jessica always wore jeans, jumpers and blouses, not *this*, a green dress with a flared skirt, falling just below the knee, and low-heeled black court shoes, her hair swept up in a ponytail and even a touch of makeup.

"Mum, you look so much like…"

Like Gran, she was about to say, from the pictures she'd studied of Gran when she'd been a much younger woman. And the dress was Sarah's, an old one kept for sentimental reasons, perhaps, formerly in the bag going to the charity shop. It was a perfect fit for Jessica. Her hair – also how Sarah used to wear it – suited her too. They were so alike, the pair of them. Like it was, in fact, Sarah standing there instead of Jessica, tears welling up in Ruby's eyes to see it, to have it brought home how much she missed her. And if it was having this effect on her…

The room fell quiet as if all of them were now caught in the in-between. Whether they'd escape it or not hanging in the balance.

Jessica, having secured Edward's attention, had to tread carefully, Ruby, alongside Theo and Ness, generating light and love. *We're with you, Mum. We've got your back.*

As if Jessica had heard these very words, she took a deep breath and then another before stepping forward. At no point did Edward's eyes leave her face.

"Sarah?" he said at last.

"It's time now, Edward," Jessica replied, "to stop with all this. We're not here to cause further harm. You've caused enough of that, to others and yourself."

"Sarah, I thought you were dead!"

Jessica shook her head.

"Oh, Sarah, Sarah, I never dared hope—"

"Edward, there is *always* hope. Open your eyes. Really open them. Understand what evil took from you, how it used you. Look at yourself, not at me, look and see what you've become. A lonely, ill old man in a halfway house. It wasn't what was promised, was it? Stop your blind devotion, put an end to the hold it has on you. *Renounce* it."

Edward coughed, an alarming hacking sound that for a moment had Jessica losing her cool demeanour. *Mum!* Ruby fired the thought at her, Jessica turning only briefly in her direction before regaining her poise. Further bridging the gap between them, she knelt in front of Edward so that their eyes were level. Ruby tensed. Would he see through her guise?

"I'm dying," he said.

"I know."

"I don't want to die."

"Why, Edward? Tell me why you don't."

"What?" Confusion entered his voice, making him sound not like a man but a child. Had no one ever asked him that question before? Ruby wondered. Had he never asked it of himself? She shook her head. All the promises he'd believed, eternal life being one of them, he must now realise how hollow they were, how *pathetic*. You couldn't outrun or outwit fate. She glanced at

Carrie-Ann still hovering in the doorway, clutching on to Saul, and amended that thought. If you did manage to outrun it, it wouldn't be for long.

With the speed of a viper, Edward suddenly leant forward, one hand gripping Jessica's arm. Ruby tensed further. They all did, Jed hopping from foot to foot.

"I can live, Sarah! I can find a host. I almost did."

"With Ruby? My granddaughter."

"No, no, a stranger! Maybe Lane, as despicable as he is. Then we can be together."

"We can't."

"Sarah! What are you saying? We can! Look at you." His hand left Jessica's arm and travelled to her face instead, stroking the skin there. "Time has been so kind to you."

Ruby shuddered on her mother's behalf regarding his touch, imagining it to be reptilian, but, to her surprise, Jessica lifted her hand too and held on to his, seeming to relish it.

"Oh, Edward," she murmured. "Dear Edward."

Ruby looked about her. Did anyone else hear it? The slight change in Jessica's voice. How was she doing it, making herself not just look like Gran but sound like her too?

"I loved you. You know that, don't you?"

"Of course, Sarah."

"With all my heart."

"I loved you too."

"There was never anyone else for me. No man could compare."

"I...oh, Sarah. If only you hadn't left me."

"I had to. You were being...dragged down."

Edward shook his head furiously, yellowish-white strands of hair dislodging. "No, no, it wasn't like that! You taught me so much, taught me what was possible, but...the things *they* taught me, Sarah! The wonders that exist, that we're capable of, how we're able to transcend."

"And yet here you are." Jessica gestured around her. "This is how you ended up."

Abruptly, Edward dropped his hand. "I thought you were enlightened."

"And I thought you were too. I thought you knew what true power was. The power of us. And yet you chose something other; you let me go. No, Edward, you never loved me."

Cash helped Ruby to sit up straighter as Jessica stood and then turned her back on him, striding towards the door.

How shocked he looked!

"Sarah? Where are you going? You can't leave me. Not again. Sarah, please!"

Before she could reach the door, it slammed itself shut, Carrie-Ann and Saul having to jump back on the far side in order to avoid it hitting them. Would they open the door? Come rushing in? Break the spell Jessica had woven?

Jessica's shoulders became rigid. The door, however, remained closed, and Ruby was grateful for it. This scenario, as precarious as it was, had to continue. Jessica – acting as Sarah – had reached a man who'd been lost for years. The only one who ever stood a chance, perhaps.

At the door, Jessica grabbed the handle, Edward

opening his mouth and emitting a roar so loud, so harsh, Ruby swore that the entire foundation of the building shook.

"YOU CANNOT LEAVE ME AGAIN!"

Jessica swung round, a fire in her eyes that more than matched his.

"THEN CHOOSE ME!" she screamed back. "CHOOSE ME OVER EVIL!"

"You don't understand—"

"No, Edward, you don't understand, even now, what it's done to you. Do you know what I loved most about you? Do you?"

There was a heartbeat of silence before she continued.

"Your intelligence, your thirst for knowledge. All kinds of knowledge. How you never once laughed when I told you what I could do, how you never once doubted me. You just…you looked at me in wonder. I remember that so well, *pure* wonder. Edward, choose me, but if you don't, then I'll have no choice. I will leave you again. You couldn't stop me then, and you can't stop me now despite your cheap theatrics. Evil can have its way with you, and you will not ascend. You will fall. And the lower planes, Edward, they are brutal, worse than even you can imagine. I won't come after you, not this time, not there. You have to choose because…because your time is close. So close."

Spittle flew from Edward's mouth as he coughed, his body doubling over, his skin, Ruby noticed, dry, almost crisp, like it was made of parchment. When he raised his head, though, the fire in his eyes was still there. But whom it burnt for, Ruby couldn't tell.

More time passed in which no one dared to move, to disturb the players.

When Jessica spoke, she sounded dreamy rather than angry, her expression wistful.

"Do you remember when we first met? At Clementine's masked ball." A girlish giggle escaped her. "You handed me a glass of champagne, and then you just…walked off."

Edward frowned, seeming as surprised as them by the sudden change in direction, expecting the fight to continue, for more harsh words to be hurled, laced with pain, bitterness and regret. Whatever game Jessica was playing, though, it was different to that.

As she'd inclined her head, so did he, frowning still, as if trying to remember. *Dig deep*, Ruby urged him, knowing how evil ate away at good memories, how, at the hands of Edward, it had tried to destroy hers. *They'll still be there.*

"The party…" he said. "Clementine…Daniel… 'Come along,' he said. 'There's someone I'd like you to meet. Someone you'll find…interesting.' Funny, really."

"What is, Edward?" Jessica asked.

"Because I don't think he expected what happened next. That from the moment I set eyes on you, I'd be…consumed."

"Oh, Edward," Jessica continued, the smile on her face indulgent. The performance she was putting on was Oscar-worthy. "We escaped into the garden, didn't we? We removed our masks, just before midnight. Rebels even then. Your face, I…never had I seen anything as beautiful, not before or after. We kissed. That kiss was our seal. All the times we met, I remember every one of them. In that curious old bookshop, full of dusty, ancient tomes, and you read to me! You swore you'd read all those books. I didn't believe you, of course, that would have been impossible, but you loved books, so much."

"Thirsty," he said. "Like you said."

"And what about the times we spent in the flat above the bookshop?"

"I remember, Sarah. Like you, every minute."

"You remember when love first blossomed?"

"Yes! It was like a tide rushing in, my heart so full it overflowed."

"And the world was such a wonderful place."

"Bright. It was bright back then."

"Everything shone."

Edward nodded, something glistening on his cheek. A tear?

"That's what love can do, Edward. *Only* love."

"Your smile, the glitter in your eyes, your laugher too, the sweetest song. Your...power."

Jessica faltered. "Edward?"

"Daniel was right. Use you, abuse you, don't fucking fall in love with you!"

"Mum," Ruby breathed, unable to help herself. His voice, from being as dreamy and wistful as Jessica's, had become something else entirely. She made to move, to interrupt further, but Cash held her back, just as Theo turned to her with eyes warning her also to stay put, Corinna leaning forward, whispering in her ear, "This has to play out."

She stilled, but she knew the power of this man, that

which belied his feeble body – she knew, and it was hard not to be frightened of it.

Edward bridged the gap this time, grabbing the cylinder of oxygen and laying it on his lap as he wheeled himself forward. When he came to a stop before Jessica, he reached up, not to touch her but to rip the nasal cannula from his face. Was it Ruby's imagination, or had he become taller, even in the chair, bigger?

"Oh shit," she breathed, increasing the flow of white light, noting the avid concentration on Theo's and Ness's faces as they did the same, and Corinna too, Jed having crept forward, ready to strike if need be.

"You speak of love, you speak of saving me," Edward continued. "You utter fool! You couldn't save me then, and you can't now. You opened up the world to me, you showed me things, and then you left me. We made promises too, remember? In the quiet hours of the night, that we'd remain by each other's side through thick and thin, that we'd explore the world and the mysteries it held, together. You said all that, Sarah, and then you left me, your promises just as empty. So who am I supposed to believe, you or evil, as you call it? Because I'll tell you something, only one of you has stood by my side, only one has ever been loyal."

If Edward was increasing in stature, so was Jessica. She leant forward, placed her hands on the arms of the wheelchair, her eyes boring into his, penetrating deep.

"My heart was always yours, Edward. Even now, despite everything, it's yours. I *was* loyal. Always. And I'm here by your side now, aren't I? Because I'm loyal. Because I'm true to my word. Because I want to save you. But you have to want to save yourself. You're not lost, not completely. The man you were is still inside. Look for him, bring him back, and choose me this time." Her voice cracking, she begged further. "You have to!"

"Foul trickster!"

"No! Edward, remember at Blakemort, the tears that you would cry? I'd listen to you in that locked room. Those tears were savage. Maybe…maybe I shouldn't have left you. But I was pregnant. And you knew, didn't you? Not then, not at Blakemort. But you got the letter I sent a few months later in a moment of weakness, the one that was returned to sender. Don't do that, don't shake your head and deny it! There it is, in your eyes, the truth of it at last. The letter was forwarded on to you from the bookshop. You must have kept in touch with Atterley, no doubt ordering those books you craved. You read the letter, and then you returned it. Oh God, I thought I sensed your hands on it. And the envelope wasn't quite sealed either from where you must have steamed it open. You returned it because…because Blakemort, as terrible as it is, didn't quite swallow you whole. There was something in you that managed to withstand it – the old Edward, the one who remembered only too well what love was and who wanted to protect me and protect his child too. Just like you'd tried to protect me the first time you left me, because you knew that, whereas I saw only the good in you, Rosamund saw what else you were capable of."

Faced with Jessica's tirade, Edward shrank. "So thirsty," he murmured.

"It was both your charm and your undoing." Again, she knelt. "You wanted to be saved, Edward."

He turned his head as if in denial.

"That's why you struck out at Ruby, once you'd put two and two together, when you realised who she might be. Not just my granddaughter but ours. That's why you connected. Finally." When still he didn't reply, Jessica reached out and turned his face back to hers. She looked younger somehow, more radiant than Ruby had ever seen her.

"Your soul is not as heavy as you think."

Chapter Thirty-Four

HELL was breaking loose. Fists banging on the door and a voice yelling.

"He's gone! Carrie-Ann has too! We have to go after them. Now!"

Corinna jumped up, so did Cash whilst helping Ruby to her feet. Jed faltered, clearly wondering whether to stay or give chase.

Jessica rolled Edward's chair backwards, away from the door, whilst Theo and Ness rushed to open it, Ness reaching it first.

"Saul, what is it? Do you know where they've gone?"

"Carrie-Ann wandered off, as if…I don't know, as if she'd heard something. Just now. Just now it happened. I followed her up the stairs to the next floor, saw her go towards one of the flats and push the door open. It was that man in there, Dave Lane. She called him Dave, anyway. He was…" Saul had to stop, take a breath. "He was a wreck, shaking like a pneumatic drill and covered in sweat. Carrie-Ann tried to calm him down, but at the sight of her, he panicked, kept saying, 'You're one of them, you're one of them.' Eventually, he jumped to his feet, pushed past her and ran. She ran after him." Having delivered this explanation, Saul spun around. "I'm going too. Who's with me?"

Cash was already halfway out the door, and Corinna.

"I'll go with them," Ness said. "Ruby, what about you?"

Edward was coughing again and gasping for air.

"I…I…"

Ness decided for her. "Stay here. You and Jessica."

"Without you? But what if…what if…"

"Ruby, look at him, really look at him. And your mother."

She dragged her eyes from Ness and the door, which Theo was also bustling out of, seeing an old man not just gasping for air. His hands were in the air also, clawing, as if trying to catch that ever-elusive oxygen and force it back inside him. As for Jessica, she was still kneeling, her attention only on him, finally managing to grab his arms, to bring them back down to his side so that she could cradle him, just…cradle him, tears running freely down her face. This was the end; it was coming.

"Oh, Gran," she said. "Oh, Mum."

"Catch us up," Ness said, a crack in her voice too.

"But how will I know—"

"Jed will know where we've gone. He'll lead you to us." Ness then reached out and placed a hand on Ruby's arm. "Families, eh?"

Ruby attempted a smile. "More trouble than they're worth sometimes."

"Sometimes," agreed Ness before taking off.

Ruby took only a few steps towards the couple in front of her, Edward's coughing having ceased, his breathing still harsh, though, as he leant into Jessica, and Jessica stroking the strands of hair on his head as though he were a child.

Jessica…or Sarah.

Ruby couldn't say. The two had merged so successfully.

"Oh, Sarah," Edward was saying, "the things I've done."

"If it's too painful to speak—"

"I must. I have to. Terrible things. I've caused so much harm, so much heartache. Intentionally. Will I…will I also suffer, afterwards?"

"In a way, you will. You'll have to experience all the pain you've caused, but…you'll learn alongside it."

"It'll be hell."

"But unlike that other hell, it's one you can escape from. When you've atoned."

"I'm frightened."

"I know you are. But the madness has to end. I'm here with you. I'll stay by your side."

"Even in death?"

"*Especially* in death. Oh, Edward, you wanted to learn, and there is so much to learn, truly incredible things. That will help you evolve, not destroy you."

"But first, atonement?"

"There's no other way."

"Oh, Sarah! Sarah!" Still there was fear in his voice, so much regret. "I was weak."

"It's human to be weak."

"I never stopped loving you."

"I know you didn't."

"But at the end, with Ruby, I couldn't resist. What if it was true? If she was who I thought she was?"

"You couldn't resist because you wanted salvation.

Oh, admit it, Edward! Just admit it."

"Only a Davis woman could do it. One in particular. Sarah, you're here. You're here!"

Tears having blinded Ruby's eyes at the exchange, at the loss of yet another man in their lives that the darkness had snatched from them, she now blinked furiously. It was extraordinary what Jessica had done, the ruse that even now she continued.

And yet…when Ruby focused on Edward, he wasn't gazing at Jessica anymore. He was staring straight ahead.

Ruby inhaled, tried to see what he could, almost as desperately. Jessica's gaze was also transfixed. But whatever was there, it was for his eyes only.

"It's magic," he breathed, hands clawing the air again but not as papery thin as before, his face not as wizened either, the hair on his head fuller. It was a glimpse, just that…of the man her grandmother had fallen in love with, his eyes still full of flames but those that enlivened rather than sucked the life from them. Although life *was* failing…rapidly. "It was always magic with us."

His eyes closed as his body slumped in the wheelchair.

As Jessica reached out again to hold him, as Ruby stood there, too amazed to move, she was sure she could hear it, the strains of a tune, an old one but familiar – *Why must I be a teenager in love?* And above it, another sound, that of tinkling laughter, low laughter accompanying it, just a quick burst, and then it was gone.

"Mum?" Ruby said at last. "Mum, are you okay?"

As Edward had laid his head against hers when alive, Jessica now laid her head on his shoulder.

"I'm fine, Ruby. Really, I am. Jed's barking." She was right. He had begun to bark, heading to the door, wanting Ruby to follow. "You'd better go."

"But what about you? What about Edward?"

"Just give me some more time with him, and then I'll phone Lee."

How could Ruby refuse? Family time before, now was solely father-and-daughter time. Oh, but the things he had done in life, the terror he had instilled in people. When she was in the darkness with him, she'd glimpsed that too, a man without mercy, who was the beast reincarnated, the stuff of nightmares. Once she came to terms with what she'd seen, would she tell her mother? Would she let her know the extent of it? Secrets. They weren't the answer. Truth and transparency were so much better. And yet...

She stood there still, ignoring Jed, causing Jessica to lift her head, a command in her voice now that Ruby dared not disobey.

"Carrie-Ann needs you. Now go!"

* * *

How Jed knew where to lead Ruby, she had no idea. He'd stayed behind with her, not followed Carrie-Ann, Lane and the rest of the team. But not once did he falter, leading Ruby out of the flat that had been Edward's, not Lane's, down the stairs of the building and onto the street, where the day was as gloomy as when she'd entered the building.

They were heading to the seafront, Ruby's heart full of so many emotions that would take time to process, maybe even the rest of her life. The strangest of days, it was far from over. What would she encounter next?

At the bottom of Southbourne Villas, she tried to cross Kingsway to reach the beach, cursing how heavy the traffic was, not one gap in it for what seemed like an age. Eventually she managed, turning to Jed. "Where now?" she said as he dashed off again.

She continued to give chase, reaching Hove Lawns, both she and Jed trampling over the grass, pastel-painted beach huts in front of them forming something of a barrier, then finally she spotted the sea, as vast and grey as the sky. At the shoreline, she could see Theo, Ness and Corinna – and Cash too, who was undressing, peeling away his jacket, then reaching down to remove his boots and kicking them aside.

He was going in the water. Because Dave Lane was in it. And Carrie-Ann.

Oh shit! "Cash!" Ruby shouted, running faster than before.

On some days the sea was like a millpond, but this wasn't one of them. The waves, although not quite crashing down upon one another, were sizeable enough. It was a rough sea, a winter sea, a strong undercurrent to it, no doubt, not a sea to enter at any cost. Cash, though, *was* entering it, the stone beach slowing Ruby's progress as she struggled to reach him. Ruby cursed it as she had cursed the traffic. "Cash, don't! It's dangerous!"

Damn it, but this kind of element, it wasn't something her psychic ability could combat. The power of the sea – the *natural* power – was just too much. Reaching her colleagues, she saw Corinna and Ness were both on the phone, Ness most likely to Lee, requesting backup, Corinna surely speaking to any emergency service she could get hold of.

"That's right," Ruby heard her saying, "we're east of the King Alfred swimming complex. Hurry! Two of them are far out. You have to hurry!"

"Theo," Ruby said on reaching her. "Fill me in."

"We were here on the beach, trying to reason with Dave, but…it was no use. Carrie-Ann was making the situation worse, pleading with him, but it was no good. He's terrified of her. And then…" The oldest member of Psychic Surveys swallowed hard. "He was so desperate to escape, he went into the sea. And although Cash tried to restrain Carrie-Ann, he couldn't. She went in after him. Oh look! Look! She's reached Dave."

Lane was splashing and flailing as wave after wave crashed over him. They didn't have to be tsunamic to be deadly. He was struggling. Badly. But Theo was correct. Carrie-Ann had reached him, Cash still battling his way through the waves to reach them too.

Having ended their calls, Corinna and Ness hurried to join Ruby and Theo, both of them assuring them help would arrive soon, 'in a matter of minutes,' Corinna said. Despite this, Ruby couldn't tear her eyes from the scene ahead. No relief in her that Carrie-Ann had hold of Lane, just further agitation.

"Hold still, Dave, for God's sake," she cried, her voice as choked as Jessica's had been back in the flat. "Just fucking hold still, will you?"

"Cash is there!" Corinna said, hope in her voice when it was entirely absent in Ruby's. "He's reached them now as well!"

Lane, though, was still struggling. He appeared to

push both Carrie-Ann and Cash away. His actions seemed to rile the sea, as if it fed off his fear, waves growing bigger.

"Cash!" Ruby screamed again as Jed, also by the water's edge, barked his warning too. "Where are the emergency services? They're all going to die!"

There was indeed the sound of sirens in the air, but not close enough.

"Oh, Cash," Ruby whispered, desperate to also plunge in. Only the thought of Hendrix stopped her. The prospect of him losing both parents.

"Wait!" It was Ness, a hand on Ruby's arm and gripping it tight. "Cash has got Dave. They're coming back. They're heading this way."

"What?" Could it be true? For a moment Ruby had averted her eyes, unable to witness any more. Never had she felt so powerless, not even when up against the might of Edward Middleton. She might be a fighter, but this was outside her remit. Now, though, something flared inside her, Corinna's determination to hold on to hope just so infectious.

It was true. Cash had one hand under Lane's chin – Lane on his back now, most likely exhausted – and with his other arm he negotiated every damned wave that crashed over them, resurfacing, taking another stroke, drawing closer and closer to shore. They were going to do it, reach safety. Ruby kicked off her boots, as did Corinna, the pair of them entering the sea but only up to their knees, Ruby feeling how greedily it tugged at her, how the ground tried to race away, but she stood resolute, ready to receive them. But Carrie-Ann, what about her? Where had she gone? A reasonable enough swimmer, despite having nearly drowned before, she was behind them, surely?

"Carrie-Ann!" Ruby shouted. "Carrie-Ann, where are you?"

The roar of the sea was incessant, easily able to snatch at her voice, gulls circling above them too, just like vultures might, emitting their woeful cries.

"Ruby, Corinna, take him."

Cash hurled Lane at them, Corinna being the first to drag him backwards.

"Where's Carrie-Ann?" Ruby asked, panic not abating but on the rise. "Where is she?"

Corinna and Lane struggled onto the beach, Ness having also waded in to help. Cash, meanwhile, was turning his back on Ruby, preparing to dive in again.

"Cash, no!" Ruby yelled. "What happened? Carrie-Ann's not there."

"I...I don't know," he said, his voice as tremulous as he was. "She...she kind of pushed Dave towards me and then retreated. Like...swam away. The minute she did, Dave calmed down and let me help him. But...she's out there still. I've got to get her."

"Cash!" Theo yelled. "Do not go in again! The emergency services are here."

He and Ruby looked behind them. It was true – ambulances and police cars were parking up.

"I'm closer than them," Cash insisted. "I'll reach her first."

"Cash, wait," said Ruby. "There's Jed. Jed's going."

"What? Where?"

"Believe me, he's in the water. He's swimming out to her."

Cash scrutinised the waves, then lifted his hand to point. "She's there. Look! I can see her...her and something else. Something black."

"It's Jed," said Ruby, staring as well. "He's already with her. And she's waving."

"Because she's in trouble!"

"No, no, she's not," Ruby replied, another strange feeling descending, a serenity, an acceptance, even as the coastguard's boat came into view. "She's saying goodbye."

Epilogue

"CHRIST Almighty," said Cash, having been discharged later that evening from the hospital.

"I know," said a solemn Ruby. "I've had better days at the office."

Cash didn't laugh, and nor did she. It was true, though. She'd experienced better days, easier days, less dramatic, but perhaps none that held quite as much wonder.

Dave Lane had also been taken to hospital and, unlike Cash, was being kept in overnight. It was Theo who'd managed to sneak past nurses and doctors to talk to him.

"There's work to be done with him," she'd subsequently told Ruby. "Quite a bit. Edward Middleton was right; he really has the most extraordinary gift. One he exploited until now, although in a relatively harmless way, via methods such as fortune-telling. Fact is, he's too damned superstitious for his own good, having listened as a young, impressionable boy to various myths and legends told to him by his great-grandfather, no less, a certain Leon Vasilescu. Right now, they're too deeply ingrained for me to persuade him they're just old wives' tales."

"So what kind of work needs to be done?" asked

Ruby, yawning. She was so exhausted.

"A shutting down," Theo informed her. "At his request. He simply doesn't want to see anymore. And, you know, can we blame him?"

"No," replied Ruby. "We can't."

"Are you all right, darling?" Theo checked.

"Yeah, yeah, I'm fine. Tired, you know."

"All that sea air."

Theo's joke fell flat too.

"You know she intended to go, don't you?" Theo continued.

"Yes," said Ruby.

"After saving Dave Lane, of course, delivering him into Cash's arms."

"I wonder if he'll ever see it that way, that she saved him."

"Possibly. One day."

"Do you think that's what she came back for?"

"To save him?"

"That, and to force him to take his talent seriously."

"Perhaps. Lane may want to shut down now, but once he's had a bit of a break from it all, once he's matured, thought about things, I mean *really* thought about them – I'll help him to shut down but I'll be planting a few seeds whilst I do so – he may want to open back up. And who knows what he's likely to achieve. Those he might be destined to help, to save too."

"Destiny," Ruby said, a crack in her voice. "No way to avoid it, I suppose. Ultimately, I mean. No matter how unfair it may seem."

"Ruby, Carrie-Ann went the way she was meant to

go. She wasn't afraid. She was finally ready."

"She was," Ruby conceded, Jed confirming that. He'd reappeared later, still drenched from the sea but wagging his tail in the widest of arcs, happier than ever. "Jed stayed with her," she told Theo. "He helped her to cross over."

"Good for him," said Theo, yawning too. "Just as Sarah helped Edward."

Thus fulfilling their destiny too, to be together no matter what.

As odd a day as it had been, it was coming to a close, Hendrix staying over at Cassy's because Ruby and Cash needed sleep.

Tomorrow was another day, and it might be a day filled with sunshine or as grey and drizzly as this one. Even if the latter, it wouldn't be a dull one. She had to answer to Lea Monaghan and resolve the case of the sad presence in the spare room. Plus, she thought, just before sleep claimed her, there were some answers that she wanted too.

* * *

"Nope, no way, you're not coming in here again!"

"But Lea—"

"Mrs Monaghan."

"Oh, right," Ruby repeated as, by her side, Corinna stiffened somewhat. "Mrs Monaghan, what happened—"

"I've thought about it," Lea said, continuing to keep the two members of the Psychic Surveys team on the doorstep rather than welcoming them in as she'd done a few days before. "And I've decided."

"Decided what?" said Corinna, her nostrils flaring slightly.

"That's it all a load of nonsense. There is no presence in the spare room. We've all just been egging each other on about it, blowing it up into something it's not. From now on, if anyone in the family brings it up, they'll get a bloody good telling-off."

"But, Mrs Monaghan," Corinna pleaded. "I think there *is* something there. And if there is, it's unfair to the spirit—"

"Unfair?" Lea repeated, her nostrils flaring too. "I'll tell you what's unfair, that you two keep coming around here and pestering me."

"This is only the second time we've been," Ruby pointed out. "You asked us the first time, and then you said you wanted answers."

"Well, I don't." Lea folded her arms. "It's nonsense, like I've said. All of it."

"Even what happened to me?" Ruby was astounded. "You saw it with your own eyes."

"Staged," Lea declared, though refusing to meet their gaze.

Corinna was about to open her mouth, protest further, but Ruby stayed her with her hand, firing a thought that she knew her colleague would catch: *Leave it.*

"Just to check, Mrs Monaghan," Ruby said, "you haven't mentioned what happened to your husband and family. Or to anyone."

Lea shook her head. "I just want to forget it. Now, if you'll excuse me." Stepping back, she promptly slammed the door shut.

SHANI STRUTHERS

"Bloody hell," swore Corinna. "Did what just happened happen?"

"It sure did," replied Ruby. "You know what I think? She knows well enough that what she senses in the spare bedroom, and what happened to me, isn't nonsense. But she doesn't want to believe it, doesn't want that insight, to have to question things."

"So she's doing a Dave Lane?"

"Yep, she's shutting down. Nothing really wrong with that. It works in our favour."

"How so?"

"Because she won't go to the papers and bad-mouth us, tell them it was staged. She'll just…dismiss it. Or try to."

"But the grounded spirit. I pity it even more if it's trapped in there with her."

Ruby thought for a moment, examined further the row of houses in front of her before reaching a decision. "Come with me."

Back on the pavement, Ruby turned right, towards the end of terrace, where there was a narrow lane.

"What are we doing?" said Corinna.

"Seeing if there's a back way into Lea's house."

"What? For real? But, Ruby, we can't just break in!"

"No, I know. Be patient."

It was as Ruby hoped. Although the narrow lane continued onwards, a side alley led off it, lined with fences and gates.

"She's twelve houses deep, isn't she?" said Ruby. "So come on, start counting."

Soon, they arrived at the rear of the Monaghan house, Ruby looking for something that she could climb

328

onto. Spotting an empty recycling box, she upturned it and asked Corinna to help her.

"What if Lea sees you?" Corinna fretted. "There'll be no shutting down then. She'll call the bloody police."

"I'll be careful," Ruby assured her. "Like you said, Corinna, that poor soul is trapped in there. We can't leave it, stuck in a moment, weighed down like that with so much sadness. We have to help. There's the window – look, right there. Shit! There's Lea, in the kitchen. Damn it, this isn't so easy after all."

Jumping down from the box, Ruby sighed in frustration as she checked her watch. "It's my turn to look after Hendrix this afternoon. Cash has got a meeting."

"So what do we do?" Corinna said, looking every bit as frustrated as Ruby felt.

"I don't know…I… Hang on. I *do* know. We come back tonight. When the family is asleep. We bring a stepladder. Let the spirit know we're here."

"Connect that way?"

"Yep. Worth a shot, huh?"

Corinna agreed. "Always."

Even now, Ruby was trying to reach out. *We won't leave you. We'll come back. We'll help. That's what we're here for.*

Without the aid of the box, only the top half of the spare-room window could be seen, but, if her eyes weren't tricking her, she saw a hand appear at the window – for a split second, no more – pressing hard against the glass. A pitiful act, desperation in it.

"Perhaps," said Ruby as the hand faded, "we'll need all the team here."

Corinna smiled. "Imagine that: the four of us, down a dark alley, at midnight."

"Whatever it takes," she replied, to which Corinna nodded.

Returning home, Ruby took over the care of Hendrix, Cash still looking exhausted from all that had transpired, but even in his world, work was work, and he had to get on with it. And sure, Cassy would have continued to spend her days looking after Hendrix, but they both wanted him back, to hold him, inhale his baby smell, Ruby especially.

In the kitchen with him, she was busy cooing and chatting to him, stroking his cheek, when Jed materialised, his eyes on the baby. Hendrix, as usual, was fussing and wriggling despite her efforts, Ruby missing Carrie-Ann all the more, not just as her friend but as someone with the magic touch.

Would her body ever be recovered? Or would the sea refuse to let go this time? Ruby felt desperately sorry for Carrie-Ann's friends and family if that was the case, although they'd never know how they'd had her for longer than was intended.

Despite Hendrix refusing to settle, she couldn't put it off any longer – she had to phone her mother, check up on her again, make sure she was as fine as she'd said she was. That what had happened with Edward, the loss of him, wouldn't drag her back into depression. And she had to ask the question burning in her mind…

"Mum, it's me. How are you today?"

"Ruby, hi. Still tired, darling. You must be too."

"Yeah, yeah, I am."

"Life goes on, though, doesn't it? Been busy today,

or have you been able to rest?"

Ruby laughed. "With Hendrix? No way."

"I can hear him, my gorgeous grandson. I can't wait to see him."

"I'll bring him over soon."

"That would be lovely."

"Mum? I really am sorry about Edward."

"Nothing to be sorry for, you know that."

True enough, Ruby supposed.

"You know, what you did, Mum, wearing Gran's clothes, styling your hair like that, and your makeup too, it was…genius."

"It was all I could think to do," Jessica said humbly. "I might have been his daughter, but it was in name only. He didn't know me. I meant nothing to him."

Ruby nodded, rocking the buggy Hendrix was lying in, in an effort to keep him placated. "You know what, though? Sometimes I thought it was Gran standing there instead of you." She cleared her throat. "Did you…feel the same way?"

"Like she was channelling me"

"Yes."

"I think…I think she orchestrated the whole thing, a plan that she hoped would come to fruition from the moment she sat down to write in that notebook, just before she died."

"Funny how it came about, that whole connection with Dave Lane and Carrie-Ann."

"We're all connected, I guess. Not only family."

True enough. Millions on the planet, and everyone a part of the same thing.

"But the thing is, he did know about you after all."

Ruby picked up the photograph of Edward Middleton, noting how faded it had become, both the picture and the writing on the back, resolving to file it rather than leave it lying around any longer.

"Sorry, Ruby, what did you say?"

"I said he knew he had a daughter. He'd received the letter Gran sent him." In a 'moment of weakness', as she'd called it. "He steamed it open, read it, and then returned to sender, stating no person at that address known. She told us she'd sent it, but not that she suspected he'd opened it. So, she admitted that in the notebook, did she?"

"What?"

Ruby frowned. "About the letter. She admitted she suspected he'd opened—"

"Sorry, I heard you. I just...so much went on, I'm still reeling from it."

"Of course."

"Did I really say such a thing?"

"Um...yeah, Mum, you did."

"Because that detail isn't in the notebook."

There was a brief silence. "It isn't? And yet...he didn't dispute it."

She sighed. "It doesn't change, though, that he was my father in name only."

"And yet it shows something. Something that Gran must have really wanted you to know."

"What, Ruby?"

"That he *was* a father in more than name only. Because what do fathers do? *Good* fathers? They protect their children. At all costs. And that's what he did in staying away from you, and from Sarah, the love of his life. Even to the detriment of himself."

"Ruby—"

"Mum, you meant something to him."

Again, there was silence, Ruby fretting that her words had caused Jessica more pain.

She needn't have worried. When Jessica spoke, her voice sounded so much lighter than before. "Thank you, Ruby. For everything."

"That's all right. Thank you for everything as well."

"I love you."

"I love you, Mum."

Simple words that held such power, that could lessen the weight of the soul.

Hendrix let out an ear-piercing scream, one little fist rubbing furiously at his eyes.

"Sorry, Mum, Hendrix has started up. I've got to go."

"See you soon, darling. See you soon."

Ruby ended the call, turning briefly from Hendrix to place the phone and photograph on the kitchen table. But when she turned back, circumstances had changed yet again.

Jed had jumped up and laid his head on the baby in the buggy.

As if he were a real-life dog, Ruby admonished him. "No, Jed, get down!"

He ignored her, settling himself further.

About to shoo him a second time, she stopped.

Hendrix was no longer rubbing at his eyelids so angrily. He had closed them instead, the most perfect little smile on his face. One of pure contentment.

"Carrie-Ann," Ruby said, watching Jed as his ears

pricked up, "are you responsible for this? Have you passed on your skills to the dog?"

A memory flashed into her mind, of her and Carrie-Ann in Theo's study, Ruby having been in tears because she couldn't soothe her baby. Carrie-Ann had consoled her, had fixed Ruby with her faded gaze and told her she was a great mother, to believe it.

It would be a dishonour to think otherwise.

Once more, tears filled Ruby's eyes, but she smiled through them.

"Thank you too, Carrie-Ann," she whispered. "Godspeed, Angel."

A note from the author

As much as I love writing, building a relationship with readers is even more exciting! I occasionally send newsletters with details on new releases, special offers and other bits of news relating to the Psychic Surveys series as well as all my other books. If you'd like to subscribe, sign up here!

www.shanistruthers.com

Printed in Great Britain
by Amazon